S0-AWM-735

Cibola

CIBOLA

James H. Cobb

Five Star • Waterville, Maine

Copyright © 2004 by James H. Cobb

All rights reserved.

This novel is a work of fiction. Names, characters, places and incidents are either the product of the author's imagination, or, if real, used fictitiously.

First Edition
First Printing: January 2004

Published in 2004 in conjunction with Tekno Books and Ed Gorman.

Set in 11 pt. Plantin by Christina S. Huff.

Printed in the United States on permanent paper.

Library of Congress Cataloging-in-Publication Data

Cobb, James H.
　　Cibola / by James H. Cobb.—1st ed.
　　　　p.　cm.
　　"Five Star first edition titles"—T.p. verso.
　　ISBN 1-59414-108-8 (hc : alk. paper)
　　1. Police—Fiction.　I. Title.
　PS3553.O178C53 2004
　　813′.54—dc22　　　　　　　　　　　　　2003064227

CIBOLA

Chapter 1

It's not hard to be in two places at the same time. No real trick to it at all.

I held back in the underlit side passage and watched myself walk by out in the main concourse. A rather well set up fellow if I do say so myself, of medium height and build and in pretty fair shape for a man who spends a lot of time in free fall. Dark hair drawn back into a short spacer's ponytail, green eyes, and a certain rakish good looks that seem to be appreciated by an adequate percentage of the female population.

The "me" out in the concourse was in uniform: the black suit liner and softboots and steel-colored armorel protective jacket of the UN International Law Enforcement Authority. The badge patch over my heart indicated the Free Marshals Service, and I was in an agitated conversation with a couple of Hindi officers wearing the tan liners and baton belts of the Maya High III security force.

For a moment I wondered what I was saying and what they were answering back. I shrugged off the question, not bothering to access the doppelganger's audio sensors. In all probability it would just be more of the same vocalized white noise we'd been getting ever since our arrival. Bo and I had been hitting resistance ever since we'd docked on the Maya High III platform. Not the belligerent bluster or the fast stab-in-the-shadows, nor even the sullen, unresponsive variety, just judicious stupidity, liberally applied. It didn't surprise me particularly. We already suspected that somebody high up in station management was wearing a collar.

For the past sixteen months, the UNILAW and the Free Marshals Service had been sharking after a particularly pernicious and well-organized band of tech-jackers. It seems that someone had been systematically marauding cis-Lunar industry, primarily targeting progressive swing technologies, i.e. the kind of stuff you need to convert expensive and complicated manufacturing procedures into cheap and simple ones.

Truth be, we hadn't been gaining much on the situation until recently. The gang was good, good enough so far to collectively fox corporate security, the top-of-the-line freelancer investigators the corporates had brought in, and UNILAW itself. Not that we'd been pushing the problem all that hard. Industrial espionage isn't a Free Marshal priority. We have other vacuums to fill.

Then the jackers tapped the Enfield-Marconi Advanced Physics facility at Clavius Minor and the package changed. This time the bad guys had scored the schematics and working prototype of a new kind of miniature liquid crystal lens array. One that just might make man-portable High Energy Laser weapons a practical reality. UNILAW can move when it has to. Every Free Marshal team in cis-Lunar space scrambled, all dancing to the same tune. Shut 'em down before that lens assembly can reach Earth.

My partner Bo and I had drawn Maya High III, a Mukurgi Combine industrial platform in near-Earth orbit. Our preliminary briefing had only indicated that we had some interesting personalities moving in and out of here on a regular basis. But after arriving on station we began to sniff the stink of large-scale buy-offs. Somebody was nest building, buying either a hidey-hole or a secure transfer point to move laundered hardware dirtside.

My doppelganger Ken moved on with its escort, climbing the perpetual upslope of the habitation wheel's concourse. I emerged from my hide and headed the other way, bumping shoulders with the slowly shuffling mob of dependents and off-duty station workers.

The air was heavy with human biological odors and metallic with ionization. Sweat prickled down my spine and under the firestorm weapons module I had strapped to my forearm, and my lungs labored a little even under the station's half gee standard gravity. Mukurgi was running the old cheapjacking stunt of cranking up the ambient temperature and humidity in their habitation spaces while pulling down the oxygen count. You don't have to spend much on recreational facilities that way because your personnel just lay around in a sweaty daze during their down time.

It worked in my favor because it made the station population too apathetic to pay much attention to any strangers in their midst. Disguise-wise I could make do with a darkening of spray-on skin dye, tinting drops in my eyes, and a thin-line moustache. A nondescript civilian suit liner and a pocket jacket with a Hindi Confederacy freightline logo transformed me into just another orbit jumper lying over between hauls.

My destination was a coffeehouse, a worker's hangout, located near one of the spoke shafts. Pushing through the flimsy formplastic door, I walked into semi-darkness. Dimmed purple lighting panels took the place of interior decoration and there was nothing in the way of human staff. A sultry female voice box, keying off your entrance, fed you one of a dozen or so greetings in orthodox Hindi and a row of self-servers ran down one wall.

A scattering of little guys in Combine coveralls occupied the place, off-duty hands from the free fall levels, trying to nurse what buzz they could from caffeine and sugar. Higher voltage intoxicants are almost universally disallowed by station managers, at least away from the tourist wheels. A justifiable fear being that some jolly slosh might try to open a window to let in some fresh air.

A few of the cheap foam aluminum tables still had functional interface jacks and some of the factory hands had visored in and were doing net porn or tonal VR, nodding and weaving to the internalized rhythms. Others talked listlessly, the liquid babble of their voices flowing around me. Still others just sat, trying to accumulate the energy to lift their cups to their lips.

I fed a plastic cash bit into a self-server and drew a small cup of theoretically Turkish coffee. Then I crossed to the very back of the room to a table occupied by one big guy in denim and suede.

Lobo, my partner, doesn't use oxygen nor does he sweat, advantages I envied under the current circumstances. At the moment he'd stand a solid sixteen centimeters over my own height and is handsome to the point of being obscene. A share and a half of shoulder to half a share of waist, shoulder-length blond hair held back with a fancy border silver clip, finely chiseled Michelangelo-class features replete with deep set, golden retriever eyes. Human females had a tendency to salivate uncontrollably whenever he ambled into a room, and you can just bet that's what he'd had in mind when he designed this particular Ken unit as his "personal."

Of course Bo can look like pretty much whatever he feels like: a sixteen-year-old Polynesian girl, a hundred-and-twenty-year-old Frenchman, me, or a Siamese cat; it just depends on what Barbie, Ken, or Critter unit he's drawn from the UNILAW Waldo pool. "Waldo" is shortform for a humanoid mobile sensor and manipulator platform operated via broadband data link. I'm kind of pleased that it was one of the old science fiction masters, Robert A. Heinlein to be specific, who came up with the concept.

You see Waldos all over the place, either as glorified store dummies doing simple sludge work under AI control, or serving as mobile representatives for cyber beings.

On the other hand, UNILAW operative class Waldos you don't see at all, at least not to know it. Our Kens and Barbies are state of the art. Not one person in a hundred can tell a well handled one from genuine meat.

As for what Lobo really looks like, visualize a chunk of silver-blue biocrystal with a hexagonal cross-section about as long as your forearm. Currently he was enclosed in an armored tank aboard his mainframe down in the Maya High docking bay.

Please make no mistake about one thing though, a chunk of crystal or not, my partner is "people" not a computer. Lobo is a true cyber being, a fully independent entity with all his sentience verifications and citizenship rights under the Recognition Compact of '65.

If he doesn't remind you of the fact, I will.

As for me, my name is Gain Chandry, butt-average human being barring a few odds and ends of steel and circuitry that I pack around under my skin.

"You know, Boss," Bo vocalized in a whisper, "I can't see this guy just walking in here like this."

"Why not?" I replied. "We figure Wassermann must be buying off somebody in the Maya High administration. We know he can ghost right through station security and we know that this club is one of his favorite transfer drops. And finally we know the timeframe is right. If they are moving hot hardware from cis-Lunar to Earth, they'll want to take it transatmospheric as soon as possible. There's a lot more hiding places down there than up here."

Bo looked dubious. "Yeah, but will they try it with a Free Marshal patrol cutter docked in the same landing bay?"

"That's why I swapped off with my doppelganger Ken. As far as Wassermann knows, the major threat against him, i.e. me, is wandering around solidly under the thumb of his bought station dogs. That prototype is white hot and Wassermann knows it. He's going to want to dump it fast. He has what he thinks is a handle on me and feels comfortable here with his known drill. I say it's safe credits he'll repeat."

Bo shook his head in the darkness. "Who can ever figure what meat's going to do next?"

"I think Gain may have a correct assessment." The nonverbal communication flowed into the back of my mind like a trickle of cool water. *"There is a suspicious vehicle currently on approach to Maya High III."*

"What do we have, Lil?" I fired my query back into my neurolink implant and out across space.

Lilith is my case officer back on Dawn City and sometimes, as now, she backstops for Bo and me. Physically, she was a good hundred and sixty thousand kays away as the comsat beams and yet she was as close as the transceiver embedded in the base of my skull.

Like Lobo, Lil is an independent cyber being. Only as Bo is an "outsider," physically interacting with the human environment, Lilith is an "insider." She lives totally within the cybernet, swimming free in the data flow like a dolphin in the Gulf Stream.

Slowed slightly by speed of light lag, the lady's response came back. *"A four-person reentry sled, a charter craft from Laker Transorbital, supposedly heading downside from L-4 Cosmoplex to their servicing facility at Rio De Janeiro. However the pilot has requested an unscheduled in-flight diversion and docking at Maya High III.*"

"*Passengers?*" I queried.

"*There shouldn't be any, Gain. According to its flight plan, the vehicle is deadheading down for maintenance with a single pilot on board. However, I've penetrated the Cosmoplex docking bay logs and I've learned that the vehicle was stocked with adequate life support consumables for two plus an emergency reserve just before its departure.*"

"*It sounds like somebody was planning on picking up a hitch-hiker.*"

"*Quite so,*" Lil replied soberly, "*and Wassermann, your person of interest, has some connections at Laker.*"

I nodded to myself. "*This is starting to sound positive, sweet one. Now leave us see if it goes all the way.*"

"*Acknowledged. I'm going intrusive into the Maya High net at this time. I'll keep you advised on further developments.*"

Lilith slipped back out of my mind, no doubt already tunneling into the industrial station's cybernet.

"You get all that, Bo?"

"Yeah. The pretty lady was running a simultaneous feed to me." He deliberately settled a little lower in his chair. "I still don't think he's going to show, though."

I couldn't tell him to shut up and drink his coffee because he couldn't.

Several eternities passed, or at least time enough for my own untouched cup to go from lukewarm to cold. Lil could feed us nothing beyond the docking of the errant sled. Then someone pushed through the coffee house doors to the tune of another synthesized greeting. My spine stiffened as I recognized Hadrah Sine, one of the local middle-management drones that I'd been introduced to when we'd first arrived on Maya High. Slight, dark, obsequious, and wearing a tan businessman's tunic and bloused trousers, he was a professional non-entity, one of those people who should just slide off your mind without registering.

Yet I'd made note of him. Maybe because he didn't seem to be doing quite as much ass kissing as an employee in his slot should be, while receiving a little more than his due. Now, he was showing his executive's face inside a dedicated workers' hangout. In a culture still as castey as that of the Hindi Confederacy, those aberrations added up to something.

Sine sat down at a table near the entrance and ignored the cup of tea he had drawn from the server. Lobo and I froze in place like a couple of hunting lizards, sticking to the camouflage of the shadows.

Wassermann walked in five minutes later, his bulk and gingery hair making him stand out among the horde of slender brunettes. Theoretically he was a Lunar-based freelance commodities agent whose profit margin always seemed to be a little too large for his trade turnover. At the moment he was wearing a spacer's suit liner with a pocket vest and a wary expression.

"Lil, we're running! Wassermann is here!"

"Acknowledged. Wait for the exchange, Gain. Remember we're not just concerned with the schematics. He has the stolen prototype assembly as well."

"But not on him, sweet one. We'll grab this pair, then burn for the reentry sled. Odds are that the prototype is being held on board. Bo, start recording this and initiate preflight-prestart on the mainframe, just in case."

"Doin' both, Boss. Audiovisual storage initiated and ready to launch in five little ones." Wassermann sat down at Sine's table. I could have linked into Lobo's augmented vision and hearing, if I'd wanted, but I didn't bother. If anything came

up that I needed to know about, he'd give me a prompt. Until then I made do with my own eyes.

It didn't take long. A short flurry of words and then came the flash of plastic as they made the exchange.

"Now!" Bo mind-shouted.

"Do it! Down 'em!"

We levered out of our chairs and charged across the room, pushing a bow wave of startled people out of our way.

"United Nations Free Marshals! Freeze!" I yelled enroute. The Sine-Wassermann connection had taken their own just-in-case precautions. They'd advanced a cover team into the coffeehouse. Two lean and agile Hindis bounced to their feet and swung into our path, both men drawing long shafted screwdrivers from the seam pockets of their coveralls.

I disarmed my man with a spin kick, swiping the *ad hoc* armament out of his hand. Then I used the momentum of my turn to drive an elbow back into his throat. Gagging, he went down slowly in the reduced grav fall of the station.

I didn't bother to check on how Bo was doing. He wouldn't need my help. I heard a wet crunch over in his direction, intermingled with an abbreviated scream, and I could guess that Bo's confronter need not be considered further.

Sine and Wassermann had shaken their surprise off in the second the fight had taken. Now, the former was groping in his suit pocket while the latter made a bolt for the door. I peeled off after Wassermann, trusting Lobo to cover my back in case Sine was drawing a more serious weapon than a screwdriver.

I'd only closed about half the gap, however, before I heard another scream behind me. I ducked as I sensed a considerable mass hurtling over my head. Sine's limp form caught

Wassermann across the shoulders, both perps exploding through the translucent formplastic of the coffeehouse door and out into the concourse beyond.

"Using a suspect as a capture and restraint weapon isn't in the books, Bo," I commented, vaulting the wreckage and dropping down beside Wassermann.

My partner grinned like a contented tiger shark and ambled over to where Sine lay wadded up under a decorative planter. "You know what my bed friends say, Boss," he replied. "I am nothing if not innovative." He dragged the Hindi station manager out into the open. "C'mon, darlin', get functional so I can read you your rights."

I ignored the growing crowd of curious onlookers in the narrow concourse and searched Wassermann's prostrate form. He turned up empty, except for his ID, a Maya High boarding pass, and a single monetary transaction card from a Bombay-based banking house. The card was privacy sealed with no amounts showing on its display, but the credit tab glowed blue, indicating it was both active and charged. "Heya! We got half the pie!" I called. "How're you doing?"

Lobo flashed something that he had found on Sine. "Data stick." He ran his reader finger across the media. "Just a second . . . there's an encryption lockout. . . . Yeah, this is the other fifty per, the lens assembly schematics."

"Righty-oh." I grabbed a handful of Wassermann's collar and lifted his head a couple of centimeters off the deck. "Okay, loser! You're burned! Where's the prototype?"

When no answer came along, I administered a couple of shakes to try and jar one loose. "Come on! Give over!"

Wassermann just goggled back at me, loose eyed and bleeding from his crushed nose and lips. Apparently being decked by a flying Hindi takes a lot out of a man.

"Gain, there's something else on this one!"

Bo held up a Day-Glo orange crisis card. It had been folded over on its activation crease. That was what Sine had been going for. Somewhere else on this station, that card's mate was telling someone else that this deal had just gone slimy.

Chapter 2

Lilith came up on the neurolink, her thoughts urgent. *"Gain, Maya High traffic control has just been ordered to clear Wassermann's sled for immediate undocking and departure!"*

"Tao! I was right! They didn't unload the damn thing!"

I whipped a loop of restraint tape around Wassermann's wrists and hauled him to his feet. "Bo, come on! The sled's bombing out with the prototype! We've got to get after it!"

"Do we turn these guys over to station security?" he asked, effortlessly tossing Sine over one shoulder.

"Frag that noise! We'd never see 'em again. We're taking 'em with us. Recall the doppelganger and have him meet us at the docking bay."

"Rajah." Lobo took over my grip on Wassermann's collar and began half-shoving, half-dragging the man down the corridor. The gawking locals parted like the Red Sea ahead of us, profoundly disinterested in getting in our way.

"Lil, what's happening with that sled launch?" I demanded into my neurolink as I followed.

"The vehicle has a pilot aboard and is powering up to get underway."

"Can you get the station to hold the departure?"

"I've tried to contact station management and I've been informed that no command authorized personnel are available at this time," she replied.

"Then can you get inside their net and bitch the launch procedure yourself?"

"I'm sorry, Gain, but I can't get access to their docking bay systems. There are man-breaks in the way."

"It was a thought. Damn it all entirely, Lil, I'm beginning to suspect that we're not getting the whole-hearted cooperation of the local authorities here."

"That's a safe estimation, Gain. Stay covered. I suspect this may get worse."

We made one of the spoke elevators and, just as the doors were closing, the other me came sprinting down the passageway. The doppelganger ducked in with us, his sardonic features stony stiff and immobile, as Bo was no longer bothering to maintain full life simulacra.

As we climbed towards the station core, my partner passed a semi-conscious Sine over to the Ken to handle, using it as a spare set of hands. Wassermann began to make a mushy protest but Bo squeezed it off with a slight but ominous tightening of the fingers he had curled around the scruff of the jacker's neck. The perp could talk to his heart's content later, but for now we didn't need any further distractions.

"Gain, the sled has undocked and has cleared the station." Lilith reported.

"Stay on him, Lil. I'm going to need a pursuit track."

"Acknowledged. Accessing SDF orbital surveillance."

Our weight fell away as we approached the spin axis and we made the transfer to the big hexagonal free fall corridor that ran the full length of the industrial complex. We headed astern, riding one of the siding handrails and towing our prisoners behind us like a couple of toy balloons.

Around us, other slide rails shunted a steady flow of cargo pods and people between the manufacturing decks and the docking bays. Beyond the occasional odd look, I didn't see any sign of interference or pursuit developing in the corridor traffic, but I didn't hold that for much. This operation was going more off-skew by the second and I couldn't call why.

We changed rails again as we approached station aft, headed out along one of the radial concourses that led to the docks and warehousing spaces. The passageway here had ports that looked out into the unpressurized hangars and onto another of Lobo's physical personas.

Bo's mainframe is a Hawker/Lockheed Aerospace corvette, the Bravo Four Law Enforcement variant with both Earth-to-orbit and deep space capability packages. A sleek and solid sixty meters in length, it was a giant gray-black spearhead cradled in the spindly arms of the service gantry. The pursuit strobes were pulsing at its needle nose and wing tips and a trace of exciter radiance glowed in the throats of its main and secondary engine bells. *"Almost home, brother,"* Bo thought to me cheerfully.

"Yeah, but not all the way yet."

They were waiting for us at the entrance to the boarding passage. Four station security men. Alert and wary, a couple of them already holding drawn shock batons.

I shifted my hand from the sliding to the fixed rail and braked to a halt, Bo and the doppelganger following suit.

"What now?" Bo inquired over the neurolink.

"I hope negotiation. Lil, what's that sled doing?"

"It appears to be setting up for atmospheric entry. Orbital Traffic Control has no flight plan filed and no destination listed."

"Shag it and related comments!"

"What seems to be the problem, gentlemen?" I said, going verbal.

The senior officer's eyes shifted uneasily between me and my doppelganger unit. Nobody had mentioned that I had a twin. "Marshal Chandry, we understand that you have taken a citizen of the Hindi Confederacy into custody and we believe there is some irregularity involved. We wish that you would accompany us to our headquarters where proper inquiries may be made."

"I'm sorry, Sergeant, but I can't accommodate you," I replied. "I'm holding UN open warrants that will be filed on both of these individuals just as soon as I can get the chance. We can sort all this out then."

The team leader bobbed his head nervously. "The rights of a Hindi citizen are involved. We must insist that an investigation be made before we can permit you to take him from Confederacy territory. We must insist that you accompany us."

"Lil, I've got a major protocol problem here. How do you want this handled?"

"You're senior officer on site, Gain. I can't second guess your judgment on this."

Tao, but I do so love modern cybercommunications. It gives your superiors the ability to pass the buck instantaneously across cis-Lunar distances.

I externalized my attention again. "Look, Sergeant, these men are suspected tech-jackers in UNILAW custody and I'm in active pursuit of one of their confederates. In short, I don't have time for swapping bits here!"

The team leader didn't reply; he just pushed off the bulkhead and started drifting towards us, his men following warily.

"So much for negotiation. Wha' do we do now, Boss?"

"Well, Bo. It worked once. Maybe it'll work again."

Wassermann and Sine hit the cluster of security guards like a strike and a spare, not only scattering them around the passageway but, given the volume of the screaming involved, apparently absorbing the charges from one or more stun batons. The Ken units and I hit the line a second or so later.

No one has yet developed a formalized martial art for free fall, so hand-to-hand in zero gee usually boils down to good old root hog or die, a primary concern being to deny your opponent leverage by prying him loose from whatever he's using as a handhold.

I dove forward, skidding along the padded corridor wall underneath the worst of the melee. Snubbing myself off, I looked around for a target. An arm in the sleeve of a security force coverall extended out of the scrim and grabbed a handrail. I hooked the toe of one soft boot under the arm's wrist and slammed my other heel down on the elbow, bending said arm in a direction nature never intended. There was another screech, then the elbow's owner was gone, tossed out of the passageway with the rest of the wreckage.

"C'mon, Bo. Grab the perps and let's move."

"Right. I sure hope we don't have to bust many more roadblocks like this, Gain. Our suspects are starting to degrade on us."

At last we had a dab of plus luck, finding no further resistance between ourselves and the soft tube out to the ship. I shoved everyone through the station-side hatch and hit the closure control. Just to make sure, I yanked my coverall sleeve back from the multiple muzzles of the firestorm strapped to my forearm. Selecting a stick of anti-materiel rounds, I burned them through the hatch's key pad and the power module below it.

Nobody was going to be paying calls on us in the foreseeable future.

As I rolled through the shipside air lock, I was yelling for Bo to get the prisoners secured.

"Done it. They're in the restraint cocoons."

His voice issued from the ship's speakers. The two Ken Waldos he'd been operating, his personal and my doppelganger, were already secured in their storage bays across from the lock entry, inert and with their aura of "alive" gone as Lobo shifted all of his processor power over to mainframe functions.

It always bothered me a little to see Pinocchio with his strings cut like that. When I visualize Bo I usually do it in humanform. Instinctively I guess because he's one of the most "human" people I know. However, this corvette mainframe is his real body and I suspect that shipform is really what he's the most average comfortable with.

I pushed through from the air lock and gear bays, through the vest pocket-sized crew's quarters to the command sphere entry. The two pilot's chairs were facing aft on their universal mount swing arm, waiting for me. They continued to wait politely until I was harnessed in before whipping around to face forward.

The full surround screens lit off and suddenly it was as if the ship's hull had gone transparent, with nothing between me and hard vacuum but the glowing readouts of the HUD displays. *"Lil, you still with me?"*

"Yes, Gain. The target has commenced a deorbiting burn. At this time I can only call a potential landing site as somewhere in the Eastern Hemisphere."

"Bo?"

"All flight systems are up and we got fire in the holes."

"Right! Maya High III departure control, this is UNILAW Cutter Golf Charley Slash Lima. Requesting pursuit traffic priority and immediate clearance to undock."

"Cutter Golf Charley Slash Lima," an unsteady voice replied. "This is Maya High departure control. We request that you go to departure hold and contact station management. There is apparently some difficulty . . ."

"Tao take it all entirely! I am declaring myself tired of this marfi! Bo, take us out!"

"Doin' it!"

Aft, hydrogen and oxygen jetted through the metastate exciters and met in the plasma arc ignition lobe of the main engine. Around us the docking bay lit with the glare of the exhaust plume. There was a lurch, a shudder, and the surge of acceleration. We fell outward through the open end of the bay, dragging a couple of metric tons of Maya High docking gantry along with us.

It's always the same. No matter how short a time you've been away from it, or how important whatever you're doing is, for a second, you've just got to look.

We were coming in on North Africa, and the browns and the golds of the Sahara were rolling over the great hazy arc of Earth's horizon. But as always, it was the blue that caught in your mind, that luminous, vivid blue of the Atlantic beneath us and the Med hooking away to the north and east, all half screened by frost-colored spiraling clouds. I don't get down dirtside too often anymore but it's always worth giving the old rock a nod, just for old sake's sake.

"I've acquired." Bo's voice snapped me back from my sightseeing. "Target is in a descending trajectory, maintaining a constant six gee decelerating burn."

"Let's see him."

A targeting recticle appeared in the lower left quadrant of the sphere screen, surrounding a spark of light just crossing the African coast below us. A second later, it windowed up to a meter-wide magnified image displaying the boat-shaped hull of the reentry sled. Running stern-forward, it was pushing a glowing bell of exhaust gases ahead of it.

"Given the way he's holding that burn, they must have topped his tanks off," Bo commented.

"Safe assumption. Let's get on him."

"Doin' it."

Bo did a fast snap roll to shake the junk off of his hide and then flipped nose for tail a hundred and eighty degrees. With our engines opposing our orbital line of flight he hit the brakes, burning back hard. The deceleration hit me across the stomach like a well-swung two-by-four. I hadn't had time to pull on a set of speed jeans so I was taking the gees straight out of the bottle. The control chair unfolded into a pallet so I could take the load flat on my back, but still, the air grunted out of my lungs as the pseudo-weight built.

The sled had a good lead on us and was running light with only a pilot aboard. He could probably match our deceleration . . . for a while at any rate. Lobo was bigger though, with a larger fuel reserve and a metastate propulsion system. He could use his propellants with two thousand percent greater efficiency than a straight chem-burner. Thus, sooner or later, we'd make intercept on this guy. The question was whether we'd have enough time and space to do it in. That sled was falling out of the sky like a debauched angel, totally ignoring the heavy traffic in the lower orbits.

In the screen window, the sled's exhaust bell flickered and faded.

"That's it," Lobo said, killing the magnification. "He just ran himself dry."

"Can we nail him before he hits atmosphere?" It was easier to think through the link than verbalize.

"Can't call it yet. Still chewing the numbers."

"Stay on it," I ordered. *"Uncage the fire control matrix and give me targeting designations."*

"You got 'em."

"Lil!"

"Yes, *Gain*," she thought back.

"Can you get me a landing point yet?"

"I'm projecting a touchdown somewhere within the Indian Ocean basin."

"He's running home to Mama."

The misty curve of the Earth was flattening and rising

ahead of us as we continued to bleed speed and altitude. Given the slightly screwball laws of orbital dynamics, to overtake an orbiting vehicle, you have to go slower than that vehicle to descend into a lower, tighter orbit. Lobo was screaming down out of space, dumping speed as fast as he could, but we still might get scraped off on the atmosphere before we could get into position to make the intercept.

"Bo, feed me! Can we take him?"

"Sorry, Boss. I've run it every way I can and we can't make a hostile hard dock with this guy before we hit serious breathin'."

"Then we gotta follow him down." That hurt. A Free Marshal is really free only out in the essentially government-less reaches of cis-Lunar space. Our authority is supposed to be just as valid dirtside. However for every kay deeper you penetrate into the atmosphere, you seem to accumulate two kays of red tape. *"Shag orbital physics entirely,"* I replied. *"Dial me up India Approach. We'd better let 'em know we're coming."*

"You're in."

I painfully sucked a talking load of air into my lungs. "India Approach Control, this is UNILAW Cutter Golf Charley Slash Lima. Requesting pursuit priority clearance into the approach basket please."

There was dead air. An unusually long stretch of it.

"Golf Charley Slash Lima. This is India Approach Control. We do not have a flight plan listed for you." The female controller had one of those irritatingly sweet receptionist-cum-cosmetics saleswoman voices.

"Acknowledged, India Approach. I repeat that this is a UNILAW pursuit priority. We are holding open warrants on reentry vehicle . . ." Bo slapped a set of numbers into my mind through the neurolink. ". . . on reentry vehicle Lima Alpha zero one six. We are attempting intercept at this time. Request clearance please."

26

"Standby, Golf Charley Slash Lima. I will relay your request to my superiors." The targeting recticle centered on the sled had crawled up the surface of the sphere screen until it was centered dead ahead of us. Even without magnification, there was now a solid dot of reflected sunlight glowing in the crosshairs. We were closing the range, but not fast enough. Indian Ocean blue was starting to show along the world edge.

"Keep diggin', Bo."

"I'm doing everything but dragging my feet, Boss, but it's getting a little thick out here. I'm going to have to reorient for atmospheric penetration in a second."

A faint vibration was starting to shudder through the mainframe. We were starting to shred through the outermost fringes of the atmosphere. The hull would be beginning to heat.

"Golf Charley Slash Lima," sweet voice was back. "This is India Approach Control. I regret we cannot grant your clearance at this time."

"What!"

"Hang on, Boss!" Bo interrupted. *"Reorienting now!"*

Bo put the mainframe through a fast skew-flip maneuver, bringing the bow around by swiveling the main engine bell. Then he cut power to the big burner, swapping deceleration over to the forward retros. I felt my eyes bounce off the back of my skull.

My control chair and the displays on the inside of the command sphere reoriented to the new thrust vector as well. We were plummeting into the atmosphere nosefirst and streamlined now, and the elephant sitting on my chest got up and went elsewhere. The bow thrusters and the atmospheric drag were a lover's hug compared to the crush of the corvette's main drive.

I got air in me again and resumed my battle with bureaucracy. "India Approach, this is a UNILAW vessel operating under UNILAW emergency priority. You are required by treaty to grant clearance!"

"Golf Charley Slash Lima," the reply shot back with no hesitation at all now. "We are not certain that a crisis situation actually exists. We cannot permit an unauthorized entry into Hindi Confederacy airspace under these circumstances."

"You've already got an unauthorized entry," I argued. "The sled I'm pursuing is coming down in your airspace whether you like it or not."

"Confederacy security agencies have been notified and will deal with the situation. If a violation is discovered, UNILAW will be notified." She was either reading a script or she had someone standing at her elbow coaching her. I could feel it. *"Lil, dammit, can you talk to these people?"*

"I'm in communication with Confederacy authorities at this time, Gain. Maintain pursuit and I'll see what I can do."

Another voice came in over the audio link: male, Hindi accented, and emotionless. "Unidentified space vehicle, you are descending into airspace controlled by the Hindi Confederacy. Execute immediate acceleration into orbit or you will be fired on."

Off to the south, a string of pulsing red dots appeared on the ocean's surface, projecting cones of scarlet light up towards us: virtual reality representations of a real-world event.

"Seychelles antiorbital defense sites are activating," Bo exclaimed. "We're being kill designated by Confederacy fire control! Gain, what's going on around here?"

"I don't know!" I snapped back. "India Approach, this is Golf Charlie Slash Lima! I repeat, we are a UN vessel, check our transponder codes! Contact your military and get those fire control systems off of us!"

The targeting recticle was finally starting to climb the upper curve of the screen and the dot of light inside it was starting to show form. We were overhauling the sled but we weren't going to make it. The hull vibration grew more intense as the atmosphere around us grew denser.

"Lil, what is this slime?"

She was slow to respond as well. *"Gain, I am still trying to talk with the Confederacy authorities. They are not being cooperative."*

I knew the feel of that deliberately formal thought phrasing. She had something she wasn't willing to come out and send open. She was instructing me to read between the lines and I could faintly feel her regret in the link sidelobe.

"Golf Charley Slash Lima," sweet voice said over the audio circuit. "Your request for an emergency approach access is being considered. Please hold for one orbit and we should be able to clear you down."

The cashbit dropped with a loud resounding click. The gee load must have been sucking the blood out of my brain or I would have caught it sooner. A tech-jacker gang might be able to buy off a station security force, or even station management, but not a whole multi-national government. "Bo, guns clear on primary armament. Give me manual fire control."

The targeting recticle went red and pulsing and one of the HOTAS grips on the command chair arm snapped upright, slapping into my palm.

You could see that there was a real ship out there now, one that was beginning to pull a ribbon of incandescent reentry plasma behind it as it interacted with the atmosphere. Just for a second, I considered trying to contact the sled pilot. Then I dropped the idea. His tanks were empty and the only direction he could go was down. He was out of the equation.

I could order Bo to do this, but I'm the senior member of the team and that means I do the ugly part. I squeezed the controller's primary trigger.

Bo was carrying a Marietta 10mm railgun on his centerline belly hardpoint. That's heavy iron for a police ship, but then he's like me. If you're going to go to all the trouble of killing somebody, you might as well kill 'em good.

The firestream touched the reentry sled and tossed it across the sky like a flipped poker chip, the spike swarm punching through its structure at multikays per second.

I don't know if the pilot lived through the first hit. It didn't matter much anyway because his vehicle integrity was gone and he was tumbling out of control when he struck serious air a few moments later.

Ever see a paper cup tossed into a campfire?

The mainframe's engines blazed and the screens went white with ionization for a second as Bo skipped us off the atmosphere. The thrust load stabilized at one standard gee as we began the climb back into orbit.

"India Approach, this is Golf Charley Slash Lima. I don't think we'll bother with that approach request after all. Shag you very much and have a nice day."

Chapter 3

Bo had consumed a lot of propellant during the pursuit and so it took him better than sixteen hours to climb out to Dawn City. That gave me plenty of time to sort out my admin. I had half a dozen different reports and depositions to file and strangely enough, considering the pooch screw the operation had devolved into, it didn't go too bad. Even the Lethal Force Review Board, with whom I have had my differences, were keeping their fangs in. I sensed that Lil might be out there doing a little checking and blocking in the scrim. And why not? She owed me monumentally.

In my loose moments I patched up my prisoners and made a half-hearted attempt at questioning them. All I succeeded in getting was a demand for a lawyer from Wassermann and a plea for a Confederacy Consul from Sine. So be it. Let the interrogation teams worry about them.

The human members of the UNILAW wrecking crew would politely ask these guys all of the pertinent questions . . . once.

If the perps failed to produce, the cyber member of the team would take over. A temporary neural access tap would be implanted and he'd drain their brains like a couple of dirty crankcases. Too bad, so sad, but we don't play light cards out here in the orbits.

We picked up Dawn City on the visuals and, like Earth, she's always worth a long look at.

Every civilization has its "Big Apple," the node around

which its society is woven. Athens, Rome, Paris, London, New York, Tokyo, Shanghai . . . now Dawn City, core of the Fourth Wave, cis-Lunar culture, rotating silently out at LaGrange Point One, dead on between Earth and Moon. Everything, and I mean everything, either lays over or transits by here at one time or another, and if you're a person who likes a little bit of variety, it's a pretty good place to live.

We planed in over the one kay radius of the huge white habitat wheel, the great connector spokes sweeping by beneath us as we followed the holographic approach lights into the combined UNILAW/Space Defense Forces fleet base at North Hub. The arms of the automatic docking gantry were waiting at the mouth of the hangar bay, ready to lock on and haul Bo into his usual berth, and we were home.

There wasn't much of a reception committee, just a constabulary team ready to take custody of the prisoners. I signed them off and handed over the hardcopy and they were out of my life, passed on up the relay that might eventually lead to justice.

There weren't even orders to contact my case officer for post-operation assessment. Only instructions to stand down until further notice. Lil was apparently a little wary of me just now. She had reason to be. I'd been short-briefed on this job and we were going to exchange some words when the time came. Lobo had fired up his personal Ken once more and was waiting for me outside of the gangway tube. He didn't have to do that; he could have just said "so long" over the speakers or neurolink. But sometimes he figures that talking is better than just communicating.

"What's up?" I inquired.

"Nothin' much, Boss. I'm going to get maintenance section started on turning the mainframe around and then I was figuring on going down and cruising the rim for a while, making trouble. You want to come?"

I shook my head. "Nah, I'm running sleep short. I'm going to go grab my rack and die for awhile. Thanks for the offer though."

"Anytime." He cocked an eyebrow. "You okay, Boss?"

I shrugged. "I'm okay. I don't much like doing the burn, that's all."

He shrugged back. "Zero choice. The Hindis were shaggin' and fraggin' with us back there and we ended up option tapped. It was either burn him or let him slide with that weapons prototype."

"I know. It's all part of the job. But sometimes that doesn't help with the feeling of it."

Bo nodded. "That is how it seems to work. I guess I'll feel the same way the first time we ever have to crack a cyber. Heya, you gonna be around to hold my hand then?"

I felt myself smile a little. "You can put cash on that, pal."

We crossed wrists for a second and then we went on our way.

I've got a month-to-month on a one-room and 'fresher down on the cheap decks. It's not too bad, barring the fact that it's on one of the windowless core corridors. I palmed the door pad and stepped through to find everything pretty much as I expected. The housekeeping service that I subscribe to had refreshed the bedding and, as per instructions, had left the rest of my slop alone.

I dumped my arms belt on the reading table at the head of the bed and my armor jacket on the couch under my art gallery. I'm kind of proud of that part of my collection. There's an original *Future Science Fiction* cover by Virgil Finlay and an original *Analog* by Kelly Freas. There's also a restored set of Chesley Bonestell prints from the old hard-copy *Life* and *Col-*

lier's magazines, and finally, a genuine, hand drawn, production sketch of Lynn Min Mei by Haruhiko Mikimoto. Good stuff all, if I do say so myself. I popped a liquid meal out of the fridge and took a pull on it, not bothering to taste if it was chocolate or vanilla; then I checked for hard mail. There was one parcel, a small plastic delivery box bearing a Newark postmark and the Redondo Brothers Media logo. I found myself sitting down on the couch and pulling the opening tab with more enthusiasm than I thought I had in me.

The Redondo Brothers aren't cheap, but they do deliver. It was one off my "really want" list, the February 1952 issue of *Astounding Science Fiction* magazine. The issue that had both the first publication of Gordon R. Dickson's short story "Steel Brother" and H. B. Fyfe's "Star-Linked," as well as the first of the James Blish Spindizzy stories. It was in fair shape too, already preservation treated and with only a couple of simulacra page inserts.

Maybe the universe wasn't such a bad place after all. I took another pull at the liquid meal, found out that it was chocolate, and then crossed over to the communications pad to fire a merchandise acceptance and a week's salary back across the void to New Jersey.

I used a nullifier towlette to get the skin dye off me and went through a double ration of shower water before hitting the bed pad. I had stretched out and had just turned the first page of my new acquisition, when I felt that cool breeze in my brain, the sensation of my neurolink activating.

"Gain, are you busy?" a tentative thought probed.

"Not so's you'd notice. What's up, Lil?"

"I need to talk to you about a few things," she replied. *"Would you like to come to my place for awhile?"*

"All right," I replied. *"Facts that be, I have a few things I need to dissect with you."*

"I thought you might. I'll be waiting."

I set the book on the nightstand and ran a hand down the light strip. Then in the darkness I gathered my consciousness and dove down into the link, beyond the basic communications level, out into the data flow where Lilith existed.

My boots crunched on raked gravel. I'd logged in down near the front gate. It was sundown and the air felt about late spring, mild and carrying the scent of growing things. This place is Lil's hobby and every time I come here she likes to show off her latest improvements. This go-round, it was the midnight blue tulips in the flowerbeds that lined the curving drive, each petal edge rimmed with silver to a perfection that any genetic botanist would cheerfully saw his left arm off to duplicate.

Upslope from me was the house, a pillared, southern mansion that would have impressed Scarlett O'Hara. Downslope was the valley, the pattern and mix of conifers and hardwoods that forested it always changing from visit to visit. Lil had added a low waterfall to the fast flowing river that snaked along the valley floor. I've always meant to hike down to that river and maybe one of these days I would.

Of course all this didn't actually exist, depending upon how you care to define existence. It was a synthesized symbology matrix intended to enhance the human/cyber interface.

Does that do anything for you? If not, try this.

Some cybers, like Bo, interrelate with we humans out here in the physical world by taking on and operating humanform Waldos. These are the "outsiders."

Others, like Lilith, prefer cyberspace as their primary plane of existence and they live their lives physically sedentary but electronically free to rove the data flow of the vast cis-Lunar infonet. These are the "insiders."

35

However, humans still relate better to humans and even the insiders usually have a personality image that they use for communication. A humanform that they can project holographically, or insert into a Virtual Reality room. For individuals like me though, who have neurolink transceivers jacked directly into their brains, they can go one better. They can write a reality pocket.

A reality pocket is a complete, cyber-generated mini-universe fed right straight into your own neural receptors. From your point of view, the place is there. You can see things, you can touch things, you can taste things. Your own senses tell you that the experience is actually happening. This is what the Virtual Reality producers and the visorheads keep groping for and what they never will reach. Only a cyber can create a reality pocket and only a cyber can invite you into it.

If you ever have the chance to experience one, go for it. It can be a ride!

Keep these points featured, however.

Point One: Even though this is all happening inside your head, this is not a dream or a VR game. What happens can count. You can be hurt there. Potentially you can even die there.

Point Two: While you are in that reality pocket, the creating cyber is God. Stay on their good side.

"Come on around the house. I'm out on the patio."

I turned off the drive near the porch and followed a flagstone path around into the deeper shade beneath the trees. Lil was waiting for me on the lawn couch.

"Hello, Gain," she said, smiling wryly. "Care for a drink before you get on with being outraged?"

One of the more interesting traits that cybers seem to have absorbed from their human role models is a streak of vanity. I have never seen a cyber use an "average" personal Waldo or telecommunications image in my life.

Lilith is no exception. She's elected to be perfect.

A perfect figure, currently sheathed in a white gown that left perfectly tanned shoulders bare. A tousled fall of diamond-colored hair that almost reached her waist. Gray eyes the tint of a clear morning sky just before the sun gets serious about rising, and a face that would make a master painter throw down his brushes in despair and take up plumbing because he could never hope get it right in a million years.

As I said, perfect.

At least that's how she expresses herself to me. How she appears to the other Free Marshals she controls, like the female ones, I don't know. Somehow we never talk about it.

Under these circumstances, it would be difficult for a conventionally oriented male to really hold a mad-on at her. I was going to give it a try but I probably wasn't going to have much luck, especially considering I hadn't been up to the Big House for awhile.

"Why not," I replied, crossing the patio and dropping onto the other end of the couch. "What are you offering?"

She tilted her head. "A good Goldendale '79?"

Tao, she was going to make this hard. "Taken."

"Calistoga or Royale?"

"Cal."

"So moot it be."

A brandy and soda materialized on the end table beside me with a soft tinkle of ice. Mad or no, I had to sit back for a moment and savor the bite of it. Lil's cyberhootch tastes the same as the real thing, and it comes with the effect as well. There's also the advantage of there not being a hangover in a tanker load.

Lil resumed her seat and tucked her feet under her, studying me with calm expectance. I took another hit of my drink and got down to it. "How long have you known that the Hindi Confederacy was backstopping that jacker ring?"

"Oh, we've suspected for about eight months," she replied promptly. "We've known for certain for four. Intelligence Division has been tracking the appearance of the stolen swing tech within the Hindi export pool. It wasn't very prudent of them to start doling those new processes out to their industrial combines so soon. The smart move would have been to sit on the material until things cooled off, but I suppose they were feeling pressure to produce results."

"Poor them," I commented.

She nodded. "That is much of their problem. The Hindi Confederacy has the world's largest population and an entrenched theocracy that fights stabilization measures tooth and nail. Their natural resources are drained and their tech levels are lagging because they don't have the capital to invest in adequate R&D."

"So they decide to take some economic short cuts by putting a tech-jacking crew on retainer?"

"More than that," Lil replied. "This industrial espionage operation was totally the creation of the Hindi Confederacy's Ministry of Intelligence. Foreign nationals were hired to make the actual acquisitions but the operations were directed by the Hindis. Mr. Sine was the senior cis-Lunar field controller."

"It sounds like UNILAW had a pretty solid handle on the situation."

She shrugged gracefully. "The Hindis weren't quite as clever as they thought they were."

"That being the case, THEN WHY WAS I SENT IN THERE STUPID?"

My explosion didn't even ruffle her hair. "Let's say I didn't want to jiggle your elbow."

"That doesn't reach me, Lil."

Lilith paused to take a long sip from a glass of sparkling water that hadn't been there a second ago. It was a pure marfi move on her part. Cybers don't get thirsty. But it was an effective stall if you wanted to derail the linear flow of somebody's anger.

"Then let's say," she continued, "that I needed a certain effect for this operation and I relayed to you all of the information I felt that you needed to produce that effect."

"And what effect was that?"

"I needed a brick hurled through a stained-glass window."

"And Lobo and I were the brick?"

"You make a very good one, Gain. You are not readily intimidated by bureaucracy and regulation, you are not above using atypical methods, and once your jaws are locked on a situation, you don't let go.

"Consider the reports I'm receiving from the Maya High platform: security personnel hospitalized, station damage from an unauthorized launch, a wild chase down into the fringes of the Earth's atmosphere, all climaxing in the destruction of the fleeing spacecraft. That's a very well-broken window."

To say that I was somewhat nonplused is an understatement. "Normally, I get called on my lack of diplomacy."

She lifted an eyebrow. "If I had wanted diplomacy I would have sent in a diplomat. Or I would have given you and Lobo a more extensive briefing on the situation. The two of you can be subtle enough when you put your minds to it. But I didn't want subtle. I wanted a nice, big, stinking mess. Which you most capably provided."

"Thank you, I think." My mad was getting undercut by intrigued. When she gets going, this little block of crystal can make Machiavelli look like a Sunday School teacher. "What was this mess in honor of?"

"You know as well as I do the unspoken protocols that UNILAW operates under. We're expected to provide law enforcement and security for cis-Lunar society in the name of the United Nations. And yet, should that responsibility lead us to discover that any of our employers are behind an infraction, it is expected of us to turn something of a blind eye on the situation. So, to produce anything close to real justice, we sometimes have to be creative."

"As in creative mess creation."

Lil nodded. "A controlled escalation of the situation to the point where it no longer can be concealed. Thanks to your actions, what had been a simple case of industrial espionage is now heavy flash. The global media is converging on the story even as we speak, and the Hindi Confederacy is frantically trying to dismantle their jacking ring and sweep the remnants under the carpet."

"So we've busted 'em."

Lil shifted on the couch, tucking her knees up under her chin, her silken gown flowing. "Not in the conventional sense. I doubt that any of the real ringleaders will ever stand trial, although the Hindis might try to increase their overall deniability by throwing a few of the mid-echelons, like Sine, into the fire.

"The real effect will be on a more subtle level. The bright young things who thought up this project have had their careers within the Hindi civil service ruined. A number of the corporates who sold out to the jackers will also likely be revealed during the investigation and they will be ruined as well.

"The corporations that were marauded will also likely

launch both civil suits and economic retaliation against the Confederacy. In short, it's probably going to be a long time before the Hindis try so flagrant a stunt again. Hopefully, other governments will be discouraged from attempting anything similar as well. It was as good an outcome as we could get."

"And what about that sled pilot that I burned?"

"I regret that, Gain, I truly do. But bugs get squashed in avalanches. Besides, the media is like a school of sharks; you have to put a little blood in the water to get them excited."

"Which I got to provide. . . ." I slammed my glass down on the marble top of the end table and it shattered on impact, the crystal shards not cutting my fingers. Sourly, I looked across from the handful of wreckage to my case officer.

"Lil, quit trying to divert me and let me get my bitch out!"

"Sorry," she said meekly. The glass reformed itself in my hand with an audible "twink" and, with exaggerated care, I set it on the table.

"As I was saying," I continued. "You set me up to burn that guy."

She shook her head emphatically. "Gain, I issued you no orders on how to handle that pursuit. I never interfere with your tactical handling of a field situation, you know that."

"No, but you sure maneuvered me into a situation where I didn't have much choice!"

"You had a fleeing felon on the verge of escape," she insisted. "To prevent that escape, you had to exercise lethal force. It's a common situation in law enforcement. You've had to deal with it before."

"Yeah, but you knew that I wouldn't back off! You used me, Lil!"

"Of course I used you." She met my gaze levelly out of those cool gray eyes. "Just as I've used you before. Just as I use every Free Marshal assigned to me. You are part of the tool kit I have available to try and mend some of the ills of society, and I will continue to use you in whatever manner I see fit for as long as you are with the Authority."

As had happened in the past I momentarily felt the chill brush of something bigger than myself or the job. Lilith is my case officer and comrade. But she's also more. More, I suspect, than even I suspect. There are some odd rumors about her, almost legends, drifting around. Some of the whispers hinting that just maybe Lilith was the first one to cross the line. The first cyber being to open her eyes on the universe and say, *"I am not a machine. I am me!"*

She's never said so in my presence. But I wonder about the name she's chosen for herself.

But one thing is certain. When she is right about something, she's right.

"Okay," I gave it up, "just as long as we both own up to it. Now get me another shot of your damn nonexistent brandy."

Lil smiled and instead of simply programming the drink into existence, she rose and went to the patio's wetbar to build it herself. It was gesture, something like Bo's *mano a mano* farewell tonight. For the moment, she was setting aside omnipotence as a kind of apology for the stinkin' end of the job that she had to uphold.

She returned with the Goldendale and she sat down next to me, just close enough for the curve of her thigh to lightly brush mine. Then we just sat for awhile and watched the sky glow fade beyond the row of cottonwoods. She was doing a really beautiful job of it tonight, an artist with a whole living universe as a canvas. Eventually I felt the soft, warm attention-asking dab of her tongue against my cheek.

"Do you really feel all that used, Gain?" she inquired.

"Oh, not really. Like you said, its all part of the package.

Heya, sweet one, you know me. I have to vent my tanks every now and again or I'll blow out."

"I do know. Intensity. I like it very much. I was just thinking that turnabout is fair play. If I've used you, then by rights, you should have the opportunity to use me."

I shot a sideways look at her. Lil had gathered herself up on the couch and was kneeling on the cushions, amused expectancy in her eyes like a going-on-sixteen cheerleader seducing her first slideball player.

"What do you have in mind?" I asked, growing a little expectant myself.

"Well, first of all, do you want to get rid of my dress or should I?"

"Lose it."

Her gown shimmered out of existence, baring honey-golden perfection.

"Now my shoes. Go or stay?"

Hm, I judged, neat little white stiletto heels like you never see off-planet. "Oh, keep them for awhile."

"Any accessories? Lingerie? Jewelry?"

"Not . . . really needed."

"How about attitude for the night? Aggressive? Challenging? Pliant?"

"Lil. Kill the checklist and come here."

Mention that you've taken a cyber lover to your average unenlightened meatball and you'll likely get a faint look of revulsion mixed with a dirty leer of expectation along with the inevitable statement of, "But that's not really . . . real?"

Well, guess what, it is "real." Those teeth that lightly rake my shoulder are "real." The vibrant body that arcs beneath mine is "real." The things that we say to each other in the warm darkness are "real."

What is reality? How do you perceive it?

Essentially for you, it's the sequential firing of electro-chemical neural receptors. Just now, for us, it's an electron storm sleeting through a crystalline cybermatrix.

Which is superior? Who can say? Tao is polyvalent.

Given that, even I have my questions now and again.

"Lil, can I ask you something?" I inquired, playing with a few silky hair strands.

"Hm?"

"How in the heck can a cyber have an orgasm?"

She chuckled softly and shifted around on the black satin sheets. After we had exhausted the possibilities of both the lawn couch and the lawn itself, she'd put us through a smooth segue transition into her bedroom.

"You ought to know by now, my love."

"No, I'm genuinely curious about this. I know that most cyber beings emulate human emotion and that you can enjoy physical sensation. But there are biological factors involved that you guys plain don't have. So, sweet one, tell me how do you go about synthesizing a climax?"

"You don't." She flumped over onto my chest so she could look down into my face. "To synthesize something, you first have to analyze it, and analyzing an orgasm is like analyzing a rainbow; it takes all of the joy out of the experience."

"So just what do you do to make the angels sing?"

"Actually we don't have a climax. We have yours."

"Oh?"

"That's why truly sharing a sexual experience can only take place between a human and cyber when the human is jacked into a neurolink." She reached up and tapped my temple with one sharp nailed fingertip. "We access the human pleasure centers and ride the experience. It's a simple feedback loop; the better time you have, the better time we have."

And she could provide a very good time indeed. I slid a hand down her spine and cupped a velvety smooth bottom.

"But just what is it that you like about it?"

"Intense physical experience, my love. We cyber beings process the input from the physical world so rapidly that we are frequently starved for simple physical sensation. Compounding the problem is that even the most sophisticated of electronic sensor systems provide only a murky approximation of the finely tuned data flow from your marvelously evolved human senses. For a cyber, accessing and sharing intense human sensual experience is like you putting Tabasco sauce on your food. It's intensely stimulating. It is, for lack of a better term, orgasmic."

"I'll be damned," I mused. "No wonder Bo maintains a harem."

Lilith chuckled again and draped herself more fully across me. She'd backed off her apparent weight to the point that having her use you for a mattress was a pleasure. "You'd better get some rest. You've got another operation coming up tomorrow."

"That's a fast turnaround?"

"I'm sorry," she said sleepily, "but it's a priority job that I had you slotted for before this other priority job came up. We can talk about it in the morning."

"Okay, sweet one. In the morning."

She kissed the curve of my neck and then rested her head on my chest. Her eyes were closed and soon her breathing began to slow. It was another bit of sophistry on her part. Just as they don't eat and drink, cybers don't sleep. In all probability, ninety percent of her faculties were off somewhere else tasking within the cybernet. But Lil was lady enough to hang around and keep me company until I dropped off. I'd wake up on my own pad tomorrow, suffering from the after effects of a catastrophic wet dream but otherwise all the better for this night. For now though, I gently stroked the silky mop of Lilith's hair and watched her made-up constellations shine through the open balcony doors.

Chapter 4

I had breakfast at Johnny the Greek's place at the foot of Spoke Four. That's the same "Watch the Worlds go by Johnny's" you see promo-windowing on the travel nets. As a result, Johnny gets a lot of tourist trade but I guess I can forgive him for that. His food's good, he has human waitresses, and I still get a kick out of the view.

Some of the restaurant's tables are set out on the top deck concourse and you can tilt your chair back and look up through the tempered glass plating of Dawn City's inner rim and watch the shipping dock at the hub ports. That morning I'd worked halfway through both a Belgian waffle and my new old magazine when Lobo dumped his displacement into the chair across from me.

"Morning, Boss. How's breathin'?"

"You'll never know," I replied. "What brings you off your grease rack so early in the watch?"

"Orders."

"Whose?"

"*Mine.*" Lil's thoughts slipped in through my link. "*Good morning, Gain. Did you have pleasant dreams?*"

"*I had a hard time telling where the dreams left off and you began, sweet one. What's doing?*"

"*That other priority operation I mentioned to you last night.*"

"*What's it involve?*" I replied, forking up another square of waffle. That's one of the minor advantages of neurolink technology; you can communicate and eat at the same time.

"Asteroid mining and we're not sure what all else. I hate having to send you and Lobo straight back out into the field without any rest, but we're running against major time restriction on this one."

"Don't sweat it. When do you want to brief?"

"Now, if possible. I'm currently with our liaison from the Johannesburg United Metals Combine and I'd like you to conference with us. Did Lobo bring an access pad with him?"

I refocused my attention back at my partner. "Heya, Tin Man," I verbalized. "I'm on the brain with our fearless leader. You got a pad on you?"

"Right here."

"Yeah, Lil. We'll be set up in a second."

"Very good. I'll be available through my standard code."

Bo flipped the access pad open and placed it in the center of the table. We could conference and image through the link, but accessing too many channels at once can give you a headache built for a horse.

As I slid my *Astounding* back into its protective envelope, I considered asteroid mining. The old-time science fiction writers knew we'd get around to it sooner or later. They were just a tad off on how we'd go about it. They visualized a kind of California Gold Rush with rocket propulsion. Long after they damn well should have known better, SF authors waxed eloquent about "hard-bitten miners ranging the wastes of the asteroid belt in pursuit of the big strike" and their "tough, freedom-loving families building a new civilization on the High Frontier." Some of them seemed to get so gone on the subject that they were practically putting spacesuits on prospectors' burros.

As usual, reality turned out to be far more mundane. Projecting and maintaining a life support base in the asteroid belt would be so expensive that mining operations wouldn't pay even if the involved rocks were solid sapphire with ruby frosting.

Instead of going out to the ore fields, real asteroid miners bring the ore fields in to them.

Prospectors were launched out into the belt. No "hard-bitten," etc., etc., etc., however. These prospectors were robotic space probes equipped with a long-duration ion drive. On flight plans that might last for twenty years, they cruised the fifth orbital zone systematically scanning asteroids for size, symmetry, and suitable mineral content.

Once a good rock was located and its orbit charted, a mass-driver tug was dispatched to make intercept. This huge automated hauler would proceed out to the belt, dock with the target asteroid, and drag it back to Earth orbit by brute force, using the asteroid's own material as reaction mass. The whole operation might take a period of years but the end result would be multi-megatons of high-grade nickel-iron ore, ready to be fed into cis-Lunar industry. The industrial clusters at L-2 and L-4 already have mining asteroids at their core and the demand for materials kept growing steadily. As the poet said, "Iron, cold iron, is master of them all."

Asteroid mining is big business in all ways: big in scope, big in capital investment, and big in profits. It also might be assumed that any problems they might be having would be big as well.

Bo tapped Lil's number into the access pad's key strip and the unit's toothbrush-sized scanner head popped up.

"All right, gentlemen," our case officer's voice came out of the empty air over the table. "I'd like you to meet Ms. Nell Rainey from Johannesburg United Metals."

A holographic image materialized on the glassy surface of the access plate. The lady's appearance shot down another popular misconception, the one about miners being large, over-muscled, and hairy-eared types. Nell Rainey was small. Small, neat, and trim with a sun gold spacer's ponytail snubbed off almost as short as my own. It was sort of hard to tell, given the doll-sized scale of her image, but I thought I sensed a dusting of freckles across the bridge of her minute, well shaped nose.

She was wearing a readily shedable white jacket and short, wrap-around skirt over a pearlecent gray suit liner and a pair of Velcro-soled softboots. A sensible rig for a moderately well-to-do spacewoman who might have to flip-flop rapidly between an executive board room and vacuum armor. She was seated in an upper-mid-level-general-bureaucracy-issue chair that marked her as being in one of the conference rooms in UNILAW's Dawn City Headquarters.

"Ms. Rainey, may I present Free Marshals Gain Chandry and Lobo. They will be the officers directly assigned to your case."

The lady soberly nodded in the direction of what must have been our images.

"Marshal Chandry, Marshal Lobo. I'm very pleased to meet you both." It was a good voice, a level and sure alto.

"Pleased to meet you as well, Ms. Rainey," I replied. *"Okay Lil, what's the word on this lady?"*

"Nell no-middle-initial Rainey. Age twenty-eight. Born in Cape Town, Union of Greater South Africa. Studied at both the Helena School of Mining in the United States of North America and at Armstrong University on Luna. Degrees in geology and zero-gee engineering. Currently employed by Johannesburg United as a field geologist and projects officer. A very bright young lady, Gain."

"Indeed."

"Ms. Rainey," Lil said, going vocal through the access board's speakers. "What I'd like for you to do is to help me bring your team up to speed on your company's problem."

"I'll be happy to be of what help I can. But as I said, we don't have very much to go on ourselves." The Joburg rep crossed her shapely legs and sat back in her seat. "Truth be, we're not even sure that we have a problem."

"How's that?" I inquired.

"Here's the situation, Marshal. In approximately one week, Joburg United will be bringing a major new project to fruition. One of our tugs, the MD-24, will be bringing a very special new asteroid into Earth orbit. We're afraid that someone may be planning to sabotage the operation."

"What's so special about this particular rock?" I inquired.

"Well, for one, Cibola isn't a belt asteroid, she's a cometary."

"You mean like what the Nemesis Watch monitors?"

"That's right."

Nell Rainey's mini-image blinked off the access pad and a neat little holograph of the solar system took her place a moment later, hovering over the projection surface. The Sun was a glowing marble at its center and the planets were singular beads strung on the thread loops of their orbits. Another sharply elliptical orbit was delineated in red, swinging inward inside of Mercury's path and then out again beyond Jupiter.

"As you can see," Rainey continued, "Cibola doesn't stay in the belt. She's a rogue in an elliptical orbit that takes her between the inner and outer systems on about a seven-year cycle."

"I didn't think you guys went after cometaries," I commented.

"This is a first, and we have a special reason for it. About three years ago, as Cibola crossed the belt, one of our company astrographers, Dr. Teague Nolan, noted that some of the other asteroids Cibola transited past had undergone a series of micro-orbital deviations, more so than a standard degree of gravitational attraction would account for. Upon further analysis, he came to the conclusion that Cibola has considerably more mass than your typical chunk of nickel-iron."

Bo suddenly produced a Cheshire-grade grin. "You guys caught a noble rock!" he exclaimed.

"Nemanahe," her disembodied voice agreed, "just so. We think that Cibola contains a very high concentration of the noble metals, gold and silver, possibly platinum and iridium. Enough so that we can expect a considerable jump in our profit margin over a standard rock. That's how she got her house name."

"Cibola, as in seven cities of?"

"Exactly, Marshal."

"How big of a profit jump are we talking about here?" I continued.

"We can't put an exact decimal place to it yet. None of our prospectors were in position to do a survey. We're operating solely on Dr. Nolan's figures. However, they looked sound enough for our board of directors to commit our company's newest and largest mass driver tug to an intercept."

"That sounds like something of a blind-shot gamble."

"All mining is a gamble to some extent, Marshal," the company woman agreed. "But if this pays off, it's going to pay big. You see, the asteroid belt can provide us with an unlimited amount of ferrous metals and we can get all of the titanium and aluminum we want from the Moon. But we still have to ship all of the gold and silver we use in our electronics and nucleonics industries up from Earth. Given its weight, that can be expensive. And even though it's not used to back currency anymore, the available stocks aren't unlimited. The company that can produce a new source of nobles in orbit is going to make a major killing."

"I can see how you would." I took a quick swallow of coffee. "How did the mission fly?"

"Initially quite well," Rainey continued. "The MD-24 was launched in a pursuit trajectory after Cibola. . . . A new orbital track appeared in the system model, a golden thread that arced out from a point on Earth's orbit to intersect with Cibola's path. . . . She successfully made intercept with Cibola and at orbital perihelion, she commenced a braking maneuver that would bring the asteroid into orbit within the Earth-Moon confluence."

The red and gold trajectories merged into an orange line that whipped around the Sun-marble and curved in to touch the blue Earth-bead.

"But then," I prompted.

"But then someone started to pay an unhealthy degree of interest in our rock."

"Define 'unhealthy.' "

"Here is an example, Gain," Lilith interjected.

The system model disappeared from over the surface of the access pad, to be replaced by glowing strings of letters.

DOOM DRAWS NIGH! THE GOLDEN HAND OF GOD IS POISED TO SMITE THE BLASPHEMER AND NONBELIEVER! IT IS THE END OF ALL FOR ALL WHO DO NOT BELIEVE! CIBOLA SHALL BE THE AVENGER! BLESSED BE CIBOLA!

"Lousy scriptwriting," Bo critiqued.

"Hundreds of inserts like this have started to pop up in public access and commercial use files throughout the cis-

Lunar net," Lil continued. "Our anti-hackers believe it to be a random-generation message program packaged as a timed-release spore virus. You understand the nature of the beast?"

"Sure," I replied. "You dump the spore into the data stream of your choice and it will free-roam along with the valid traffic, replicating itself whenever it enters a suitable hard system. Then every once and a while, a spore will blossom and introduce a randomized variant of its core message into the stream. They're a pretty sophisticated program to put together."

"Very much so," Lil agreed. "When designed correctly they are almost impossible to backtrack to a point of origin. This one was designed correctly. What do you think?"

"I think that if this is all you've got, all we've got is a prankster or a socio-religious nut case with too many cyber skills for his own good."

"There's more." Nell Rainey's hologram reappeared on the surface of the access plate. "To the population at large the asteroid we have under tow is known only by a catalog number. Cibola is our house name for the project and no one outside of the company should know it. Because of that we brought in the security firm of Kent and Verrick to do an access audit of our primary computer systems."

"They're a good outfit," I commented, nudging the table's spice server aside to get a better look at the holo.

The sleek little image nodded. "Yes and they found that we were tight except for one aberration, a series of minute time-log variants on one particular file. Their evaluation is that for the last six months someone has been penetrating our system, accessing that particular file, and then carefully attempting to erase the evidence of the access."

I asked the obvious. "What was in the file?"

"All of the navigational data downloads on the Cibola/MD-24 combine."

The statement hovered in the middle of the table for a long moment, too heavy to disperse right away. It brought to mind all sorts of interesting images: a desperate government that might look upon a flying mountain as a cheap alternative to an orbital weapons arsenal. A terrorist outfit looking for the ultimate boot to put on the neck of society. Or maybe just some pious individuals who thought that maybe the Supreme Commander was dragging his feet a little when it came to declaring Judgment Day.

"How good a screen do you maintain around your systems?" I asked.

"First rate," the lady miner replied. "Joburg United has the state of the art in commercial protection. Overwatch grids, infinite random variable coding, roving hunter-killer programs, the best package on the market. Whoever invaded our net must have been a royalty grade hacker. He ghosted right through all of our lockouts as if they didn't exist."

I nodded to the doll-woman on my table. "You got a problem. What are you doing about it?"

"Everything we can think of. Inserting asteroids into Earth orbit is high-risk macro-engineering. We can't afford to take any chances at all. We're totally revamping our security setup and we've isolated the Cibola projects block with as many man-breaks as possible. We're also putting a team on Cibola itself to monitor the final phase of the orbital approach and rendezvous. Just in case there is a need to go hands-on."

"Interpol has been alerted," Lil interjected, "and we are in communication with the security agencies of all of the major supra-nations. All known terrorist organizations and quasi-religious radicalist groups are being placed under increased surveillance. We're also increasing our spot checks on surface-to-orbit passenger service as well as initiating anti-virus and anti-hacker sweeps within the general access info and communications nets. In addition, cis-Lunar Traffic Control has made the Cibola/MD-24 combine a tracking priority and the UNSDF has been advised of a possible Nemesis event."

Nemesis, to the uninitiated, was what the science Johnnys ended up calling the rock that smacked Earth some umpty-five million years ago, simultaneously creating both the Caribbean ocean basin and the mass extinction that put the dinosaurs out of business.

Part of the charter of our sister service, the UN Space Defense Force, is to maintain a sufficient base of fusion firepower to destroy or divert any errant asteroid or comet that might try and repeat the process on the human race. Even a near miss was something to be avoided. A multi-gagaton wanderer plowing through the heavily traveled orbits of cis-Lunar could be a catastrophe in its own right.

"Okay, Lil. What's our part of the deal?"

"I want to put you and Lobo out on Cibola itself."

"And the mission intent?"

"Maintain on-site security and stand by to cope with any untoward events, operating on the assumption that someone, somewhere, is planning to somehow interfere with the Cibola-Earth rendezvous. This may not be the case at all. This could still be a hoax or a propaganda ploy of some nature but, as Ms. Rainey indicated, we can't take any chances."

The mentioned lady looked somber. "Just what's happened so far has made the UN Space Safety Commission leery. If a real situation develops, we could get our authorization pulled. That would mean having to dump the rock and aborting the rendezvous. That could cost Joburg United billions."

"What all would we have to cover out there?"

"The MD stack of course," she replied. "Then there'll be the towboat and survey barge combine we're sending out. It launched out of our L-2 facility and it should be touching down on Cibola within the next few hours. The team on board is led by Dr. Nolan and includes his wife Rana; she's another of our company astrographers. There's also one of our field engineers, Gavin Wilcox, and the two-person towboat crew." Ms. Rainey's image looked up at me. "It was supposed to include me as well, but I held over here at Dawn City to consult with the authorities. I was wondering if I could hitch a lift out with you?"

I hesitated for a second to see if I heard any objections, either verbally or over the neurolink. When none came, I gave an agreeing nod. "No problem. Glad to have you aboard."

And I was. Not only would she provide me with a good data source for the flight out, but Ms. Nell Rainey seemed like good potential company and she did thought-provoking things to a spacesuit liner.

"When can you move out, Gain?" Lil inquired.

"Bo?" I passed the inquiry on to my partner.

"All primary servicing programs have been completed on the mainframe," my partner replied. "For this deep a run, I'm going to need to mount and top-off a set of ferry tanks and I'd like to draw and load a little extra just-in-case ordinance. Give me two hours. Oh yeah, and if we're going to execute a rapid transit flight plan, I'd like for a yard tug to give us a shove. That'll help to put us on station with the primary tankage still full."

"Ms. Rainey?"

"I just have to collect my kit bag and suit, Marshal, and I'll be ready to go."

"Fine, T minus two hours it is. And Ms. Rainey, if we're

shipping together, it's Bo and Gain. It just works better that way."

She gave me a quick flash of smile. "Then call me Nell. That works better too."

The briefing broke and all the involved parties got on about their business. As Lobo and I crossed the concourse to the four-spoke elevator bank, I found myself compelled to ask a certain question.

"Bo, let's say we bitch this job and some nasties end up dropping this rock on humanity. What are we looking at here? Night all?"

"As in the end of the world?" He considered for a second, crunching numbers at full cyberspeed. "Nah, I don't compute it as coming to that. This rock's too small and the potential kinetic energy involved is too low. This sucker's on a convergent orbit and it's been braking steadily for better 'n six months. We couldn't get a full-blown Nemesis event out of it."

"So what could we get?"

He shrugged. "A lot would depend on the exact point of impact. For sure the global weather patterns would be shagged up for a couple of years. The continent that took the hit would be pretty well hashed. . . . Oh, I'd call it a quarter of a billion casualties, give or take a few hundred thousand."

"Well, Tao. That's hardly worth paying attention to."

Chapter 5

One hour later, we had a full load of life support consumables on board. We were maxed-out on fuel with Bo's mainframe studded with four massive drop tanks. We had a tug standing by to give us a bonus velocity boost on launch. We had ordnance, eatin', and all of the other odds and ends necessary for a deep space mission.

What we didn't have was a passenger.

"Heya, Boss," Bo said reproachfully through the control sphere speakers. "We're ten plus on our departure time and the Port Master is having a hemorrhage. When are we going to get out of here?"

"Don't ask me," I replied, tilting the pilot's chair back. "Any sign of Rainey dockside?"

"Not that I can see. A couple of lock dogs delivered her spacesuit awhile back but no sign of the lady."

"Ah, Tao and a half entirely. Get me the Port Security Office."

"You got it."

A communications window opened up on the surface of the surround-screen and filled with the disinterested face of the watch officer.

"This is Marshal Gain Chandry aboard UNILAW GC slash L. I'm expecting a passenger here presently, a Ms. Nell Rainey from Johannesburg United Metals. Is she hung up at one of your checkpoints?"

"Ahh . . . negative on that, Marshal Chandry. I'm not

showing anything about her on my screens."

"Thanks, Lieutenant."

He windowed out.

Somewhere in the back of my brain, a little yellow light went on. I didn't know all that much about Nell Rainey but I was willing to put cash on the probability that she wasn't late for many space ships.

"Bo, access the station com net and give our Ms. Rainey a buzz."

"Rajah."

I rapped my fingertips on the chair arm and counted off twenty-two seconds.

"Uh, Boss. She's not answering. Directory services indicates that her phone isn't active."

That little light went red. If she was at all like any of the other corporates I knew, she'd rather sacrifice a major organ than have her communications cut off.

"Bo, what hotel was Ms. Rainey staying at?"

"The High Concourse Hyatt."

"Get me the front desk."

This time, the com window filled with a hotel logo and the voice that answered had the measured, artificial pleasantness of a service AI. "Good morning. This is the front desk. How may we help you?"

"This is UNILAW Free Marshal Gain Chandry and this is an official inquiry," I replied to the computer. "Do you have a Ms. Nell Rainey registered there?"

"I'm sorry, but Ms. Rainey checked out approximately forty-five minutes ago. May we be of further assistance?"

"Negative."

"Then have a nice day."

"Yeah, you too."

Forty-five minutes. Big as it is, no place on Dawn City is

more then twenty minutes away from anyplace else.

I reverted to my neurolink. *"Lil, we've got a problem here."*

"What is it, Gain?" she replied. *"Has there been a change of plan with the Cibola operation?"*

"No."

"I was about to contact you to see why you hadn't taken departure yet."

"It's because my miner forty-niner tra-la-la-la Clementine has disappeared on me. She checked out of her hotel three-quarters of an hour ago and she's out of communication at this time. Has she been in touch with you?"

"No, and I agree, we may have a problem. I am notifying station and port security."

"Right, and I'm getting out there too." I began shrugging out of the seat harness. "Bo, we're going into the field, but have the Port Master hold the mainframe as number one to launch."

"He ain't going to like it, Boss."

"We all have our problems. Meet me at the air lock."

I pushed aft, pausing at the gun safe to augment armament.

I already had my favorite carry, the little Ruger Starlite V firestorm, strapped to my right forearm. But now, I added a tactical belt studded with my "outside" gun, a big Norinco recoilless 10mm and a couple of spare barrel clusters. I also tucked a pair of combat gloves into an inside pocket. You never know when you might need that little something extra.

Bo's personal Ken was standing by at the outer air lock door. As usual, he wasn't carrying a gun. He preferred a pocketful of ball bearings as his primary personal armament. If that doesn't sound too impressive, then you've obviously never seen a human skull struck by a two-centimeter steel sphere thrown at two hundred and fifty meters per second.

"Let's go," I commanded.

Bo didn't ask where. He just dropped into his familiar flanking slot and followed.

At the moment, I wasn't too sure exactly where we were going myself. I was just drifting in towards where the action might be while I studied the developing situation.

"Gain, I've talked to Johannesburg United and they haven't heard from Ms. Rainey either," Lil reported. *"I have also checked with station security and emergency medical services and they don't have anything on her. I concur that we may have a possible hit or kidnapping underway."*

That being the case, there is one question you always have to ask whenever you're aboard a station or a ship. *"Lil, access Dawn City's operational logs for the past forty-five minutes and check for any unusual or unauthorized air lock usage."*

"Accessing . . . None recorded." That was something anyhow. Nell Rainey had been a pretty little person. I hadn't liked the visualization of her spewing boiling blood from all of her body orifices.

"How about ship departures?"

"None within the given timeframe."

Okay, then let's assume she's still inboard somewhere.

The key to a good search operation is to eliminate all of the places that you don't have to look before you actually start looking. As we cleared the checkpoint at the entryway to the Fleet Base, I realized that we could probably eliminate the hub section for a start. There was too damn much security around the ports for anyone to realistically hope to make a quiet and successful touch.

That left the rim and the spokes. I headed us down the slide rails towards the rotation transfer corridor. The habitation rim wasn't too likely either. Too damn crowded. Dawn City is a big place with a permanent population in excess of thirty thousand. But still, it's more like an Earthside village than a major metroplex. If somebody yells for help, people respond. If a struggle or anything else unusual takes place, people notice and do something about it. Spacers have to be that way. Ask not for whom the bell tolls, it tolls because there's a shaggin' pressure blow-out in the next frame and if we don't all hang together we could all end up breathing vacuum. That left the spokes. Above and beyond the elevator cores, a lot of the station's secondary systems are strung out along them. Sewage and water treatment, air revitalization, storage and consumables; lots and lots of little service decks and bays, all heavily automated and all seldom visited.

We reached the transfer corridor and stepped across the red warning line from the fixed hub section to the rotating spoke collar, swaying a little with the first tug of centrifugal force. For some reason, people seemed to be scrambling to get out of our way. I guess they must have thought that we were going somewhere important.

Now, let's work on this spoke premise. Where could I best put the bag on someone if I wanted to take advantage of all of those lovely hiding places? At the foot of the spoke of course, right at the elevator banks. Right where you could whip your victim up and out of sight in a hurry. Which one though?

"Lil, give me a map of the promenade deck, showing the location of both the hotel Ms. Rainey was staying at and all the spoke bases."

I paused for a second as the required map materialized in front of my mind's eye, the requested locations clearly outlined. Spoke Two was the closest to the Hyatt. That would have been the logical one for our lady to use. I started moving again, aiming for the same place.

"Lil, have station security start checking around the base of

Spoke Two. See if anyone suspicious has been seen hanging around down there."

"Acknowledged."

Now that we had what we thought was the right spoke, how'd they get up into it? Dragging either an inert or a resisting body up a narrow emergency access ladder wasn't too likely. They must have used an elevator.

But not any of the big passenger or cargo lifts. Those were all expresses, running straight between hub and rim. Stopping one of them on a spoke level would set off alarms in both security and maintenance. That left the smaller service lifts. They all had card locks on them to prevent their use by anyone but authorized station personnel. But I knew that there were a lot of extra key cards drifting around out there.

"Lil, access the station logs again. Cross-reference service lift activity with any scheduled maintenance for the Spoke Two subsystems. Within the last forty-five minutes, have any of the service lifts stopped on any decks where maintenance was not scheduled?"

"Three stops listed within your parameters, Gain. Decks two oh two, sixty-nine, and seven."

"Right. Stay with me, Lil. We're closing in on them." We reached the elevator head and went for one of the service lifts. I pulled one of those drifting key cards out of my jacket pocket and flipped it against the reader plate.

"Get that golden nose of yours ready, Bo. We're going bird dogging."

We tagged them on level sixty-nine. I covered Lobo as he circled the small maintenance vestibule beyond the elevator doors, sniffing the air suspiciously like one of his four-footed namesakes.

When you see or hear a Ken or Barbie "breathe," it's not all just for show. They're getting rid of the waste heat from their systems by using a set of internal bellows to draw air over a radiator. In Bo's case, he was also drawing air over a set of sophisticated atmospheric chemo-sensors.

"Four, maybe five of them," he murmured. "A short time ago . . . one of them a young female . . . Yardley body shampoo and bath powder, and she uses a Jezelle Gamin Mist cologne brush on her hair . . ."

"That sounds about right," I commented, panning the quad-muzzles of the Norinco across the dimly lit mouths of the side corridors. "I think we found our baby."

"Yeah," he agreed. "Especially since I'm getting a real strong fear smell in here."

"Can you track it?"

"No, the ventilators are spreading it all throughout this level."

"Lil," I thought. *"We think we're on to something on sixty-nine. Are there any security sensors up here?"*

"Negative," she replied, *"fire, leak and pressure-loss only."*

"Okay, then I guess we go looking ourselves."

"Do you desire backup?"

"Not yet, Lil. Just cut all elevator service to this level and seal all access hatches to levels sixty-eight and seventy."

"Done."

I slid the Norinco back into its holster for a second and pulled on the pair of armorel combat gloves. I also closed the front seal of my jacket and flipped up the collar to protect the back of my neck. Across from me, Bo went through the same cladding-on-of-armor ritual.

"We're non-verbal from here on out, Bo."

"Rajah. You want right or left?"

I jigged on my feet a little, getting the feel of the gravity and corolus effect on this level. *"I'll go left. I've got a hunch on who these guys might be, and I think we can take them alive. Let's stay non-lethal if possible."*

"Ah, you're no fun anymore. Break a leg, Boss."

"Burn out a resistor, pal."

We moved out, counter-circling through the tight maze of curving passageways. Lil was feeding us a gridded mental deckplan of our surroundings and Bo and I called it off as we moved.

"Corridor one, frame three, clear."

"Corridor one. frame twenty-four, clear."

"Compartment nineteen left, clear."

We were alone on that deck. Or at least just us and the bad guys. But there was activity, sound, movement, scent. The living guts of the habituate station. The soft roaring of air in a duct. The vibration of a heavy fluid pump. A faint foulness leaking from a sewage junction. You had to try and push your senses out beyond all that to seek out sign of the enemy.

"Corridor one, frame nine, clear."

"Compartment thirty-three right, clear."

"Moving on to corridor two, outboard."

I hugged in close to the dull green bulkheads, taking what advantage I could from the low-light shadows. For the ten-thousandth time I had to admire the old-time law dogs who had to go into situations like this really alone. My partner was only a thought away and Lil was closer than that. I could feel her presence through the neurolink, peering out through my eyes, listening though my ears, ready to call a warning or the cavalry if needed. A guardian angel perched on your shoulder is a damned nice accessory to have at a time like this.

"Corridor two, frame twelve, clear."

"Corridor one, frame thirty, clear."

"Compartment forty-one le . . ."

The door lever I was reaching for lifted before I could touch it.

"Contact!"

I slammed the pocket-panel door open, startling all Tao out of the individual on the other side. I took in the split-second image of a garish suit liner no real spacer would be caught dead in, a pigtail braided in copper wire, and a blank, juvenile face. With my expectations met, I reacted, driving the muzzles of my Norinco into his gut with all of my strength.

He gagged and buckled over and I completed the job with a short chop across the back of his skull with the heavy vacuum-proofed butt of the pistol. I couldn't wait for him to finish falling over on his own, so I shoved him aside and charged into the compartment.

There were three others in the locker-lined space, all marked with the same youth-culture conformity. They all started to move as I burst in on them, one bolting for the farside hatchway and escape, the other two coming in my direction.

"Bo, you got one going around your way; intercept!"

My lead attacker fancied himself as a Kung Fu man and came off the deck to launch a flying kick at my throat. Unfortunately for him, the idiot forgot to compensate for the fact that we were half-way up the spoke. In the reduced-gee environment, his kick carried him almost to the ceiling. I ducked under it and clubbed him aside with a sweep of my forearm, the Starlite weapons module I had strapped to it adding to the impact. He piled into the bulkhead behind me with a considerable crash.

Attacker number two was a good old-fashioned boy. He lunged at me with a length of pipe upraised over his head, intent on busting in mine. I parried with my forearm again, taking the hit. The kinetic energy of the blow triggered the armorel smart fabric of my jacket sleeve and it went rigid for an instant, deflecting the pipe with no more damage than a

burst of pain and the promise of a pretty good bruise. I replied with a knee to the groin, bouncing him off me for a
second.

A hunk of pipe qualifies as an official deadly weapon, and
at that moment I had an open card to shoot the little slimer. I
didn't want to be bothered with the paperwork though.

Attacker number one was struggling to get up, so I threw
the Norinco at him to keep him diverted for the few seconds
I'd need to finish number two.

I moved in again on the pipe swinger. As he lifted his
weapon for another go at head busting, he left himself wide
open. I fired a right cross at his jaw and I felt bone give and
teeth break, my armorel gloves being a vast improvement
over the old-time brass knuckles. He started to haze out and I
gently lifted his club out of his hand.

Whipping it around into a two-handed horizontal hold, I
gave him a couple of finishing shots, one across the forehead
and one across the breastbone. No longer operational, he
sagged to the deck. One left, and that guy was up on his knees,
leveling my own gun at me and squeezing the firing stud.

Of course the Norinco's internal safety didn't recognize
the hand holding its grip, and thus all he was getting out of
the deal was a series of dry clicks. I went over to the kid,
kicked him in the face, just once, very hard, and reclaimed my
property.

Bo appeared at the rear door, shoving another terrified
teenager ahead of him. "Heya greedy-guts," he said. "I
thought you were going to give me even divvies."

I shrugged. "What can I say, they were impatient."

My partner looked around at the biological wreckage scattered around room. "Boss, I sure hope these guys are who we
think they are. 'Cause if they're not, we're probably really
going to get yelled at."

Bo needn't have worried. We found Nell Rainey trussed up in one of the big wall lockers. She was totally zeroed out and her wrists and ankles had been sloppily taped together. Her jacket was also wadded up in one corner of the locker and her suit liner had been peeled down to her waist, leaving her bare-backed and bare-breasted. A row of dermal absorption patches charged with a potent over-the-counter sleep inducer had been plastered down her spine. Easing her out onto the deck, I peeled the patches off and scrubbed what drug residue I could from her skin with my sleeve. Her pulse was slow but regular and when I checked her eyes with a pocket light, I found them dilated but even. She also moaned softly as I lifted her eyelids. She wasn't down too deep. With as much detachment as I could muster while cradling an attractive, semi-nude, and semi-conscious female, I gently re-sheathed her in her liner and ran the seal back up.

"Bo, take over here. Give the lady a thermographic scan for concussion and access a medical data base for information on . . ." I checked the active compound on one of the dermal patches. ". . . Lipinol B overdoses and the treatment of same."

"Okay but wouldn't it be better to get her to medical services?"

I shook my head. "Not yet. Have you picked up a make on these guys?"

"Yeah, I've just been running a feed through Lil into the Dawn City citizens' files."

He pointed out our clients around the room. "Bleeding-heavily-through-the-nose over there is Kevin Chen. Curled-up-and-moaning-softly is Karo Malemba, and flat-on-his-back-and-oblivious is Richard Yager. And this sweet forget-me-not here is Norby Green. Say hello to the nice man, Norby."

Bo rattled an incoherent gurgle out of his prisoner.

"All of them are dependents of station personnel and all of them have infraction records not quite heavy enough to get them flushed dirtside."

Like I figured, typical station snotties; old enough to get into trouble but not old enough for the company to have sunk the responsibility hook of a high-paying job into them.

I got to my feet and took over with Mr. Green, shoving him back against the lockers and pinning him there with a forearm across his throat. It helps at times like this if they think that you might be just a little bit crazy.

"Hello, Norby," I said from a range of about ten millimeters. "I trust that you've noticed that no one has read you your rights yet. There's a reason for that. You see, I have two options involving you and your little slimer buddies.

"Option one. I can turn you over to station security. In which case, the company will probably just shrug their shoulders and ship you back to Earth at Daddy's expense.

"Option two. I can invoke the UN enforcement mandate and bring you crudballs up on charges that will include kidnapping, criminal conspiracy, felonious assault, resisting arrest, and assaulting a police officer. I'm not sure about attempted rape but, heya, we can give it the old college try.

"I can guarantee you, and I mean I . . . can . . . guarantee . . . you . . . a minimum of ten years on a desert reclamation gang in Central Africa. What I decide depends solely on how much you tell me, right now, about who got you to put the grab on this lady and why. You get one chance, one . . . chance, at this. Clear? Okay then, my little asshole, start shitting."

The snotty was so pale he looked a liter low on blood. He was just at that age when they think that nothing in the universe can touch them and he wasn't enjoying the fact that this assumption was turning out to be erroneous. Frantically he rolled his eyes, looking for someone, anyone, who could free him from this mess.

I leaned into his windpipe a little harder. "May I construe this hesitation as a desire for a long residence in a hot, dry climate?"

"No!" he strangled.

The gates opened wide.

"We got paid to do it! A thousand cash apiece! Half before and half after we did it!"

"Who bought you?" I demanded.

"We dunno. We never saw 'em. I swear! He contacted Kar through the infonet a couple of watches back. No access point listing. No name."

"You say he? Was it a male?"

"I dunno. We dunno. It was just copy on a screen and a printout of the spin's picture."

"Meat had to be there for the payoff!"

"No, he left cash under the hand wash in the 'fresher down at the Red Stripe Club. We never saw anybody!"

"What were you supposed to do for that cash?"

"Just put the spin under plastic for a few watches. We weren't gonna burn her or shag her. I swear it!"

I scowled. Tao take it all but I suspected that this patch of low-grade vacuum is telling the truth. I'm reading him as too scared and brainshort to lie effectively.

"Thanks." I unleaned and let the blubbing kid sink down to the deck. *"Lil, we can use that backup now."*

"Station security is enroute. A very swift and astute piece of police work, Gain."

"Yeah, for what it's worth, which isn't much. Buzz the Port Master for us, Lil, and make sure we're still clear for immediate departure."

"Done."

71

I turned back to where Bo was kneeling beside the unconscious girl. "How's she doing?"

"Thermoscan doesn't indicate a concussion or any major internal injuries," he replied, studying her in concern. "I think she's just zoney. The med base indicates that this Lipinol stuff is fairly safe even in overload dosages. She'll suffer lassitude and intermittent nausea for a couple of days but that should be it."

"Can she travel?"

"Rest and professional medical supervision is suggested, Boss."

"Bo, the question before the General Assembly is: Yes or no, can she travel?"

Bo wasn't happy with the answer he had to give. "Well, I guess she can." There isn't a single molecule of human DNA in Bo's physical structure but still the big lug can be one titanic bowl of mush when it comes to cute ladies and kids.

"Okay, then let's get her aboard the mainframe."

"What's the rush?" he protested.

"Somebody really is trying to jack around with this Cibola operation, Bo. Zero doubt. And, for some reason, they want to keep Ms. Rainey here from getting to her asteroid. Such being, I think it behooves us to get her to that rock just as fast as we can. Maybe that will bitch somebody's works."

He thought about it for a couple of picoseconds. "I'll buy that for a dollar," he agreed, scooping Nell Rainey effortlessly off the deck. Cradled in Bo's massive arms and with her head resting on his shoulder, she looked a lot more like a weary and ill-used child than she did a smart, young business exec.

The Dawn City security team appeared at the compartment door and their lead man raised his eyebrows at the carnage.

I nodded to him. "Hi, Sarge. All of these guys are yours to

keep and cherish. The charge is kidnapping plus a whole bunch of other stuff that I'll get around to telling you about as soon as I can get the reports filed. In the meantime, my partner and I are moving."

"Just a second, Marshal," the station cop protested. "You can't just walk away and leave us with this mess. We have to take these people back to HQ . . ."

"Sarge, let's break it here. The last guy I had this tedious conversation with is still in traction."

Chapter 6

We left Dawn City a shining star in our wake and blew past the Moon close enough to see both the lights of the farside colonies glowing on the surface and the space-born artificial constellation of foundries and shipyards out at LaGrange 2. Then, with Bo conducting intermittent engine burns to keep us tweaked into a rapid transit trajectory, we headed out into the double-dark beyond lunar orbit.

Not many manned ships get out this far. Just a scattering of deep probers and survey vessels and the big long-haul barge sticks that maintain the Mars and Venus science colonies. We were just dipping our toe into the edge of serious space, but still, it's something to be able to reach out to a view screen and cover your entire civilization with one hand.

The flight out gave us the chance to get to know Nell Rainey.

Well, maybe "get to know" is the wrong set of words, considering that the lady spent most of her time either laying around in a drugged torpor or being deathly ill. "Get comfortable with" might be a better term.

Medical caregivers are familiar with the phenomenon. A certain bond of intimacy forms between two people when one of them holds the other steady as they throw up everything they've eaten for the past six months.

Be that as it may, our lady miner wasn't really operational 'til morning watch of our fourth day out. I was having breakfast up front in the control sphere when Bo informed me that our passenger was up and around.

"Invite her forward."

"Okay, but it'll be a minute," he replied through his ship's speakers. "She's back aft in the 'fresher using the bath bag."

"How's she seem?"

"A little ganted up after the past couple of days but still toothsome. And a natural blonde."

"And how did you find that out, you warped and perverted block of cybernetics?"

"I didn't violate the lady's privacy if that is what you are insinuating," he replied loftily.

"Then how do you know for sure that she's a natural?" I insisted, enjoying our daily bout of hassletime. "The body stylists are getting very good at that kind of thing."

"I have powers far beyond those of mortal man, meatball. Out of pure scientific curiosity I shot a flash spectrograph of her hair. She's pure genetic gold right down to the follicle. Maybe a leedle bit of enhancer tint but not enough for the referees to call a penalty. Oops, here she comes." The entry hatch to the control sphere sliced open and Nell Rainey pushed through, looking seal-sleek in a fresh suit liner and trailing a thin, glinting haze of water droplets from her newly washed hair.

Bo had to be right. It had to be the genuine biological article. "Good morning, Ms. Rainey. In a mood for breakfast?"

"Much to my surprise, yes." She did a neat zero gee roll over the back of the copilot's chair. Settling into it, she tacked herself down with the seat belt. "After these last couple of days, I didn't think I'd ever want to see food again. What's being served?"

I rummaged around in the warmer bag I'd clipped to the arm of the pilot's seat.

"Well, we've got a couple of bacon bars, coffee with the accessories, and bagels."

"Bagels?"

"Tao yes, bagels, the Jewish culture's gastronomic gift to the spacefarer. They keep. They don't crumb worth mentioning, and they put up enough resistance so you actually think that you've had something to eat. Plain or with raisins?"

"Oh, I'll splurge," she dimpled. "Raisins."

I got the feeling that her standard settings were "happy" and "friendly."

We swapped grins and I started passing her rations.

"How soon will we be reaching Cibola?" she asked, popping the sweetener and creamer ampoules in her coffee pouch.

"We're on approach now. We'll be making rendezvous inside the hour."

"Is everything still going all right?"

"As far as anyone can tell," I replied. "UNILAW is maintaining open channels with both your people on Cibola and your corporate headquarters. To date, the pixies haven't put in any further appearances."

"Have they learned anything more about the people that kidnapped me?"

I shook my head. "No."

"Didn't they put them through, what do you call it, a memory survey?"

"That's the polite name for it," I replied. "Sure, they ran their cerebellums through the juicer, but nothing of interest drifted to the top. Those snotties that nailed you were nothing but very low-grade hired help. Whoever did the hiring was careful to put enough man-breaks between us and them to prevent a net backtrack. Dead lead."

"Damn," she shuddered lightly. "I wish something good could have come out of that experience."

"Something did," I replied. "We learned that we have a real problem with a real criminal conspiracy and not just a hyper-hacker with a perverse sense of humor. It's easier to fight a real enemy than the supposition."

"I'll take your word for it," she replied, dubiously eyeing her bagel. "I'd prefer that whoever it is would stay a supposition until we get Cibola into orbit."

I bit off a chunk of bacon. "We'll soon see if they'll be that obliging."

Breakfast was about gone when Bo heated up his overhead speakers. "We're going final on Cibola and we should be visual in another couple of minutes."

A glowing virtual reality warning basket appeared in the upper right quadrant of the surround screen, delineating a tube of apparently empty space.

"What's that designating?" Nell inquired.

"The exhaust plume from the MD, pretty lady," he replied. "We have to watch it or we could end up getting sandblasted to death."

"Mmmm," she nodded, "very valid point."

Valid indeed. Essentially a mass driver tug is gigantic linear accelerators that use the iron of the rocks they push around as reaction mass. Grinder heads sheer surface material off the asteroids and reduce it to a metallic powder. This powder is then boosted down a magnetic conduit that runs the full length of the vehicle, producing thrust.

When that dust clears the end of the conduit, it is *moving!*

Consider this. An accumulator-powered military rail gun can fire a spike out of a ten-meter tube at thirty thousand meters per second. The linear accelerator of an MD tug is twelve kilometers long and is powered by a solar energy array that could light a major city.

"Better let 'em know we're coming, Bo," I said.

"Have done and I've acquired their guidance beacons. Beginning final phase braking burn now."

The control sphere oriented so we wouldn't hang from our seat straps as the mainframe's retros fired.

"There she is!" Nell exclaimed, pointing "forward" on the surround screens.

What had been just another star out in the ultranight had begun to grow and take on form.

What does an MD tug and payload combine look like? At a distance, visualize a lollipop built on a scale for God, with the candy part having the lopsided massivity of a creek boulder and the handle the fairy-light structure of a snowflake's linedance.

Closer in, you just keep re-evaluating your definition of the word "big."

As the combine was in braking mode, the tug was aligned ahead of the asteroid and Bo maneuvered to make an observation fly-by down its full length.

Coming in past the MD's stern, we ghosted past the stadium-sized steering bell with its ranked banks of variable power magnets used to bend the exhaust plume. The mainframe's thrusters thudded as Bo countered the field pull and then we trailed on down the great central thrust member.

The main dive field coils ran through the center of a hexagonal, girder structure. Above and below this structure were spaced the black, glassy solar power arrays. Hundreds of them. Each a vertically mounted rectangle the size of a football field, all trimmed to catch a maximum amount of sunlight.

Back-lit like a spider's web in the dawn, a network of KevlarX cables, similar to the standing rigging of an old-time sailing ship, interlaced the structure, bracing and supporting the whole.

As the array files kept flowing past, I couldn't help the exclamation that boiled out of me. "Tao, but that's a big son of a bitch!"

"I know," Nell commented soberly. "I work with these rigs all the time. But still, every now and again, I'll look at one of them and my brain will just short out. Solar power sats may have more surface area and LaGrange orbital habitats may have more displacement, but the MDs are the biggest things ever built by man that can move under their own power."

We'd been running down the shadow side of the tug and now Bo rolled the mainframe's belly in towards the rig's flank and activated the landing lights, playing the twin circles of illumination across the structure's macro-scale complexity.

"Gain," he said dubiously, "granted that someone is going to try and take this thing out. How in the whole fraggin' universe are the two of us supposed to spot a sabotage point in all of that?"

"Well, we can start with the process of elimination," I replied. "Like we won't worry about any system that's covered by multiple redundancy or any structural member not critical to the design integrity."

"Great. I figure that'll reduce the odds from flatly impossible to merely requiring a personal favor from God."

We started coming in on the rock itself. At one time Cibola had been roughly in the form of a stumpy cigar, a good shovin' shape as the asteroid miners call it. Now it was closer to spherical. Two-thirds of its bulk had been eaten away to provide the reaction mass needed to bring this last third to Earth. The facing, where the MD's bow plate was planted, was faceted like a huge gemstone. Spaced around the perimeter of the facing were the circle of kilometer-long guylines that converged on the mooring collar of the tug's main thrust member, bracing it in position.

There was also something moving down there. A cold chill rippled across the back of my neck and, just for a second, I was living between the pages of one of my old science fiction novels. For it looked as if Cibola's surface was infested with giant spiders. Then, sadly, reality re-engaged. Those things were just the tug's mobile cutter and manipulator heads. Now I could see the magnetic conduits they pulled behind them, channeling the iron dust they produced into the linear accelerator. The four multi-legged mechanisms trudged perpetually across the surface of the asteroid, producing reaction mass, maintaining the rock's symmetry and balance over the thrust axis, and shifting and tightening the tug's mooring lines as the surface was consumed.

As we transited around to the far end of Cibola, we picked up the blue-white flare of a ship's marker strobe. The flat, octagonal form of the Johannesburg United laboratory barge was down on the surface, still docked with the utilitarian brick-with-drop-tanks silhouette of the Husky class towboat that had brought it there.

"Okay, Bo, pick us out a nice place by the lake and not too far from the volleyball courts."

"Doing it, Boss. But keep your suit on. This is going to take awhile."

Bo popped the mainframe's landing gear and eased down towards the surface with bare minimal thruster bursts. As he did, we could hear him muttering theatrically to himself.

"Compute for a point oh-oh-five gee field, compensate for deceleration variant, compensate yet again for the shaggin' transient effects from the shaggin' MD's accelerator coils. God, I hate operating in shaggin' micro-gravity . . ."

For all of his pissing and moaning, Bo touched us down feather light. Even so, the minimal recoil of the undercarriage shock absorbers almost bounced us back off the surface. He threw a magnetic field out from the gear trucks however and anchored us down.

"We be there, Boss."

"Thanks, Bo. Pretty landing. Okay, Nell, allow us to see you to your door."

As we bumbled aft towards the air locks, I found myself agreeing with Bo on the shortfalls of micro gee. Cibola wasn't big enough to produce a decent gravitational field, just a whisper of a one. Barely enough to be annoying.

In zero gravity, you can let go of an object and it'll just hang there in mid-air. In positive gravity, you can let go of an object and it'll fall. In micro gravity, the object will still fall. It just won't land until sometime that afternoon.

You lack the total lighter-than-air freedom of honest free fall and yet you also lack the traction and solidity of real gravity. It was the worst of both worlds and I found that it was already starting to set my teeth on edge.

We suited up. Like just about every other free fall engineer or miner in cis-Lunar space, Nell used a BAC/Leyland hard-suit. Hers was an expensive, customized Mark XII Skymaster with a chest plate slotted to take spare power packs and the sleeves studded with power take-offs and smart-tool jack-in points. Lobo stuck with his standard UNILAW issue Sanyo Aerospace. It may seem funny that a Ken unit would need a spacesuit, but their systems can use the extra thermal protection and Bo always complains that hard vacuum is hell on his complexion.

Besides, having an extra untapped life support pack around can be handy at times.

As for me, I use a patch-together. A Marine-issue skin suit under a camouflaged armorel coverall, mated with a York Model B long-duration life support system and a Bell close-fit pilot's helmet.

We all clipped magnetic sole plates onto our boots. This was the first time I'd ever had the opportunity to use that old sci-fi gimmick. Most ships and stations these days are made out of non-ferrous alloys and composite materials.

We cycled through the lock and dropped out of the belly hatch, taking our first close up look at the eternity just beyond the five-millimeter thickness of our helmet visors.

Steel sliver stars and a sun like an incandescent coin in a jet sky. The rock itself presented a dull gray-black surface that all the light in the universe couldn't brighten, its terrain features softened by eons of meteoroid erosion into low swales and hollows. The horizon so close it seemed as if you could stretch your arm out and reach over it. And you damn near could too.

"Heya," Bo inquired over the suit radio. "I thought this rock was supposed to be the mother lode. So where's all the gold?"

"We didn't exactly expect to find a quartz reef drifting around out here," Nell replied, lightly tapping the asteroid's surface with the edge of her boot. "Dr. Nolan's theory is that Cibola is primarily the same nickel-iron base material that most of the rocky-type planets, moons, and asteroids in the system are composed of. This particular rock just happens to have a particularly high concentration of noble atoms in it. We'll have to refine this stuff before we'll actually see any gold."

"So you don't actually hands-on know that there's gold here?" I said as we started to pick our way across the hundred-odd meters to the laboratory barge.

"Not really. The MD-24 wasn't outfitted with a survey package because she was only supposed to be sent out after rocks that had already been scanned by a prospector probe. We're still running on Dr. Nolan's density estimates."

"So what if this rock turns out to be weighted down with, say, lead or tungsten instead of gold or silver?"

She didn't sound worried. "Then we still stand to make a lot of money. Those elements are almost as valuable on the cis-Lunar market as the noble metals. Our rule of thumb is: if its heavy, it's valuable."

The barge was up on its landing jacks and as we passed beneath it, the belly hatch of its air lock swung open. Someone was expecting us. Actually a number of someones.

Just by looking at Dr. Teague Nolan, you could tell that he had been cast perfectly as a scientist. Not of the high-domed hyper-intellectual variety, but of the enthusiastic young-college-professor subspecies. Hair straw-colored and a little shaggy, eyes gray, and he likely would have been wearing horn-rimmed glasses if optical corrective surgery hadn't reached such a high state of proficiency.

"Nell, we're so glad to see you," he exclaimed, assisting the lady in question through the inner air lock door. "Company headquarters informed us about what happened on Dawn City. Are you all right?"

"A little hung-over but tolerable," she replied, lifting her helmet off its locking collar. "Mostly thanks to these gentlemen. Dr. Nolan, these are Free Marshals Gain Chandry and Lobo of the UN International Law Enforcement Authority."

"A pleasure to have you aboard, Marshal Chandry. And you too, Marshal . . . uh," Nolan hesitated for a second, ". . . Lobo?"

My partner smiled genially. "No family name because there's no family. I'm not of the protean persuasion."

In response to the blank look he received, Bo continued gently. "I'm a cyber, Doc."

Most of the population these days know that cyber beings are out there, but it's still a little startling for your average citizen to actually shake hands with one. Especially when they find that they can't tell the difference.

"Oh, well," Nolan fumbled on. "Let me introduce you both to the rest of our team. This is my wife, Rana, Dr. Rana Nolan."

This other Dr. Nolan was a cat of a different color, specifically a rich coffee-with-plenty-of-cream shade, with warm brown eyes and black hair tucked into a tight knot at the back of her well-formed head.

"I'm happy to meet you, gentlemen. I'm glad you are here."

I contented myself with shaking her hand. Bo bowed over it. For a skinny professor type, Teague Nolan had done pretty good for himself. "Glad we can be of assistance, Dr. Nolan," I replied.

"Since there are two Dr. Nolans, please call me Rana."

The other introductions went rapidly as we shed our vacuum gear.

The combination tug captain and towing master of the operation was called Lee Tran, a lean, graying Asian with an air of intense capability about him. He acknowledged us with a quiet nod. His co-pilot, a young woman called Donna Torveska, was quiet, too: quiet, pale, and plain. That isn't all that common in a world where body sculpting is available in any neighborhood shopping mall. She had much the same aura of solid competency about her as Captain Tran and she moved in his wake like a small, alert shadow.

The fifth barge passenger hadn't bothered to come to the air lock. He was waiting for us in the barge's central dining area cum lounge/office space. Or at least nine-tenths of him was. Somewhere along the line, Field Engineer Gavin Wilcox had reached for something without asking, "Mother, may I?" He was short a right hand and forearm.

At one time, this might have been a serious consideration. But these days, when constructing an entire artificial humanform is possible, a mere forearm is child's play. He could have had a fully functional artificial limb that you wouldn't have been able to tell from the real thing, any more than you could have with one of Bo's arms.

But Wilcox had opted differently. His right arm now ended in powerful rotor cuff. Currently he had a multi-purpose gripper head, a massive set of metal pinchers, mounted in it. It looked damn intimidating and I suspected that was just how he liked it.

Big and blocky with a beginning of a gut bulging out the front of his suit liner, his beard was the color and texture of rusty steel wool. His hair was the same, shagged off shorter than was the norm these days.

He was lounging negligently at the serving bar and, as I approached him, our eyes met.

I recognized him then. Our association went back for a long time. Centuries in fact. Back to the day when human civilization had first developed laws and had selected members of its society to enforce them. Gavin Wilcox was a cop-fighter. I also suspected a cop-hater.

It's hard to call just how I knew this. Chalk it up to ESP (Extra Sensory Police). When the time came to shake, Wilcox extended his prosthetic arm, silently daring me to risk a handful of fingers to his machine tool hand. I smiled back and accepted, silently daring the shagass to try it. Oh, I could already tell we were just going to get along magnificently.

"Heya, Gain. Who's this other guy?"

Bo's neurolink call disrupted my stare-down with Wilcox. There were supposed to be six people on the Joburg team. Count Bo and I and there should be eight. So how come there were nine people in the lounge?

Nell was apparently taken by surprise as well. "Paul?" she exclaimed. "What in the world are you doing here?"

"Just watching out for the company's investments," he grinned back. "What do you think?"

"That it's a miracle," she replied, bouncing herself off the deck so she could pull on her Velcro boots. "I was sure that nothing short of demolition tape could blast you loose from company headquarters."

I could buy that statement. The newcomer wore the same snug fitting suit liner as the rest of us, but on him, it didn't ride right. Those shoulders would be more comfortable under a wageman's jacket. They probably would have come off squarer as well. He was dark haired and good looking, with that carefully customized, non-controversial handsomeness you get with some face rebuilds. The face job also blurred his age to anywhere between twenty and forty.

Nell seemed to know him pretty well though. Well enough so that she went up to rest a friendly hand on his arm. "Gain, this is Paul Zane, the assistant operations director for the Cibola Project."

"It's a pleasure, Marshal," he emoted. "And on behalf of Johannesburg United, I'd like to thank you for the rescue of Ms. Rainey here. We are in your debt."

I shrugged. "That's what you pay taxes for, Mr. Zane."

"Since you're on the team now, you can call me Paul."

"Sure." I was getting a little bit tired of shaking hands by this time so I kept my distance.

"Now that the introductions are over with," Nell asked Zane, "how does it look?"

He arched his eyebrows. "We don't know yet."

"We've been very busy setting up the past couple of days, Ms. Rainey," the male Dr. Nolan said, crossing the compartment. "The specific gravity figures we're getting match up with my estimations but we decided to wait until we had our geologist here to run the actual assaying tests."

He sheepishly ran his hand through his disordered hair. "Truthfully, I've been a little bit scared to try."

"Well, there's no reason for us to be standing around in suspense," Nell replied. "Show me where I can stow my suit and kit bag and I'll get to work."

"You've got a cubicle to yourself. The farthest one forward on the port side."

"I'll just be a second then."

Nell went to collect her gear, her softboots scrunching on the Velcro flooring. Nolan turned back to me. "Will you and your associate be needing quarters, Marshal?" he inquired politely.

"Negative, we're set on our ship."

"Breakfast? A pouch of coffee?"

"Already taken care of, Doc. While you're waiting for Ms. Rainey, I'd like to get on with my part of things if we may. Your company HQ has indicated to us that you haven't had any problems out here so far. Expanding on that, has anyone on your team noticed anything unusual or unexpected since landing on Cibola?"

"Nothing at all, Marshal. Captain Tran and Engineer Wilcox have checked out the MD and it's functioning perfectly. Our flight path is dead-on as well. Things couldn't be better."

"No indications of possible tampering or of any other human presence?"

"That would be highly unlikely, Marshal Chandry," an unemotional baritone interjected. Captain Tran came over and joined us. "The MD-24 has been in deep space for over a year. During that time, the nearest transit distance with any other manned ship was twelve million kilometers. No one could have been here."

"Theoretically, no one could have gotten into your company's computer system either, Captain," I replied. "Speaking as a law enforcement officer, I've found that sometimes it works out better if you assume that your opponent is just a little bit omnipotent. It helps prevent nasty surprises."

Nell re-emerged from the habitat bay a few moments later. "Okay, where's the lab?"

It was port side from the lounge, beyond a transparent safety bulkhead. It was cramped but well equipped, as far as I was any judge. Nell looked pleased as well, as she drift-stepped inside.

"There are a number of ways we can go about this," she said over her shoulder. "But as I'm an old fashioned girl at heart, we'll try the acid test."

Like any decent free fall or micro gee lab, this one had a glove box set up for handling hazardous materials, as a cloud of active corrosive can ruin your whole day. As we looked on, Nell moved around the compartment, stocking the transparent plastic cube with various chemical vials, a small table-top centrifuge, and a couple of mean-looking hypodermics.

"Do we have any ore samples on board?" she inquired.

"That we do." Wilcox brushed past me; the brush turned into a low-yield shoulder block that almost disengaged me from the flooring. Oh, this fine fellow and I were definitely going to have some interesting times together in the days ahead. The engineer indicated a rack of sample tubes, each partially filled with a grayish-black powder. "These have all been tapped straight off the grinder heads. Any preference?"

"No, any one of them will do for a start." Wilcox lifted one of the tubes from the rack with his prosthetic, displaying a considerable deftness and delicacy of control with the manipulator grip. Nell accepted it and gave it a knowledgeable look.

"Yes, this will be fine." She placed the tube in the box and sealed the lid, then slid her arms into the handling gloves. As we looked on, she charged a hypodermic from one of the vials.

"What I'm doing here is a classic method of verifying the presence of gold and silver," she said, injecting the hypo's load through the permeable but acid-proof cap of the sample tube. "This is aqua regia, a mixture of sulfuric and nitric acids. It's pretty furious stuff, the only acid that will dissolve the noble metals."

She shook the tube vigorously and the powdered ore fizzed into a rust colored semi-liquid.

"We wait a second while the ore breaks down completely." She set the sample aside and charged the second hypo from a second vial. ". . . Then we kill the acid with an alkali-based neutralizing agent." She injected the ore sample again and snapped the tube into the small lab centrifuge. Switching it on, she continued to speak over the muffled buzz of the motor. "As the acid neutralizes, it can no longer hold the gold molecules in suspension, so they'll form crystals and precipitate out. These gold crystals will clump at the bottom of the tube under the influence of positive gravity. Granted, of course, that there is any gold."

The centrifuge whirred to a stop and I moved in to peer over Nell's shoulder as she lifted the sample from the unit. There was a two-centimeter plug of dark sediment at the base of the tube. The bottom-most layer glittered like the black sky beyond the hull of the barge.

"A hit at the first try," she whispered almost passionately. "Gold, a very nice concentration. We've got valid ore."

Nell's pronouncement set off another round of hand shaking, intermixed with a certain amount of hugging, kissing, and joyful noise. Bo and I just faded back a little and observed. Sometimes it's amazing what you can learn by pretending to be a patch of paint on the bulkhead.

The Doctors Nolan embraced, laughed, and maybe cried a little, like a set of parents whose child had made it through a tricky round of surgery. Paul Zane had deftly maneuvered himself into position to "spontaneously" embrace Nell Rainey. She in turn, with the skill learned early on by attractive females, deftly maneuvered to get un-embraced. Captain Tran and his co-pilot also just looked on with that same near-eerie synchronicity of expression and posture. As for friend Wilcox? Well, he was watching me.

"Teague," Zane said, giving up on Nell, "God love you, you delivered! The company is not going to forget this!"

"Speaking honestly, I don't think I will either," Nolan replied, swiping his wrist across his forehead. "I was sure about what we'd find here on Cibola. I was absolutely dead sure right up until the board of directors agreed to go after her. Since then, I haven't been certain about anything."

"I've been certain enough for both of us, darling," Rana Nolan said, her face buried against her husband's chest.

"We all should have had as much faith in you as your wife did, Doctor," Zane continued. "On behalf of Johannesburg United, we thank you."

"Heya, Boss. You notice how this guy Zane brandishes the Joburg banner as if it was his personal house flag?"

"Yeah, I'd love to hear him at work on his superiors. I bet he kisses ass so hard you can hear the pucker at a half-a-kay range."

"Bet not taken."

"Nell," Zane continued jovially, "what do you think we're going to clear on this operation?"

"I have a long way to go before I can make that kind of estimate," she replied. "But, if this gold concentration is close to any kind of average throughout the ore body, this intercept will have been more than worth it. Granted, that is, that the separation and refining works out."

"Don't worry about that," Wilcox rumbled. "The new processing stack'll work fine on low grade."

Nell shrugged. "I know that's what the computer simulations say, but let's face it, no one's ever tried to separate and refine gold in orbit before. We've never even had the chance to test your process on real ore."

Wilcox looked dark. "We had this discussion before in the planning sessions, Rainey. Refining Division has the problem covered."

She dismissed him with a flip of her ponytail. "Well, I hope so, Gavin. Our stockholders are not going to appreciate our dragging this rock halfway across the solar system just to learn we can't crack it."

"I said that my division has it covered!" the engineer retorted irritably.

I received a mental snicker. *"Poor Mr. Wilcox. Three new people in town and none of 'em'll bully worth a damn."*

"It's just not his watch, Bo."

"Look," Teague Nolan interceded, "from the start, this whole project has been beset by a lot of unknowns. To date we've been able to overcome them all. Let's just assume that we're going to continue to do so."

"That's right," Zane added, joining into the peacekeeper role. "We'll take this one step at a time. Our primary concern right now is to get Cibola into Earth orbit."

Across the way, I noticed an odd expression come across my partner's face. "Pardon me," he said, "but in relation to that last statement, was your MD tug supposed to turn itself off just now?" The entire compartment went absolutely dead still.

"I'll take that as a no," Bo sighed.

The paralysis broke and everyone, and I mean everyone, scrambled for a computer terminal, including me.

"How'd you spot it, Bo?"

"The navigational sensors on the mainframe detected the deceleration drop. It's way too mild for meat to detect."

"Somebody give me an access clearance!" Nell yelled as she reached the workstation in the mineralogy lab.

"Your company code plus 6827, slash, star, star," Rana Nolan called back from the lounge terminal. "That will give you the tug's primary systems menu."

"Why aren't we getting any malfunction warnings?" Teague Nolan demanded. He'd jacked a portable access pad into his wife's station and he was playing it with all the intensity of a teener with a new VR game.

"I don't know!" Wilcox replied, leaning over Mrs. Nolan's shoulder. "No systems are red-lining. They're just shutting down."

"We have just received a transmission from company headquarters." At first I didn't recognize the feminine voice issuing from the overhead speakers. Then I realized it must be Torveska, the co-pilot. She and Captain Tran had headed aft to the barge's control center when the lid had blown off. "They are asking why we've initiated power-down sequencing on the tug."

"That's it," Nell raised her voice slightly to activate the microphone of the compartment intercom. "This isn't a malfunction. The tug has gone into its post-mission power-down mode."

"How could that happen!" Nolan demanded.

"I don't know!" she replied. "This can't be a malfunction! Someone must have entered the initiation command into the system."

Nolan looked up at the intercom speaker like a desperate sinner might look up to God. "Captain, can we stop this?"

"The book says no, Dr. Nolan," the towing master answered. "We'll have to let her run through the entire power-down and then initiate a re-start sequence."

"How long will that take?"

"At least sixteen hours, given the re-start checklists we'll have to work through."

"We can't afford to lose better than half a day's deceleration this close in," Nolan exclaimed.

"We may not have any choice."

I looked across at Bo. *"Do we?"*

"I dunno, Boss. I suppose I could get in there and shag around to see how much of a mess I could make."

"Do it!"

I launched my thoughts across space, relaying through the neurolink, to the mainframe's transceivers and on to Dawn City.

"Lil, big problem!"

"I've been alerted by Joburg headquarters." Her mental coolness returned. *"What is your situation?"*

"Someone's initiated a premature shut-down command on the tug. According to Dr. Nolan, we can't afford to lose the braking time at this phase of the approach. Bo thinks that he can catch the crash if he can get in system fast enough."

"Correction on that," my partner interjected. *"Bo thinks that there is a minute possibility that Bo might actually be able to do something constructive, granted that he's given more luck than he deserves."*

"How may I help?"

"I'm going to need a data dump of the MD-24's entire core software package. Then I'm going to need you to back-stop me as I restructure the operations program." I knew that Bo and Lil were actually saying a whole lot more to each other a lot faster than my, or any other meat mind, could comprehend. They were feeding me a much abbreviated humanspeed summary to keep me in the events loop.

"Accessing the Joburg database and standing by to transmit."

We managed all that in the few seconds it took to cross the lounge space to the workstation. "Pardon me, Doc," I said, brushing past Wilcox and dropping my hand on Mrs. Nolan's shoulder. "My partner thinks he can help. Can he get in here for awhile?"

Looking at us hopefully, she let Bo take her place at the workstation. Before he even settled into the seat, his fingers were flowing over the keyboard, commanding and cajoling the system.

"I'm going to need direct interface, Boss," he said, his full concentration focused on the data flow on the screen. "I've got a set of jacks in my hip pouch. Set me up."

He didn't pay me further attention as I opened the shoulder zip of his liner and socked the contact prongs of the jacks into the skin indentations that marked his output ports. A moment later and his Ken was plugged into the console.

"You're set, Bo."

"Okay, everyone listen up!" he called, raising his voice. "I'm going to be peeling programming blocks off for each of your stations to cover. Nell, you've got the auxiliaries and solar collector subsystems. Hold the power levels!"

"Right."

"Captain Tran, you and your co-pilot are going to have manual thermal control. Watch the transformer banks and the coil superconductors. Don't let anything overheat or cool off. Mr. Wilcox, you'd better get back there and give them a hand."

Tran acknowledged and Wilcox grunted his assent, moving aft.

"Dr. Nolan, overview for system malfunctions and yell if you spot anything we miss."

Teague Nolan nodded, silent and taut.

Bo's fingers had never for an instant stopped their

lightspeed flicker across the keyboard. "All right, I'm going inside now. Wish me luck, Boss."

Bo cut the neurolink. He was going where my human mentality couldn't follow, boosting back up to full processing speed. What he and Lil were attempting to do was impossible by conventional wisdom or human capability.

The huge mass driver tug was made up of literally hundreds of thousands of interconnected sub-systems that were powering down in a cascade effect; one system affecting ten systems that affected a hundred systems and so on in a precise, pre-calculated sequence.

The two cybers were going to try and interrupt that sequence and reverse it without blowing too many fuses and/or gaskets. It would be an off-the-cuff rewrite of a macro-program while the program was still up and running, the equivalency of knocking over a house of cards and then grabbing all of the cards out of mid-air and re-stacking them in place before any of then could hit the floor. Very diverting work.

Slowly I watched the "aliveness" fade from Bo's Ken. He was channeling everything that he was into the problem. Likewise, all I was getting from Lil was dead air.

"How are they doing, Doc?" I asked Nolan.

He shook his head. "I don't know. I don't even know what they're doing."

A very long few minutes followed, giving me plenty of time to play the old cop's game of whos, whys and hows. There was a set of questions I needed to ask but I didn't have access to the answers, at least not until Bo and Lil resurfaced.

I couldn't call how we were doing until I saw the animation start to return to Bo's face. A grin formed. For the first time his right hand came slowly off the keyboard to flash a thumbs-up.

"Just possibly I think we're back in business," he said. "All stations, report. How are you looking?"

"Green board," Nell called.

"All functions nominal, Marshal." Tran's calm voice issued from the overhead.

Teague Nolan's head bobbed nervously. "Yes. I think the same."

"Okay," Bo continued. "I'm re-integrating your program segments now . . . and let's try for an engine restart. . . . Re-integration complete. . . . All systems cycling through final phase checklists. . . . Reactivating primary propulsion system . . . now!"

Nell broke the bad news. "We do not have power up."

"I concur," Nolan added, staring into his hand deck. "Primary accelerator coils have not energized."

Bo's brows creased. "What in Tao? I'm not registering any malfunctions here, Doc."

"I'm not either," Nolan said looking up, "but we still don't have thrust."

"I am now indicating a system failure," Captain Tran's disembodied voice sounded in the lounge. "I have a red warning in the mid-ships switching relays."

"I've got it now too," Bo reported. "Where did that come from?"

"I do not know, Marshal. I can't call up a specific on this. I'm just showing a general block failure. And the automatic repair remotes are not picking up on it. They aren't seeing the malfunction for some reason."

Bo shook his head, perplexed, "We'll worry about that later. For now, let's just get some way on this thing. By-passing to secondary power busses . . . secondaries engaging."

"We have power up!" Dr. Nolan reported.

"No," Bo was scowling now. "No, we have greens but we don't have thrust."

"I'm getting split readings here," Nell called in from the lab. "Engine instrumentation says that the mass driver is on-line. Navigational read-outs indicate that it is not."

"I can confirm that," Captain Tran added. "I'm getting a restart acknowledgement but I'm not getting any field readings off the primary coils. We do not have thrust."

"Boss, something seriously strange is going on here."

"Tell me about it."

"Captain Tran, could you come forward please?"

The towing master emerged from the passageway aft a few moments later.

"Okay, Captain," I said. "You know more about MD tugs than anyone else here. In your best estimation, what's happened?"

Tran scowled. "I do not know. This is not any kind of standard listed malfunction. The re-start must have stressed something and brought on an engineering casualty."

"No," Bo shook his head emphatically. "I was in there, Captain. I can testify that I got her put back together all right. Nothing busted."

"He's right, Gain," Lil whispered in my mind. *"I cross-checked Lobo and I couldn't spot any overloaded systems."*

"How about sabotage?" I asked aloud.

"I suppose the possibility must be considered," Tran said slowly. "It's very odd that the remotes aren't engaging if there is actual physical damage. Be that as it may, we aren't receiving enough telemetry to make any kind of a solid judgment call on the problem."

"Pardon me, but this is all secondary to the fact that we must get Cibola back under deceleration!" Teague Nolan pressed his suddenly damp hair back out of his eyes. A tiny globule of sweat broke loose and arced ever so slowly towards the deck. "We're wasting our time reserves!"

Tran nodded impassively. "You're right, Doctor. We need to go and take a direct look at the problem. Mr. Wilcox and I will execute an EVA and check out the involved systems block."

"I'll go with you, Captain," I said.

"No sense in that, Marshal." Wilcox emerged bearlike from the aft corridor. "We can handle it. There won't be anyone to arrest out there."

I tucked the corners of my mouth up into something that resembled a smile. "You never can tell."

The barge's air lock had exit hatches on both its upper and lower decks. We went out the topside hatch to a rack of waiting thruster packs and harnessed up. A few minutes later, we were lifting off on thin jets of metastable hydrogen peroxide steam.

"Our first check point will be Transformer One, about three kilometers up the thrust member," Tran said. "Let's go."

Wilcox and I held formation on the towing master as we began to climb away from Cibola. "Climb" was a valid orientation term for the moment because the asteroid's feeble gravitational field still produced faint, intermittent sensations of "down" as we maneuvered.

We drifted along parallel to the shadow-side of the MD, a scattering of stars on our right hand and the frame of the tug on our left, back-lit by the light of the sun like the skeleton of the Midgard serpent.

Captain Tran kept our speed low so I had the time to work on some of those questions I'd come up with.

"Lil, could that deactivation code have been transmitted over the Joburg vehicle command frequencies?"

"It could have been, but it wasn't. Ever since we received this case, I've had a monitor on all of Joburg's radio traffic to and from the Cibola Combine. That code was not transmitted from their operations center. That doesn't mean it couldn't have been beamed in from some other source though."

"Nope, that's a buster as well," Bo cut in. *"I've had my own frequency scanners up ever since we reached Cibola's space. That code didn't come in from anywhere outside."*

"Could it have been time-bombed into the system programming earlier on?" I thought.

"Possibly, Gain," Lil replied. *"Or we must consider the possibility that it was done by someone right on Cibola."*

"There is that."

Bo mentally snorted. *"They have great timing then. Doing it just as the cops show up."*

"Maybe it's not timing, Bo," I mused. *"Maybe it's an agenda."*

"What do you mean, Boss?"

"I'm not sure myself."

"Transformer One, this is it." Captain Tran's voice sounded in my helmet earphones. The towing master braked and then veered off inside the tug's girder structure. Wilcox and I followed.

I lagged back a little deliberately, taking stock of my surroundings. The transformer bay itself was a massive rectangular block wedged in between the thrust member framing and the coils of the accelerator.

I could see one of the tug's automated repair and maintenance remotes crouching atop the bay like a metallic Tinker toy caterpillar. The little semi-autonomous drone had a dataprobe inserted in an access port in the transformer shell, but it wasn't moving. Designed to seek out and deal with hardware failures in the tug's systems, it obviously wasn't "seeing" the problem. Either that or it wasn't recognizing it as coming within its zone of responsibility.

Tran and Wilcox touched down on one of the coils at the base of the bay and I landed on the next loop aft, separated from them by the four-meter gap between the big electromagnets. I looked on as they activated their suit lights and began to play them across the shell of the transformer bank and the cable clusters that fed into it.

Have you ever had that funny sensation of having someone's casual comment or action trigger something in your mind? Something that you can't quite pull to the surface. I was having that sensation now and I wasn't much liking it. We were all missing something.

And frequently, the thing that you miss is the thing that doesn't miss you.

"Outer casing looks intact," Wilcox commented. "I'll check the conduit connectors." His hard-suit had a modified sleeve that locked in around his manipulator arm and I could see his grip claw outlined against the glow of his chest lamp. "There's no sign of scorching or spalling."

"No internal explosion then," Tran replied. "Some kind of a mechanical failure in the liquid state make-and-breaks maybe? We'll see."

Shuffling across the surface of the coil on his magnetic boot plates, Tran went to the end of the bay just beyond the coil gap from me. I watched as he struggled with a cold-welded cover plate, eventually popping it open to reveal a monitor panel. The lights from the read-outs reflected in his helmet visor. A couple of meters off to his far side, Gavin Wilcox began to undo a second access door into the bay.

"Just a moment, Wilcox," Tran said. "Donna, what kind of propulsion status are you showing currently."

"No change, Captain," the copilot replied. "Main power

busses are off-line. Secondaries read engaged, but we still aren't getting a charge in the accelerator."

"Right, that's what I'm reading here. No indication why yet. Let's be safe just the same. Shut down the secondary busses."

It all clicked in my mind then, just half a second too late. I knew what was going on now. I knew what had been done to sabotage the tug. I knew what was about to happen. But I couldn't stop it. I couldn't get that one word out fast enough. "No!"

The tug's engine fired.

Suddenly there was a new "down." The big magnets of the accelerator reached out and grabbed the metal in our suits, yanking us off balance. I'd made one of those instinctive and totally futile lunges forward and, as I fell, I caught a fragmentary glimpse of Wilcox reaching out to snag a grab bar with his human hand. Tran twisted sideways and he toppled into the coil gap, the focused magnetic fields drawing him in. His scream overloaded the communications channel.

I landed on my chest with my helmet extending over the edge of the coil and I found myself looking directly into the core of the mass driver engine. Unlike a Metastate or nuclear drive, there was no pillar of flame, no unholy radiation glow. There was just a sooty little pencil streak running through the center of the coil focus. A jet less than a meter in diameter and yet made up of billions of tiny iron particles, all being boosted to hundreds of kays per second by the modulated magnetic fields of the mass driver. Those same fields had reached out and seized the towing master, snapping him into their nexus.

The human frame was never intended to have congress with that kind of kinetic energy. Tran touched the particle stream . . . and exploded.

He was blown to the molecular level and sprayed out across a universe's worth of space before even he could acknowledge his own destruction. After awhile, I noticed that someone was yelling into my mind. *"Gain! Gain! Talk to me, Boss! What's happening out there?"*

"Captain Tran has just been killed." I shook some of the shock fuzz out of my skull and tried to swallow the bile in my throat. *"No, correction on that. Captain Tran has just been murdered."*

Chapter 7

I edged back from the coil gap and got to my feet. The drag from the electromagnets wasn't all that intense outside of the core accelerator assembly, less than one standard gravity. It had been the sudden onset that had put me on the deck and toppled Tran to his death.

Immediately across from me Gavin Wilcox stood gazing down into the coil gap, his hand still on the grab bar that had saved him. There was a gabble of voices in my helmet phones but I ignored them, internalizing on my mind-to-mind with Bo.

"Propulsion status on the mass driver? What do your boards say?"

"Boards now indicate driver thrust is off-line and on safe."

"Right. Engage the secondary power busses and fire the driver."

"But, Boss, it's already . . ."

"Do it, Bo. Run the start sequence."

"Doing it."

The stream of iron particles snapped off like a torch beam. A couple of beats later, so did the magnetic fields.

"That's it then," I shot back. *"Somebody's inverted the drive command sequences in the propulsion programming. On is off. Off is on."*

"Wait a minute, Boss," Bo protested. *"I scanned that entire software block before I tried the restart and it matched the pack-up copy at Joburg headquarters exactly. I mean it was pristine!"*

"*Then somebody was a fast worker, Bo. What's your status back there?*"

"*We're pretty much okay. Most of us anyhow.*"

There was something odd in the way he thought that. I mentalized the access geometrics that let me link into Bo's optical systems and I peered out through the electronic eyes of his Ken unit.

I found myself looking at the mission co-pilot, Donna Torveska.

My first impression of her had been that she was a lady with almost an over-abundance of personal control.

It was gone now.

She was curled up in a fetal position, clinging to one of the lounge couches and weeping with the hard-edged intensity of someone who couldn't get the grief out fast enough to ease the pain. Nell Rainey was kneeling beside the crouch cradling the brown haired co-pilot in her arms and wearing the despairing expression of someone who gives a damn but who doesn't have anything really constructive they can do.

Bo's vision panned across the other three members of the team. The two doctors and Zane were all wearing the appropriate expressions of shock and unease the average individual gets when suddenly exposed to terminal-grade violence. "*You got any further orders, Boss?*"

"*Yeah, are you updating Lil on the situation?*"

"*I'm running a continuous real-time feed to her.*"

"*Good enough. Then dig into that programming block again and figure out how the bad guys got past us.*"

"*Doin' it!*"

Someone spoke my name over the voice circuit and I drew my attention back into myself. Wilcox was looking at me from across the coil gap. "There's nothing more we can do here," the engineer repeated. "Let's get back to the barge."

"Wait a minute." I took advantage of our restored state of free fall and took a couple of steps forward. Breaking magnet contact with the coil surface, I let my momentum carry me across the gap. On reaching the other side, I socked a boot down and re-anchored myself in front of Wilcox. "You came out here to check that transformer block. You haven't got it done yet."

Wilcox shook his helmet. "Oh, for Christ's sake. We came out here to see if the hardware had been sabotaged or not. It should be pretty obvious that it hasn't been."

"How do you know?" I asked levelly. "For all we know, bitched software could cover up bitched hardware."

We faced off for about half a minute. I couldn't see what was going on behind his faceplate and he couldn't see what was happening behind mine. When that field had hit, Wilcox had managed to snag that grab bar and stay on his feet while Tran and I had both gone down. Maybe he had good reflexes, or maybe just dumb luck.

Or just maybe he'd been braced and waiting for it.

"What do you want me to do?" Wilcox asked heavily.

"Check out the transformer block, just like the plan."

"And what are you going to be doing?"

"Watching you, just like the plan."

We returned to the laboratory barge about two hours later to find that my boss had come aboard, at least in the cybernetic sense.

Bo had brought a genie box over from the mainframe and had it deployed in the crew's lounge.

A genie box is a vastly uprated form of the little 3-D computer access plates you see everywhere. Closed it merely looks like an expensive vacuum-proof briefcase. Open, it deploys an array of sensor heads and holograph projectors that link into the cis-Lunar infonet, permitting an insider cyber like Lil to establish an on-site presence in the field.

As we exited the air lock, I found Lil already in conversation with the others of the Joburg crew. I noted that my case officer was using her Avenging Angel variant. Clad in a simulacra of a severe white pantsuit, she was a little taller, she had a few less curves, and she had more steel than mist in her eyes.

"What did you find, Gain?" she asked, her image pacing a couple of steps toward me. The genie box was throwing a good 'graph and she couldn't be told from solid. At least until you noticed that her boots didn't rasp on the Velcro carpet.

"Nothing much," I replied, arming off my helmet. "Mr. Wilcox over there verified that no one has been hands-on with the transformer block."

Wilcox grunted an acknowledgment. He was half out of his vacuum gear and he looked like a violent collision between man and robot, his rusty wool hair and flushed face clashing with the dead white composite of his hardsuit.

"All components were functional within specs," he said, "and every access plate and door in that unit was cold welded tight. If the system was bitched, it had to be through the programming."

My boss nodded. "Just so. As you suspected, Gain, the propulsion programs had been rewritten, reversing the secondary drive initiation protocols and incorporating a false transformer failure to force their usage."

"I still don't understand how I could have missed it," Bo said unhappily. "I scanned that entire software package before attempting restart and those modifications just weren't there."

"Yes, they were, Lobo," Lil replied. "They just weren't in a format that could be readily recognized. I scanned the tug's software package myself and I missed them as well. The program rewrites were incorporated into a camouflaged spore virus caged over the propulsion control program, keyed to blossom when anyone tried a drive restart."

"A very sophisticated bunch of slimers," Bo commented. "It was like the old chess ploy, one attack unmasks a second. The attempted engine shutdown unmasked the spore virus."

"A spore virus?" I twisted the lock rings on my suit cuffs and tugged off my gloves. "Where have I heard that before?"

Lil nodded soberly. "The feel of this piece of programming is very similar to that of the spore virus used to propagate the Cibola religious propaganda through the infonets."

"That closes the circle then." I unharnessed my life support pack. "The same outfit that popped the propaganda likely also invaded the Joburg computer net and arranged for Ms. Rainey's kidnapping. Now they've attacked the MD. The assumption we have to make is that whoever is behind this plot has also physically infiltrated this operation and that they have one or more agents here on the barge."

Paul Zane looked up sharply from the communications pad he'd had cradled in his lap. Ever since Wilcox and I had gotten back aboard, Zane had been caucusing intermittently with his company headquarters. Now his concerns abruptly localized. "You can't mean one of us?"

I hooked the pack onto the gear rack and connected the oxygen and power recharge lines. "Point me out somebody else."

"Just one bloody second, Johnny Law," Wilcox growled. "We all knew Lee Tran."

"And your point?" I replied. "The statistics read that if you're ever murdered by somebody, it will likely be somebody you know."

"Marshal Chandry," Dr. Nolan cut in. "Everyone here is a long-term Johannesburg employee who has been involved with the Cibola Project from its conception. I hand-picked this team and I can't conceive of anyone on it being a saboteur, much less a murderer."

Up until then, the Doc and his wife had been huddled together in the far corner of the lounge like the little lost Waifs of the Woods, as if a meter or two might distance them from what was happening.

"Doc," I replied patiently, "at one time or another you have probably stood shoulder to shoulder with thieves, killers, rapists, any kind of criminal or sociopath you can name." I unzipped my coverall and popped the pressure seal on the skin suit underneath, letting in a welcome puff of cool air. "You've shared monorail cars with them. You've eaten with them in restaurants. You've said hello to them on the street. You just never known it because the bad guys seldom advertise who they are.

"Someone had to insert that rewrite virus into the MD's computers and somebody had to key that premature shutdown command. I say again. Who else is there?"

"The virus could have been inserted over our telecommunications links at any time by anyone," Nolan replied, valiantly defending his state of denial.

Bo shook his head. "Maybe the virus, Doc, but not the shutdown command itself. I've been monitoring the full communications spectrum since we landed and that command didn't come in from outside."

"That could have been a pre-planted spore as well," Rana Nolan said, moving up to support her mate.

"Possibly," Lil replied. "But I know what to look for now and I can find no residual signature of a second spore within the tug's software package. I concur with Marshal Chandry. The shutdown command was likely keyed into the tug's systems via the hardlink you've established from the laboratory barge."

"Wait a minute," Nell spoke up. "Gain, that can't be right. We were all either right here in the lounge or in the mineralogy lab, in full view from the time you and Lobo came aboard until the tug's powerdown started."

The little blonde rose from the couch, swaying a little as she balanced in the micro gee. She was no longer tending to Donna Torveska.

Come to think of it, the co-pilot wasn't even present.

"Whoever entered in the shutdown command could have set up a personal work pad to execute the command dump," I replied. "It could have been programmed to activate, access the barge's network, download the code, erase itself, and then shut down. That would have allowed the perp to be up front and looking innocent when things went to pieces."

"Hell of a funny time to do it, just when a couple of lawboys come walking through the door," Wilcox snorted.

Bo shrugged and gave Wilcox one of his more charming shark's smiles. "Heya, the boss and I aren't exactly unknown out here, friend. Could be your spook, whoever he or she is, got more spooked when us two keen guys showed. He or she hears our call sign while we're turning final and figures that he'd better spring his little hackjob before we shagged up affairs."

Wilcox looked sour, shifting his eyes between Bo and me. "Sounds like you lot are planning to set somebody up nice and solid. But answer me this. Why? Why would one of us set up to kill Tran and wreck our own company's operation? Why?"

"I don't know yet, Wilcox," I replied, keeping my voice level. "Do you?"

Wilcox's prosthetic manipulator closed with a decisive metallic click and he took a step towards me.

Bo caught the move and he bounced in on his flank. Lil

was faster though. She derezzed and re-materialized in front of the burly engineer so rapidly that he almost walked through her. "I advise restraint Mr. Wilcox," she said. "Marshal Chandry is only doing his job."

"She's right, Wilcox," Paul Zane added coldly. "We've already had more then enough hysterics out here. But I have to say, Ms. Lilith, the marshal does seem to be a little overfocused on the potential guilt of our personnel here. I hope there are other alternatives being considered?"

Lil nodded. "There are, and those alternatives are being investigated. However, Cibola itself is Marshal Chandry's zone of responsibility. I am satisfied with his methodology."

Praise Tao for a boss who is not only perilously good in bed but who will back you up when the shoving starts.

"You still could be a little less blunt about things, Gain." Lil's mental interjection was a little rueful.

"Heya sweet one. You're the one who labeled me a brick."

She did have a point however.

"Look," I said, going back to verbal. "Everyone here is a suspect, but in a closed event environment like this, that should only be expected. But we're not accusing anyone of anything yet. The investigation is ongoing and we're a long way from coming to any conclusions.

"If you feel you are being leaned on a little," I continued, "I regret the effect. I won't apologize for it though because that's an aspect of the situation. Sabotage and murder aren't fun to be around."

"Nice speech, Boss," Bo commented.

"Yeah, but will it play in Paducah?"

Apparently it did because the tension thinned out slightly.

"All right, Marshal," Zane said. "You're the professional here. I do hope you understand that we're just not used to this kind of thing."

"I hope you never get used to murder, Mr. Zane. I never have."

"One thing though," the corporate continued, "when it gets out that we've had both a murder and a major act of sabotage on this towing combine, the UN Space Safety Commission is bound to go into session on our operations permits. I hope you were speaking figuratively about having a long way to go on this case."

"We're trying, Mr. Zane. That's all I can say."

"I'll be speaking to the Safety Commission as well," Lil added. "I think they can be held off for a time longer."

"I hope you are correct, Ms. Lilith."

The corner of my case officer's mouth quirked up in a perfect mimic of an involuntary half-smile. "I usually am, Mr. Zane. And now, if you will excuse me, I have other matters that require my attention. I leave you in the capable hands of Marshal Lobo and Marshal Chandry."

"Good hunting, Gain." Lil's image snuffed out like a candle flame and her genie box retracted its sensor booms and snapped shut.

There was a general self-conscious pause in the compartment, the kind you sometimes get when a high-tension situation suddenly goes limp, leaving the involved parties at a loss for what to do next.

That wasn't a concern of mine. I had a whole list of things I needed to get done. My challenge was which to tackle first.

"Nell, where's Donna Torveska?"

She pointed aft. "She went aft to the control center. She said she had some work to take care of."

"Is she all right?"

Nell looked uncertain. "I don't know. When we learned about Captain Tran, she disintegrated into total weeping hysteria. Then she seemed to catch herself and get it back together again almost as fast as she came apart. I'm not sure what kind of shape she's in, Gain."

"I'll find out." I gave Nell a pat on the shoulder and then headed down the passageway aft.

As I did so I accessed my personal fount of all knowledge.

"Bo, what do we have on Torveska?"

"Age twenty eight," he fired back. *"Birthplace, Karwia, United Baltic Republics. Educated at the University of Warsaw and the Star City Institute of Cosmonautics. Limited operations tickets for light orbital transfer craft and light and medium deep space tugs and towboats. Tabs for nuclear, chem., and ion drives. Employed for four years by Joburg United. Record clean."*

"Specifics now. Anything on her relationship with Tran?"

"Company crew profile indicates a high degree of professional compatibility with Tran. As a crew they buried the needle on their company efficiency ratings. Two mutual requests over the past two operational years to remain together as a team."

"That's all?"

"One other thing, Boss. Tran had a current marriage contract. He left a wife and two children in Singapore."

"Interesting."

The co-pilot was in the joint vehicle control center, a workstation-studded compartment on the rear rim of the barge just forward of the docking collar occupied by the bow of the towboat. The pressure hatch of the trans-ship connector tunnel had been latched open and a warm draft flowed through, the #5 "mountain pine" scent of the towboat's air revitalization system mingling with the barge's #8 "wildflower meadow."

Overtly at least, it seemed as if the co-pilot had pulled it together again. She was working her way around the terminals, running systems checks with a tight-lipped concentration, burying the grief she must be feeling in duty and routine. An escape I suspected she had used often before, the redness of her eyes being the only reminder of her previous breakdown.

"Excuse me, Ms. Torveska, but I need to talk to you."

She looked at me, some new inscrutable emotion flaring in her eyes for a moment. "Of course, Marshal," she replied. "Whatever you wish."

She drifted down into one of the console seats and I followed suit, cinching myself in with the light duty Velcro restraint belt. It's a funny thing, in micro-gravity there is no real reason to sit, but you still do, just for the instinct of the thing.

"Okay," I began. "I'm sure you understand that we've started an investigation into Captain Tran's death. As an aspect of that, a lot of questions are going to have to be asked and answered."

She nodded. "I understand fully."

"Then can I start by asking about your relationship with Captain Tran."

"What about it?"

"Was it something more than professional?"

She met my gaze level-eyed and with no hesitation in her response. "Yes, Lee and I were lovers. We were so for some time."

"And were you aware that he had an active marriage contract, with a wife and two children dirtside in Singapore."

Again she nodded. "Of course. He'd frequently read his children's letters aloud to me. His daughter Leu Bin was accepted into her educational district's honors program last week. That pleased him. He was very proud of his wife's handicraft work as well. Co is very much into traditional Asian silkwork and she's done some lovely things."

Her responses weren't quite what I had expected. "Was his wife aware of you?" I probed.

Torveska shrugged. "I would presume she was. I never

113

asked. Lee was a chronically honest person. I don't think it was in him to conceal something as big as a relationship from someone he truly cared about."

I didn't say anything. I just studied the young woman without speaking. Sometimes that can be the most effective interrogation technique of all. You just let the suspect fill in the silences in their own way, much like a psychotherapist might work.

After a moment the poker-faced silence got to her. "You must understand. Lee spent eight months out of the year in space and four on Earth. He lived in two worlds and I was part of one of them. His wife and his family were part of the other. I didn't intrude into that world. Lee and Co and I had put together an ambiance and I was content with my share."

I drew it out a little longer and her voice lifted slightly, tension creeping into it. "I was happy and it worked!"

"Good," I said finally. "What's bothering you about it now?"

She hesitated. "Isn't the 'other woman' usually considered a prime suspect? I had the opportunity and the skills. And now there is Co for a motive."

I had to nod in agreement. "That is a classic. One point of a love triangle burning another in a fit of jealousy or because they were afraid they were being discarded. It's worth keeping in mind, and I will. However I suspect I have more likely probabilities in this case.

"I'm still pretty sure that I'm still tracking on a conspiracy that's trying to sabotage the Cibola operation. I think they're the ones responsible for Captain Tran's murder."

I lifted my hands. "Again that's not saying, of course, that you couldn't be a cold-hearted bitch who not only sold out her company but availed herself of the opportunity to kill an extra bird with the same stone. But heya, I'm a big fan of

Occam's razor. That seems a little overly complicated to me. I think I've got some other options open for consideration."

Even under the circumstances she managed a ghost of a smile. "What can I do to prove up one of these other options?"

"Off the top, you can keep talking to me. On the run out here, did you or Captain Tran notice anything unusual or out of place?"

Torveska tilted her head back thoughtfully. Given the chance to study her more closely, I could see that maybe she wasn't all that plain after all.

"No," she said finally. "Our departure from L-2 station, our flight here, our landing, everything was a totally routine, right up until your arrival. I can't even recall a bad instrument reading."

"What about your passengers? Anything unusual about them? Did they do or say anything off-skew? Was there anything noteworthy about the way they behaved toward each other?"

"Nothing that comes to mind," she replied. "I know most of these people, like Mr. Zane and the Nolans, only by company reputation. I couldn't say what is normal for them or not. What active discussions there were seemed to be about purely professional matters. Beyond that everyone seemed to keep to themselves."

"Even after the landing?"

"Again I can't recall anything outstanding. We simply touched down and set up housekeeping. I managed the powerdown of the towboat and I've been maintaining the systems watch. Lee worked with Mr. Wilcox quite a bit on the initial inspection of the MD-24 and Dr. Nolan, the male one, went outside a number of times as well. Rana Nolan and Mr. Zane hardly went outboard at all."

"How about any unusual communications. In or out."

She paused and brushed at her eyes for a moment. "Nothing except routine company traffic and mission telemetry on both the data and voice channels. The only thing that caused any stir at all was the report of Ms. Rainey's kidnapping."

"Any ship sightings? Unidentified radar contacts? Anything at all that might indicate that you've had company out here?"

"Nothing at all. We haven't a military grade sensor suite on board but to the limits of some very good civilian systems, we have not detected anything beyond the occasional random meteor since we cleared lunar orbit."

I kept trying to stretch the parameters of the case to incorporate some outside influence but it kept cycling back to the here and now and my present list of suspects. As it read I was likely sitting within twenty meters of my primary perpetrator right now and the knowledge didn't do me a solitary microbyte of good.

Donna Torveska read my mind and filled in the gap in my questioning once more. "I suppose that places me back on the list of suspects again." She stared into one of the inactive flatscreens on the console before her. Whatever images she was seeing she was placing there herself.

"Like I said, not necessarily," I replied, gentling my voice. "Even though I suspect you'd be very happy just now if I did slap the tape on you and proclaim to the universe that you were our saboteur-cum-murderer." My words cut through her internalized hurt and she looked up at me, half anger—half anguish in her eyes. "What are you saying?"

"The truth," I continued. "We both know that you really did kill Lee Tran and it would be a great relief for you to have someone else say it out loud."

"No," that lifted a strangled cry out of her. She tried to

rise but I gripped my chair arm and her shoulder, bracing her down.

"The truth, Ms. Torveska," I continued with a soft mercilessness. "Better to confront it now than let it fester. I was listening in on the circuit when it happened. You killed him. Tran gave the order. You keyed the sequence and Tran died. You killed him, but . . . you . . . didn't . . . murder . . . him. You were set up by the real murderer. Like Tran was set up. Like we all were set up. No one except the bastards behind this knew that the system had been sabotaged. They are the ones responsible. You were only used. The guilt that's eating you alive doesn't belong to you. Unload it. Captain Tran would have understood this. He wouldn't want you to chew yourself up for something you were never responsible for. So don't, for his sake."

She caught a sob and choked it back down. I figured that was enough for now and I unstrapped and started to leave. But the lady caught my arm. "Marshal, do you know if they have notified Lee's family yet?"

"I don't know. I can find out though. Why?"

"I was just wondering if I could be the one . . ."

I rested a hand on her shoulder. "That might be a good idea."

"Thank you. Even if they have been informed, I think we may still have some things to talk about."

One by one I cycled through the other members of the lab crew, isolating them, interrogating, judging, getting their feel. The preliminary stuff of an investigation.

The responses varied. Bewilderment, the Nolans. Enthusiastic cooperation, Nell. Studied wariness, Zane. Sarcastic belligerence, Wilcox.

They all had one thing in common however. None of them could provide me with anything concretely useful.

Bo sniffed around the tug and barge combination as well, checking the life support consumables and doing a degree of forensic eyeballing. His conclusion: if there was a stowaway on board, he didn't breathe oxygen or leave fingerprints.

Of course, as he would be the first to admit, that doesn't necessarily mean much these days.

After a couple of hours Bo and I suited up and stepped outside for a breath of fresh air. Well, not air exactly but privacy. We had our silent chat line via the neurolink, but for awhile I didn't want a lot of other presences around to jam up my thinking.

I had to start analyzing what I'd learned about this case so far and what I was feeling about it. As any working detective can tell you, first comes the feel, then you start matching the facts to it to see if it all holds on the same bearing.

We clumped across the natural steel of Cibola until we were roughly in the center of the lopsided triangle formed by Bo's mainframe, the lab barge, and the cut face of the asteroid. We were right on the day-night terminator line of the little world with the sun blazing on black velvet off to port. The Earth and Moon glowed in mellow blue and white comparison to starboard and the tower of the mass driver stretched off ahead of us like cold fate.

Bo parked his Ken unit on an iron outcropping and I just went limp, my suit's internal pressure keeping me upright while my boots kept me anchored.

"Okay, Bo," I began, *"so we know that the shutdown code didn't come in over the tug's telemetry band. So where was the input point? Where would the system access be here on the rock?"*

"So I don't know," Bo thought back.

"You don't know? Elucidate me on this failing, old friend?"

"Let me re-run that. It's not so much that I don't know as much as it doesn't." Bo gestured toward the geowork skeleton

of the mass driver. *"Cybernetically speaking, this damn thing is an extremely sophisticated cracker box. Other than the company access coding lockouts and firewalls on the command channels, the tug's net has no internal security assets whatsoever. Not even elementary access logs. The operational assumption built into this system is that once you get let in, you're supposed to be here. The primary action memories record that the command was fed into the tug's computer network from a valid net access point but they didn't record which one."*

"How many potential access points do we have to choose from?" I demanded.

"Promise you won't slug me, Boss."

"No promises. How many?"

"Counting the terminals and workstations aboard the lab barge and towboat, plus the service jacks on the mass driver itself, one hundred forty-six."

"Joy for fragging ever unconfined." I hooked my gloved thumbs under my suit's harness belt. *"I guess it's understandable. This rig was designed to operate in deep space, umpty-five gajillion kays away from any potential hands-on interference. The assumption would be that you'd only have to be concerned with hacking on the telemetry and guidance links."*

I glanced down at my partner. *"If we ran our own hardlink from your mainframe over to the computer core of the MD, could you monitor its operations as well as maintaining your own?"*

"Sure. It might slow me down a little but you wouldn't notice it at humanspeed."

"Right, that ought to stave off any more program skagging by the bad guys."

"Maybe," Bo thought dubiously. *"What's our next move?"*

"We hope that Lil geniuses up some leads for us cis-Lunar side." I glanced toward the angular bulk of the lab barge. *"Beyond that, we keep our eyes open and we wait for his, her, or its*

next move. We're still behind the curve out here, Bo. We're still totally reactive."

"Well, we've got at least one bright blip anyhow," Bo was trying to be positive.

"What's that?" I replied, not willing to be positive at all.

"There's one pup in the litter we don't have to worry about. Our delightful, golden Ms. Rainey."

"Sez who?" I mentally grunted.

"Hey, she's been with us all of the time."

"Oh really, my cybernetic innocent? It seems to me that in the interval between our arrival aboard the lab and the tug's shutdown, she was the only one actually out of our sight. Remember when she went to stow her gear in her quarters?"

Of course he remembered. He just didn't want to. Well, neither did I for that matter.

"Tao, Gain," he grumbled, *"it was only for a couple of minutes."*

"Hey ho, how long would it take to feed a pre-prepped data card into the terminal in her sleep cubicle? A couple of seconds? And consider the fact that all hell didn't break loose out here until she arrived on site."

"But the perps tried to have her kidnapped!"

"And a pretty pathetic job of it they did too. Twenty minutes after they grabbed her, we grabbed her back. And if it hadn't have been us, it would have been station security in another half an hour. It strikes me that if someone was serious about diverting suspicion from themselves, being the guest of honor at a flubbed kidnapping would be a great way of going about it."

"Ah shag it all entirely, Boss," he thought in disgust. *"You meatballs are really devious, you know that?"*

"Bear that in mind, my cybernetic innocent. We have two million years of evolutionary sneakiness on our side. That's why we're still on top of the heap."

He mentally sighed. *"The thing is, Boss, I rather fancy that little spin. If she was only link equipped . . ."*

"I know, Bo. I like her too. That's why we have to be spookier about her than anyone else." I thumped him on top of the helmet. *"Come on, let's get that hardline rigged."*

Chapter 8

Aboard the mainframe next morning, Bo blasted me awake with his patented synthesizer version of "Ride of the Valkyries." I reviled his name appropriately and asked if I'd missed anything.

"Negative, Boss. No new developments to report. The time is 0700 hours and everyone and everything is still present and accounted for. The rock is on trajectory and on the deceleration curve and will be entering Earth orbit in sixty-one hours and eighteen minutes, give or take your odd millisecond. As for the neighbors, I've been monitoring them through the box and they're up and stirring around."

Last night, we'd casually left Lil's genie box clipped to a work surface in the barge's crew lounge. I wondered if any of the Joburg team realized that the box's sensors were as effective and as readily accessible with the box closed and apparently inert as they were when the box was open and overtly operational. As we weren't going to mention it, I'd guess we'd never know.

"Good enough. Anything else?"

"Yeah," Bo replied smugly. "I am required to inform you that you are running a half hour short on your low gee calisthenics this week and if you don't do something about it I'm gonna tell Lil, na nana na na nahhhh."

I could think of nothing adequately foul to call him, so I got up and got at it.

I went through half an hour's workout in a resistance harness, working the burn until I was inhaling a haze of my own sweat. Then I hit the bath bag in the 'fresher. I was in the middle of my clean-up when Bo hailed me again.

"Heya, Boss, company coming. One suit headed this way from the barge."

"Do the honors. I'll be out in a short."

I shaved and pulled on a fresh suit liner, then went forward into the habitat space. There, I found myself looking at myself seated across from Nell Rainey in the galley dinette.

The expression on the poor innocent's face as she caught sight of the other me was classic. "I didn't know there were . . . two of you," she said feebly.

"Two of us? I have no idea what you are talking about." I replied, sliding into the dinette and gently bumping her over into the center between me and myself.

"Me neither, you've obviously gone crazy," the other Gain commented.

Your own voice sounds odd enough to you when you hear it in a recording. When somebody else is actually using it, it really sounds strange.

Brows raised, she looked from one of us to the other. Then she grinned. "I understand. One of you is Bo using a duplicate . . . what do you call it . . . Ken of Gain."

"Why would anyone waste good circuitry on making a copy of that lost cause?" my good friend replied.

"Beyond that," I countered, "why would anyone risk his reputation by letting a crashed program like Bo run it?"

"This is exceedingly weird," Nell laughed. "Which one of you is the real one."

"Define real."

"Come on! Be fair, who's who?"

"You come on," I said, thoroughly enjoying myself. "You're a pretty capable individual. You should be able to figure out the difference between the real thing and a cheap copy."

"That's a canard! They ran over budget when they built me and I'm damn proud of it!"

Nell bought into the challenge, leaning forward to study us intently.

"Five cash she can't spot the difference," Bo chortled.

"Taken!" I shot back. *"Meat will out."*

After a few moments, Nell pounced, reaching for and grasping our wrists. She looked smug for a few seconds, then her face fell.

"Nice try," I said, "a fake pulse is part of the standard accessory package."

"Damn," she frowned, thinking hard. Then, after a few seconds, she started to smile again. Deliberately she leaned across the table and kissed Bo full on the mouth. Then, to my considerable interest, she repeated the process with me.

Up to this point in time I have to confess that I'd seriously underrated geologists. There was a pressure of warmly velvet lips, a brush of soft hair carrying her Gamin mist signature scent, and a sudden urgent biological realization that Nell Rainey could be a very inspiring young woman if she put her mind to it.

"Different," she judged, drawing back. "About on a par, but different."

"I don't know if I should be relieved or insulted," Bo commented from across the table.

"That's my line."

"Let's try that again," our lady said slyly. She carefully twined her hand around Bo's wrist. This time, when she leaned forward to administer her kiss, she took her time about it.

Then it was my turn and this time it was full compression

and minimum shielding. A small, warm tongue was deftly used and somewhere in the middle of things the back of my hand was accidentally on purpose guided against the smooth curve of a liner sheathed breast.

She chuckled and drew back a little, grinning into my face. "It's you. You're the human, Gain."

"How did you know," I asked, taking a moment to get my vocal cords back under tension.

"Because your pulse speeded up when I kissed you."

"Aaaagh!" On the other side of the dinette, Bo slapped the heel of his/my hand against his/my forehead.

"That's five you owe me, you inattentive wad of crystalline carbon," I beamed at him. *"If you'd paid attention to the details, no telling how far we could have pushed this."*

"Now will somebody please tell me what is going on?" Nell asked, reorienting to business.

"I don't know myself. Why do you have my doppelganger Ken fired up, Bo?"

"As a spare set of eyes," he replied. "While preserving my own far more dashing and debonair personal for the important stuff, I intend to use short, dark, and repulsive here as a recon unit. I can use him to check out high vulnerability points on the mass driver and to keep an eye on things outside of the range of the mainframe sensors."

"What about the tug's remote servicing manipulators?" Nell asked. "Aren't they good for that?"

He shrugged expressively. "I already am, to a degree, but I'm not sure just how far I can trust the little buggers. They're semi-autonomous, operating on an updating command link from the tug's primary control matrix. We know that our perp is a master hacker and I can't be totally sure that the remotes haven't had their programming cooked to ignore sabotage or even to do more of it."

125

I had to agree with him. "Good point, but can you timeshare both Kens, run the mainframe, and monitor the MD's computer blocks all at the same time?"

"Not a problem. I can shunt a lot of the routine stuff off to the mainframe's auxiliary AIs. But since I'm doing all of these simultaneous jobs, maybe I should ask Lil for simultaneous paychecks."

"Why not? She could use a good laugh. But getting back to reality, what can we do for Ms. Rainey here?"

"The question is more like what can I do?" Nell replied. "I mean I've never been in the middle of a murder investigation before. How should I be going about things?"

"Pretty much the way you normally would, just be aware of anything off the wall."

She lifted an eyebrow. "That will be a challenge. Things are rather crawly over on the barge at the moment."

"What's been happening?" I asked. We already had a pretty fair idea thanks to our friend, the genie box. But it would be good to pull in her personal POV.

"It's just that everyone is so wired up that they can hardly breathe. I don't think anyone slept last nightwatch. I know that it was the first time I ever used the lock on a shipboard sleep cubicle."

"How is everyone handling it?"

"As I said, most crawly. Donna seems to have gotten over her grief, after a fashion. When she's not aft in the control center she just sits in a corner of the lounge looking as if she's waiting for an excuse to cut somebody's throat. The same with Wilcox, only he looks like he's willing to make his own excuse."

"How about Paul Zane?"

"I'm afraid Paul is a little out of his depth," Nell replied. "I've worked with him before and he's a very capable manager, albeit a bit 'eager,' if you know what I mean. But he's an office hand and not really adapted to fieldwork. The same with the Nolans. I know this is their project but they really shouldn't be let out of their observatory without a keeper."

Interesting. I wondered if she could be forthright about other things as well. "How about Nell Rainey?"

The lady in question displayed a dimple. "She is a quivering mass of raw nerve endings but she'd still like to get some work done. Dr. Nolan wants us all to just fort up in the lab barge until we reach orbit, but I've got an ore survey to do, murder and sabotage be damned."

"What's on your agenda?" I asked.

"I'm going out on the surface to burn a few deep core spectrography readings."

"Need a hand?"

"Not really, but I certainly wouldn't mind a bodyguard."

"You've got one. Let me get a pouch of coffee in me and we'll be on your way."

Outside, the sky had changed. The Earth and Moon had grown larger as we had closed the range. Soon, we'd be tipping over the edge of the cis-Lunar gravity well, starting the swing into Earth orbit that would end with Cibola holding in geo-sync over the equator at thirty-seven thousand kilometers out.

As we clumped toward the lab barge, I noticed that someone else was outboard and moving around. A bulky figure in an engineer's hardsuit was setting up a laser rectiliniator. I didn't have to see either the name on his helmet or to see his manipulator gripper hand to recognize who it was.

"Hello, Gavin," Nell called over the suit circuit. "I see you decided to get to work as well."

"Yeah," he replied. "I'm getting started on the installation site surveys. You can shove the sabotage and the rest of that whole damn program."

"Nemanahe!" Nell agreed, giving a thumbs-up.

"And that includes the damn doctors Nolan too."

"Cut them a degree of slack, Gavin," Nell objected. "They're sweating it out just like we are. Only it's more so for them. After all, it's just another job for us but they have their careers riding on this one."

"Then they'd better back off and let us get on with it." Wilcox hunkered down beside the rectilineator and made a minute adjustment to its frame, the massive power gripper on the end of his left arm again working with an uncanny deftness.

He'd studiously ignored me throughout the conversation.

"No argument there. Come on, Gain, the testing rig is over here."

Nell's equipment was stowed in one of the barge's exterior storage bays. It consisted of a fairly fierce-looking industrial laser and power cell combination, a collapsible tripod mount, and a short collection of vacuum-sealed instrument cases and control units.

The weight didn't matter for carrying, of course, but the balance and inertia of it did. As we loaded up, I asked, "Was that a square count? What you were saying to Wilcox back there about the Nolan's career riding on this?"

"Well, I couldn't say for absolutely sure," she replied. "But this operation is definitely Doc Nolan's baby. He produced the numbers that indicated Cibola was a noble rock and he talked the board of directors into going for the intercept. If he can bring it all home, he'll be the company's fair-haired boy for a long time to come. But if Cibola aborts, his standing in the company just might do so as well. His name will be bonded forever to a catastrophic multi-billion cash flop. Not good. Is that riding okay?"

I tried and failed to shake loose the tripod assembly. "Yeah, that's okay. Cinch it down. How about the others on the team? Do any of them have any personal stake in Cibola?"

She thought for a second. "Well, Gavin led the design group that put together the special ore smelting and separating stack we'll be using on Cibola. That's a bit dodgy because no one has ever tried to crack gold ore in orbit before. He's tested very small pilot models but he hasn't had a suitable large ore body to feed through the big unit."

"You mean you might have hauled this thing clear back to Earth and you might not be able to get the gold out?"

"Oh, of course not," she replied. "If it's here, we'll figure out a way to get it out somehow. It's just a matter of profit margins. The faster we can get Cibola producing, the faster we can get our stockholders their investment back and the happier those stockholders will be. The delays involved in another round of R&D on the processing stack would not be appreciated."

I glanced toward the hulking space-armored form working over at his survey site. It had suddenly occurred to me that Nell and I had been speaking unscrambled on a general access EVA channel. If he was interested, Wilcox could have been listening in on our conversation. For that matter, so could anyone on the barge.

A mistake on my part. Maybe. Too late to worry about it now.

"As for everyone else, our stake is in simply not making a hash out of things." Nell peered around my shoulder and into my visor. "And that includes me."

"Acknowledged. Let's go."

We moved out across the asteroid's surface, a ten-meter tether connecting our suit harnesses, a safety precaution to augment the pull of our magnetic boots.

"I want to get a look at Cibola's core," Nell explained as she led out. "So I want to go down on the exposed facing of the rock."

A few minutes and half a kay later we were at the edge of the forward end of the asteroid, near one of the mooring line anchors. "Below" us, the tower of the MD tug rose out of the center of the forward facing, the asteroid's smooth natural topography giving way to the angular planes carved by the tug's cutter heads.

One of those units was trudging past about fifty meters off. From this angle it looked considerably more benign than it had from above, less like a spider and more like a six-legged mechanical cow grazing its way along. Each of its articulated metal limbs ended in a powerful magnetic footpad, the combined pull of which kept the "head" with its three-meter-wide grinder clamped firmly against the surface.

In turn, the spinning grinder wheel's synthetic diamond facing peeled powdered nickel iron off the surface, channeling it through a flexible umbilical duct to the mass driver.

On Earth, the grinding process would have produced a scream like a buggered dinosaur and a spray of sparks that would have been seen twenty kays off. Out here, in hard vacuum, the process was dark and silent, Cibola's bulk absorbing even the vibration.

My companion called up a surface map projection on her faceplate and keyed her transmitter. "Control Center?"

"Control 'by."

"Donna, this is Nell out on the edge of the cutface. I want to sink my first burn on radius nine at about sector twenty-four. How does that match with the sweep pattern of the cutter heads?"

"A moment, Nell, I'm checking it. . . . That should be

good. None of the heads are patterned to cover that area for about the next two hours. Will that be enough time or should I reprogram?"

"Negative. That should be more than enough time. Thanks."

Another voice cut in on the circuit, Rana Nolan's. "Nell, Teague and I do wish you'd hold off on these tests and return to the barge. They can be done under more controlled circumstances after we reach Earth orbit."

That conversation told me a great deal about Teague Nolan. A real expedition leader doesn't coax, he orders. Nell Rainey was right, the Doctors Nolan shouldn't be let out without a keeper, at least not out here.

"Really, it's okay, Rana. Marshal Chandry is right here with me and nothing is going to happen."

I do hate it when some trusting soul applies omnipotence to me just because I happen to wander around wearing a badge patch.

"That's right, Doc," I added. "I'll be keeping an eye on things."

"Very well," the female Nolan didn't sound happy. "But please be careful, both of you."

We crossed the cut line and trudged on. The sun, low angled on the left, shot streams of sharp-edged shadow across the facing of the asteroid. We hadn't gone to far before I broke step for a moment.

"Are you all right?" Nell asked.

"Yeah," I replied, looking back over my shoulder. "My neurolink just went down. We must have too much mass between us and the mainframe."

"Is that a problem?"

"Not really, it's just that Bo and I usually keep an open link."

"You mean you hear each other thinking all of the time?"

"No, to transmit across a neurolink, you have to deliberately key it. A human has to visualize a sequence of geometric shapes and colors to activate the transmitter. It's a mentalization technique they teach you in training and it takes only a fraction of a second after you've practiced it awhile. It's just that I'm used to having Bo's carrier wave buzzing around in the back of my brain. It's one of those things you don't notice until it isn't there anymore."

You can't really see someone shudder in a hardsuit but I had a hunch Nell was going about it. "Excuse me, but I don't think I could ever let somebody else have access to my mind like that."

I smiled and thought about Lil. "Don't knock it until you've tried it, as they used to say. I guess it all depends on who the somebody else is and what you're used to."

"How long have you and Bo been partners?" she inquired as we moved on again.

"About eight years I guess. We linked back during the last Unification conflict: combat operations and special forces work, that sort of stuff. Afterwards we decided to stick together and we transferred to UNILAW. We've been working as a Free Marshal team ever since."

"And its never bothered you being that . . . close?"

I had to think about that for a moment. "Not really, although when Bo was first initialized he had this thing about mirroring my word and behavior patterns. That's pretty common with a newly booted cyber being and it did set my teeth on edge a little. But eventually he began to spin off his own personality and it was okay after that."

"And what about now?"

I felt the corner of my mouth quirk up a little. "Now we've been working together for so long that we're beginning to blur around the edges. Sometimes it's sort of hard to tell where one brain begins and the other leaves off."

She was carefully casual with her next words. "So if anyone else was around you very much, Bo would be part of the package."

"Pretty much."

"Well, Bo isn't so bad," she mused. "What about Ms. Lilith?"

"She's the one who brought Lobo and me over to UNILAW and she's been our case officer since. She's a prime lady. What about her?"

"Well, nothing really. She seems to do . . . female very well."

"She has the knack." I grinned.

Even without a neurolink I could sense that Nell had a couple of hundred other questions, mostly pointed ones about Lil, that she wanted to ask. Certain aspects of female vs. female relations remain constant, even when one of the females is human and the other a sentient biocrystal cybermatrix.

We reached the burn site Nell desired and we started unharnessing the gear. Under her direction, I set up the laser unit's man-high tripod and anchored it in place with magnetic clamps. Then I clipped the projector in place at its center, aimed downward.

"What does this glitterwompus do anyhow?" I asked, running the power leads over to the energy.

"It's a deep-core spectrographic analyzer," she replied, kneeling beside one of the equipment cases. "We use it to survey ore concentrations. This high-energy laser burns down into the surface and a special camera equipped with a spectrographic grid scans the incandescent mineral vapor that comes boiling back up the shaft. We can then cross-reference this recorded image with a time hack and the depth of the shaft and come up with an accurate cross-section of the asteroid's internal makeup."

"Don't you already know the gold's here?"

"Mmmhum," she continued absently, screwing a fiber optic connector into the side of the laser. "But my superiors are going to want to know more about how much. Approximate percentages per ton and such. If I can sink about a dozen of these burns, I should be able to graph that out pretty well. What do the indicators read on the power pack?"

"Uh, three green lights."

"Okay, press the safety switch and move away a bit."

A control pad held in her gloved hands, Nell stepped back about four meters and I followed suit. She tapped a glowing touch point on the pad. "Ready?"

"Heya, you know what you're doing, I don't."

"Here we go then." She keyed another touch point and the analyzer fired.

For the first couple of seconds, the laser was invisible. Then, as metallic vapor began to boil off the surface, the beam became incandescent, as did the vapor itself.

A plume of purple-gold ghostfire flowed around the drill rig and rippled upward ten meters from the surface before dissipating, a strip torn from the aurora.

"Tao!" I said, appreciating.

"It is a pretty thing, isn't it?" Nell commented. "Looks like a pretty fair burn too. We should get a good read on this. We'll take it down about twenty meters."

Our helmet visors darkened in response to the flare of the laser, cutting out the stars beyond the plume. Its wavering light, combined with the ionization hiss in our earphones, created a near-hypnotic effect, like the shimmer and rush of water in a creek bed. It was one of those things you could have stood and watched for hours. Or at least, as Nell and I did, for a long time.

I don't know what it was.

Maybe I picked up a faint, subliminal vibration through my boot soles. Or maybe it was that instinctive urge to "check six" that warriors and cops develop. Or maybe the Universe just leaned over and whispered in my ear. For whatever the reason, I glanced back over my shoulder.

"Sweet befraggin' Tao! Look out!"

I just barely had time enough to grab Nell's shoulder harness and throw her aside, then I dodged myself.

The massive grinder wheel slammed down where we had been standing. The safety tether fouled in it and for a single crazing second, I thought I was going to be dragged back underneath it. Then the heavy gauge Kevlar strap was chewed through and I could scramble clear. The MD tug's cutter unit lifted and swung its grinder head again like a huge hunting beast seeking a scent.

That was more than just a colorful description. This wasn't just a developing industrial accident; the damn thing had veered off its programmed path and was coming for us! Even as I watched, it hunched its way forward a few meters more and brought its grinder plate slamming down on the analyzer. Shredded fragments drooled out from under the edges of the disk like blood and saliva.

Slowly it backed off and started to turn, seeking a new target. And then I heard Nell scream.

I spotted her beyond the bulk of the cutter unit. By rotten chance, the vectors of my toss-aside and the yank on the tether had almost exactly canceled each other out and the geologist was "hung" almost motionless about a meter off the asteroid's surface.

In a few seconds, the pull of her boot magnets and

Cibola's minute gravity would have drawn her back down to the deck, but she didn't have that few seconds to spare.

She was living the realization of a classic nightmare, the one where the shambling god-awful is bearing down on you and you try to run but nothing happens. She twisted and writhed helplessly, trying to get traction on anything and screamed again, the despairing cry of a trapped animal.

I had the Norinco in my exterior suit holster and I clawed for it before realizing the futility of the action. There were probably a dozen places where I could put a gyrocket round into the cutter head that would kill it. But I didn't know where those places were and I wasn't going to have time to find out. Likewise there wasn't anything anyone back at the barge could do in time to help us.

Somebody back there had to be doing this to us!

All I could do was to run. So I leaned forward until I was near parallel with the surface, dug in my toe magnets, and I ran. Actually it was closer to flying low, each raking stride building my acceleration.

I cut around the berserk machine and charged for Nell. I didn't know if there was enough time or space left to make it. Its grinder plate had lifted and was holding over the girl like a malignant child might poise a rock over a crippled mouse, just before the last smash down.

We plowed together with a tooth-jarring crash and my accumulated momentum carried us out and clear. I don't know by how far the grinder plate missed us. I was just content that it did.

Cibola's surface fell away below. Not only had I thrown us clear of the cutter unit but I'd kicked us beyond Cibola's near non-existent escape velocity. We were arcing out into an unsteady orbit around the little world. That didn't disturb me a whole lot just then. I was content to catch up on my backlog of breathing and to hold Nell in the awkward way spacesuits mandate while she cried out her shock and fear. There was a babble of voices over the suit radio that I ignored, focusing on the neurolink. Two minutes after I regained line-of-sight on the mainframe Bo picked us up.

Nell was curled up in the dinette, her suit liner and hair sweat darkened. At the same time though, she was shivering and cupping a pouch of coffee as if its warmth was the most important thing in the Universe.

She wasn't busted however. She looked up at me and tried a wavering smile. "First a kidnapping, then an attempted murder. Do I sense a trend here?"

"Maybe." I pulled another pouch out of the hot box and anchored myself in place by bracing a foot against the far bulkhead. "Then again, you just could have been a good target of opportunity in both instances."

"That's not all that comforting, Gain," she replied. "I don't know which is worse, to be deliberately targeted for murder or to be killed just because you're . . . convenient."

She shuddered again and Bo swiveled one of his cabin ventilator vents around and gently blew a stream of warm air over her. Actually, that was a pretty good question. What reason would there be to single this lady out?

"*Bo. Reference available Joburg databases outside of the current Cibola operation. Any cross-connections or past relationships noted between Nell Rainey and any of the other members of the team.*"

"*Accessing . . . Her name shows up along with Paul Zane's on a couple of minor committee and task group rosters. The same with Gavin Wilcox. She has flown on vehicles crewed by Torveska and Tran before. Nothing outstanding.*"

"*It was a thought.*"

I rested my hand on Nell's shoulder for a second and then I went forward into the command sphere.

Bo was holding us in a parallel flight path to Cibola, about two hundred meters over the surface, and the surround screens gave me a God's-eye view of the Joburg barge, its immediate environs, and the site of the cutter head attack.

I sat there for awhile and brooded over the vista.

"How'd he do it, Bo? How'd he beat us this time?"

"The slimer cut me out of the loop," Bo replied flatly. *"I was running anti-tamper sweeps throughout the MD's software every ten seconds and he must have managed to spot my intervals.*

"During the down time between my sweeps, he not only got in-system and switched that cutter head over to manual remote control but he initiated a dummy feedback from its semi-autonomous AI. I'd keep asking it what was doing and it kept answering 'nothing special.'

"The first warning I had that something was wrong was when he must have bailed out of the system. All of a sudden, the position track on that cutter head gave a big jump as it stopped reporting where it was supposed to be and began telling me where it really was. A few seconds later, I heard you yell for pickup.

"I'm sorry, Boss," he added miserably. *"I let 'em get past me."*

I reached out and thumped the side of the control sphere with the end of my fist. *"Forget it. We've been one orbit behind this guy from the start. Before we arrived on site, he had a couple of days free time to wire things up his way. No telling how many systems he's gimmicked or booby traps he's rigged. Our perp is smart, Bo. He doesn't just think he's smart, he is smart."*

"Too smart for his own good, Boss. And you know what? I'm going to help him with that problem. 'Cause when we nail him, I'm going to wrap my hands around his head and I'm gonna

squeeze, and I'm going to keep on squeezing until his fraggin' frontal lobes squirt out through his sinus passages!"

It's kind of humbling to have someone else get that worked up about your attempted elimination. It kind of makes you wish you were more worthy of the concern.

"Take it easy, pal, and let's go at this from a little different angle. Query, which one of the Joburg team has the technical expertise to do the kind of hyperhacking we've been seeing?"

"None of them do, but all of them could."

"You want to clarify that a little bit there, Bo?"

"Sure. What I mean is, nobody down there has that kind of training listed in their file. None of them was a combat hacker in the military and nobody has done any software design or cybernetic security work. However, all of these people are extremely computer literate. Given a while, any one of our suspects could potentially have self-taught themselves how to do this kind of stuff. Especially from inside of the company firewalls. Having the accesses they'd need as senior project personnel puts them halfway there."

"Abso-shaggin'-lutely marvelous."

An attention tone chimed on one of the verbal communications channels and Bo caught the call.

"It's Dr. Nolan, Boss. He wants to talk to you . . . again."

"Tell him I went into town for some beer and a pizza. No, negative, cancel that. . . . Tell him to have all of his people inboard and waiting for me in ten minutes. I'll talk to him then and explain what's going on."

"Rajah. . . . What is going on anyhow?"

"This. Up to this point, our perpetrator has had the edge because he's had the home court advantage. Well, now we're going to go evens by changing the rules on him."

I hit 'em hard the second we got aboard the barge.

"Bo, search the ship. Access and scan every byte of

memory existent on this pop can. You know the kind of thing you're looking for."

"Yes, sir," he responded, playing formal. He headed forward toward the Joburg team's living quarters.

"What is this, Marshal?" Teague Nolan demanded as Bo brushed past him.

"As I may have mentioned before, it is a murder investigation, Doctor. And a sabotage investigation and an attempted murder investigation and an assault on a law enforcement officer investigation, and I could go on but I'm not going to because you should have the image by now."

"There's been something else?" Rana Nolan asked anxiously.

"There has," Nell acknowledged, removing her helmet. "A short while ago, someone tried to kill both the marshal and I with one of the cutter heads. They just about succeeded too."

Nolan's wife whipped her hand to her mouth. "Oh no, no! Not again!"

"Too right," I added. "And it was someone aboard this barge who tried it. Hands on, up close and personal. This time, there's no question." I glanced over the small cluster of people around the air lock door and noticed someone missing. "While we're on the subject, where's Wilcox?"

"Still outside," the male Nolan said impatiently. "I tried to recall him but he said he was busy. But what's this about a files search?"

"Just that. Our perp likes to play computer games. So, maybe he's left some of his toys laying around: hacker packs, combat 'ware, stuff like that. That's what Marshal Lobo will be looking for."

"But what about our research files?" Mrs. Nolan protested. "Our business documentation, our personal correspondence?"

"From this moment on, there is nothing 'personal' aboard this ship. I wouldn't worry though. Bo doesn't talk stuff around."

"Just a second, Marshal," Paul Zane called in from the back of the pack. "I know that you have your job to do but you can't just come in here and start crashing through our private affairs this way."

"Can and am. And Doc," Doctor Nolan had started to turn away after Bo, "don't get out of my sight or fool with any computer access for a while, please."

"As you wish, Marshal," he replied stiffly. "But I would like to see a warrant before you or your associate start going through our personal possessions."

"I think we could say the same about this entire ship," Zane added. "Look, Marshal, Johannesburg United is the firm being victimized here. I can't see how rousting our personnel . . ."

"Mr. Zane, it is one of our personnel who is doing the victimizing!" Donna Torveska's voice cut in. Suddenly, some of Tran was back with us in the command presence that had settled onto her shoulders. "And Marshal Chandry will not be needing any warrants. I am giving him full authorization to search this craft and everything on board."

"Ms. Torveska, do I have to remind you that I'm leader of this expedition?" Doc Nolan began.

"That is Captain Torveska, Doctor! And I should not have to remind you that I am now command pilot of this space vehicle and that I make the final decisions about what goes on aboard it! Marshal Chandry has my permission to do whatever he believes is needed for his investigation. And we will cooperate . . . fully."

Zane was not pleased. Hell hath no fury like senior management thwarted.

"And maybe you should keep in mind that your status in this company can change, Ms. Torveska!"

She looked at him coldly. "And maybe I am not concerned with my status in the company, Mr. Zane. But until we dock at home base, I make the decisions regarding the operation of this vehicle."

"Paul, wait! Wait a minute." Nolan raised an interceding hand. "She's right . . . he's right. I guess the best thing we can do is to get this craziness over as quickly as possible. Go ahead, Marshal."

"Okay. While my partner conducts his search, let's go into the lounge and do a little more talking."

"Bo. Tap into my hearing and timeshare this with me."

"I'm in."

"Thirty five minutes ago, where? You first, Doc." I aimed a finger at the team leader.

Teague Nolan settled onto one of the lounges. His wife, as seemed to be her thing, huddled close. No more Waifs of the Woods now, they looked like a pair of weary thirty-somethings who had both acquired a maxed-out load of frayed nerves. I suspected the tight handgrip they shared was the primary fixture holding them both together.

"I was right here in the lounge, Marshal, using the work-station to cross-check some of the figures on the upcoming orbital insertion."

"Bo, can you verify?"

"Yeah, the workstation was active. I used the genie box to make a sweep of the lounge during that timeframe and I can fix Nolan there."

"Right."

"Mr. Zane, how about yourself?"

"I was in here as well." The corporate replied with the self-consciousness of a man who senses that recently he just might have made an idiot of himself. He gestured toward a lounge chair with a computer workpad tucked into its side holding pocket. "I was catching up on some business correspondence. Dr. Nolan can verify that, just as I can verify the fact that he was here."

"Me too. He was in the lounge as well. Does that mean we can eliminate them?"

"Nope. We're talking death-by-video-game here. Both of these guys were fooling with computer access. Unless you were physically looking over their shoulders, you'd have no idea what either of them were really doing. A real ballsy mark could commit remote-control murder in front of the UN General Assembly and you'd never know it."

"How about you, Mrs. Nolan?"

She shook her head. "If you are asking for an alibi, Marshal, I'm afraid I don't have one. I was up forward in our sleep cubicle, alone, taking a nap. I can't say that I know of anyone who can verify that for you."

"Bo?"

"Can't prove it by me. She wasn't within my sensor range during the assault timeframe. On the other hand, I didn't sense an active terminal in the Nolans' quarters either. That may be noteworthy. Then again, it may not, given the way our perp can juice a computer system. . . . Oh my goodness, what have we here?"

"What do you have?"

"Our Mr. Zane has some very interactive software in his personal collection. I might just have to make a copy of this stuff for further perusal at a later date . . . in the interest of public morals of course."

"Quit shaggin' around, Bo."

"Rog."

"I can't give you an alibi either, Marshal," Donna

Torveska said. "I was back aft in the towboat, running a reactor core check. I didn't see or talk to anyone."

Bo didn't make me ask. *"The reactor was being run through a core test cycle at that time. Beyond that, the present deponent knoweth not."*

"Okay," I said to him, them, and myself. "That leaves Wilcox."

"He's been outside all morning," Zane offered.

"He also had a field access pad with him and he was out of my line of sight during the time of the attack," Bo seconded.

I turned back toward the gear rack. "Thank you all for your cooperation. I will be going back outside again for a while. Please remain here in the lounge until Marshal Lobo has completed his search."

"You want some cover?"

"Negative, finish your search and keep an eye on these guys through the genie box."

"Okay, Boss. Play nice with the other kids."

My suit came back under pressure tension as the air lock's scavenger pumps began to pull the atmosphere from around me.

"Read me what you've got on Gavin Wilcox."

"Interesting stuff," Bo replied. *"New Zealander; born in Christchurch some thirty-two odd years ago. Not the mellowest of childhoods either. A couple of brushes are recorded by juvenile and school authorities. Nothing major but all related to fighting and a bad temper.*

"Then we have a stretch of International Emergency service. He had a good war record, barring a certain propensity to forget who the enemy was supposed to be. Busted in rank twice for busting inappropriate heads."

I caught the reflection of my smile in my helmet visor. *"No wonder we can't stand each other. We sound too much alike."*

"*I suspect that you put a skootch more youthful exuberance and light-hearted joy into your ass-kicking than Wilcox did. When he went spaceside, his personality scan indicated a chronic aggression problem along with a definite hitch in his mental gitalong when it came to authority figures. Not quite enough to get him a psycho-downcheck but enough so that I bet they thought twice about him. And that was even before his little incident.*"

"*And what little incident was that?*"

"*The one that earned him the permanent nickname of 'Lefty.'*"

"*Proceed.*"

"*Wilcox was working Moonside for the Artimus Group when the mine he was stationed at was hit with some labor troubles. Things apparently devolved to the point that some jackhead felt the need to plant a bomb against the outer wall of the mine administration center. According to the file on the incident, it wasn't all that much of a bomb, but the mine's security chief hit the panic button. He notified UNILAW but the sector bomb squad was delayed in deployment. The security man then ordered his site demolitions engineer to try and defuse the device, even though said engineer didn't have bomb disposal training or the proper equipment.*"

"*Wilcox?*"

"*Yeah. Wilcox wasn't wild about the notion but the security boss held his job over his head until he agreed to take a shot at it. He almost pulled it off too, but then a detonator tab went off in his hand and breached his suit glove. The emergency blow-out cuff at his elbow joint kept him from losing all of his air but it didn't do anything to keep his right forearm from being exposed to hard vacuum. The tissue damage was so extensive that the docs had to amputate.*"

"*Hm. If a cop was directly responsible for my arm getting freeze-dried, I might have a grunt on with the law myself.*"

The lock finished cycling. The deck hatch swung open and I dropped down to the surface.

"Thanks for the update, Bo. If I end up having to push Wilcox's face in, I'll do it in a much more sympathetic and understanding manner now."

Wilcox was quartering an area adjacent to the far side of the barge, marking off a survey grid with the tip of a crayon wand. It's hard to read body language through a spacesuit but I sensed that the big man was running taut.

"Whatever it was, I didn't have anything to do with it," he said over the open circuit.

"Who says anything's happened?" I replied.

"Easy to figure. A short time ago, your ship bounced off the surface, going somewhere in a hurry. Then Nolan starts yelling over the radio link, asking what was going on out at the cut facing. Then you come steaming out here looking for somebody to share trouble with."

I nodded my helmet in response. "When you're right you're right. There's been another sabotage event and murder try. This time I was included."

"I gather they missed."

"Don't be too disappointed. It wasn't by much. Nell Rainey was in the cross-hairs as well."

That seemed to get his attention. "Did Rainey get hurt?"

"No. She was lucky too. Doctor Nolan called you in. Why didn't you come?"

"I had things to do," Wilcox replied, turning away.

"Such as . . ."

"I've been finding a site for my ore processors." He replaced his ground marker in an equipment rack and gestured towards the flats beyond the barge. "We need a large, level area for the heat exchanger banks."

"But that's only if you get this rock into orbit, of course."

Wilcox paused and turned back towards me, half-lit and half-shadowed in the knife-edged light of the distant Sun.

"Yeah. So?"

"So I'm thinking about a comment Ms. Rainey made a while back . . . something to the effect of how the refining process you've developed hasn't been tested in the field."

"So again?"

"So what if this refining process doesn't really work? So what if Joburg, in fact, does get this asteroid all the way home only to find that you can't squeeze the juice out of it as promised, that your refining process doesn't work on the real stuff? So what if management decided to blame the cost overruns onto you? That would not look good on a resume."

His suit visor had gone reflective in the sun so I couldn't see his face, but his voice made me think of a tight feral grin.

"Is that an accusation, Lawboy?"

What could I say? "I'd be lying if I said that the thought hasn't made a pass."

"What are you going to do about it?"

"I'm going to ask you to convince me I'm wrong," I replied. "Were you using computer access out here?"

"Just a field terminal pad."

"Mind if I have a look at it?"

"Why not?" He slid the terminal out of the case clipped to his suit harness and held it out to me.

But he reached cross-body to do it. With his human left hand.

We looked at each other over the extended computer pad, both of us knowing this was an incredibly stupid thing we were about to do. I don't know how many times I've crossed vectors with guys like Wilcox and it always seems to end the same way. It's not the best way to handle the situation and I know it, but I'm me and he's him and there's nothing for it but to blame the shaggin' Universe and get it over with.

I reached for the terminal, and Wilcox's right hand, the tool steel one, pistoned out, targeted on my gut.

I broke my mag boots loose from the surface and blocked the punch with crossed arms, the armorel cloth of my defense coverall keeping the bones from breaking as I rode the impact of the blow. Slamming my boot soles back down onto the rough nickel-iron of the surface, I braked to a stop and drove forward again, ducking under Wilcox's second swing. I felt his manipulator peel paint off the back of my helmet, then I drove my elbow into his flank and it was his turn to ride the impact.

I pivoted and went low again, diving for his feet with the hope of breaking him loose from his contact points and hanging him up off the surface. For all of my good efforts, I was rewarded with a kick in the chest with a metal-shod mag boot. Wilcox was not only big but he was fast too.

Not fast enough to beat the laws of physics however. His boot magnets fixed on my steel harness buckles and fouled him as he tried to haul back for another kick. I got one hand on Wilcox's ankle, the other on the leg of the equipment rack, and one foot braced on one of the barge's landing pads, then I heaved. The engineer sailed over me and crashed into the barge's hull in a slow motion flail of arms and legs.

The problem was that for all of our kicking around, we really weren't accomplishing all that much. The drawback to hand fighting in vacuum gear is that the modern spacesuit is built to be tough and durable to the extreme. A conventional sock in the face doesn't account for much when both of the combatants involved are armored like Sir Lancelot.

The obverse side is that if something does bust, someone may die.

I got to Wilcox before he could get himself upright and oriented and I tried to lock one of his arms up behind his back. I heard him snarl/grunt over the radio band and he powered out of my hold with sheer muscle. Tao, this guy was strong! I tried a commando chop next, aiming for the soft neck joint between his helmet and breastplate. That didn't work either and Wilcox's manipulator hand whipped up and closed on my forearm.

Armorel works great for protecting you from sharp kinetic impacts but it isn't much good against constant pressure. I could make out Wilcox grinning behind his visor as I tried to break free, and I could feel his grip claw jerk and tighten as he shifted its gear ratios and bore down. A band of agony wrapped around my arm as my flesh was crushed against bone, and in a few seconds more, the bone itself was going to collapse.

Frag this slime! If you are up on twentieth century popular literature, it was time to play Superman.

Back when I had my neurolink transceivers implanted, I also had a couple of other accessories installed as well and I opted to use one of them now. I mentalized an activation pattern and a subcutaneous injector capsule fired.

I felt the hot flush roll through me as the Wardrug reached my bloodstream and my biological afterburners lit off. The pain in my arm faded out like a bad dream and the whole world seemed to go slow, giving me three seconds for every one everybody else had. There would be a price to pay for it eventually, but for here and now, it felt good!

I tried the commando chop again with my free hand. This time, the neck joint of his suit dimpled in and Wilcox gagged at the blow across his larynx. His grip slacked for an instant and I yanked free. I got a grip of my own then, shooting my hand out and curling my fingers under his helmet ring. We were still near that landing leg and I drove him headlong into it, my surge of muscle power overriding the inertia of Wilcox's considerable mass. At the last instant, I down-angled his helmet enough so that he took the impact across the impervious crown instead of the slightly more fragile faceplate.

Maybe I could have left it at that, but that's another problem with Wardrug. It has a tendency to make you a bit cranky.

I made use of the landing leg again, or specifically, a grab bar mounted on it. Wilcox still seemed to be operating in slow motion as I grabbed his artificial wrist and slammed his manipulator down over the bar. Then I went for the sheath clipped to my right boot.

Last time I was dirtside, I'd spent some time in a little town down in the Mexican Republic, a place where fighting steel is still understood and appreciated. There, I'd had a knife maker custom-run me something special, a narrow, heavy triangular blade with a T-grip instead of a conventional handle, a modernized equivalent of the old punch dagger.

Back in ancient India, they used them to penetrate suits of armor. I figured it could do the same to a spacesuit.

There wasn't a need for that yet, so when I struck, I targeted the point down into the housing of Wilcox's artificial hand, below the pressure junction of his suit.

It worked pretty much as I figured. The razor-edged alloy of the blade pierced the plastic shell of the manipulator and committed various atrocities inside. He didn't loose any blood or breathin' but the short circuits feeding up the connectors into his nervous system likely didn't feel very good.

Wilcox convulsed and roared in agony and his manipulator locked up around the grab bar. I yanked the punch dagger out of his forearm and angled it across the faceplate of his helmet, letting the unfiltered sunlight shine on the polylubricant smeared along its cutting edges.

"Ever since I landed on this rock, we've both been wondering how this would end out." My jaw muscles were locking up from adrenaline tension and I had to work them carefully to get the words to come out right. "Well, now we know, don't we?"

Wilcox sank to his knees, hanging his bulk from his ruined manipulator. "Shag you, you lawboy bastard," he muttered back over the circuit.

The engineer's work pad still dangled from its elastic safety lanyard and I collected it with a slash of the punch dagger. "Thank you for your cooperation, citizen. We'll be contacting you if we have any further questions."

I re-sheathed my knife and left the engineer sagging against the barge's landing leg. Dr. Nolan's voice sounded querulously in my helmet phones as I walked away. "Marshal Chandry, what's happening out there? Do you require assistance?"

"Negative. I don't need assistance and nothing worth mentioning is happening. . . . You might send someone out to help your Mr. Wilcox however. He might need a hand."

Pissed and juiced both, I still couldn't pass up that line.

I was just clearing the bow of the barge when I caught movement in the down-sun-side shadows. My hyped nerves had my gun out and leveled before I realized I was even drawing.

"Ho, Boss. Just me." Bo's voice sounded in my head. The figure that came out of the dark towards me was wearing a spacesuit identical to my own rig. It was my doppelganger Ken, the unit Bo had activated that morning for snooping and

scouting. I should have figured he'd keep me covered, even when I hadn't asked for it.

"You okay?" he inquired.

"Yeah," I said, re-holstering the Norinco. *"I just had a brief yet pointed discussion with Brother Wilcox. He came out of it on the down side, in case you couldn't guess."*

"I guessed. Your suit okay?"

"Yeah, I'm tight and green."

"Excuse me for saying," he probed cautiously, *"but your bio read-outs are looking a little bent."*

I suppressed another shudder. *"I popped a shot of Wardrug. I just have to walk it off."*

The Ken swung into step alongside me. The strength and reflex boost were already fading. Soon, they'd be replaced by the crawling gut, the aching muscles, and the cold sweat of the backlash. There's no such thing as a Wardrug addict. The designers made sure the stuff makes you feel too fraggin' rotten to promote such a thing.

"You had to charge up just to take one measly little engineer? Pathetic, Boss."

"I'm getting old, Tin Man."

"You want me to get started on booking Wilcox?"

I shook my head. *"Negative. Let it lay."*

"He tried to take a chunk out of you!" Bo protested.

"I'm calling it as not on company time, Bo. Private affair, so just let it lay. Now, how are things going inboard?"

"I've scanned through all of the personal files I could scare up and now I'm going through the system memory banks of both the barge and towboat. Nothing worth mentioning so far."

I shrugged. *"That doesn't mean that they couldn't have held their hackerware in active memory and then dumped it after using it. Or, they could have it stored on a data card that's been hidden somewhere. Ten minutes after you finish your search, our perp* could be up and spooking around in the Mass Driver's systems again."

"Hey ho. Not arguing."

"We've got to cut him off, Bo. We've got to isolate him from the tug systems."

"No arguing again. But how? I could upload some standard anti-hacking programs into the MD's software block but I don't know how much good that'd do. If this guy is as good as he seems to be, he could bugger your sister through her digital watch."

I stopped for a second and looked out at the eternity-tower of the MD tug. "Maybe we're going about this the wrong way. Maybe we should be treating this as a hardware problem."

"How's that, Boss?"

"I mean, why not try physically cutting our perp off from access to the MD's systems?"

"How? By bodily ripping every terminal and workstation aboard the barge out by the roots?"

"Uh uh," I thought back, shaking my head. "We work from the other end. We disable the MD's existing computer control matrix and we replace it with a system that can't be hacked, spooked, or penetrated in any known way."

Inside the visor of the doppleganger's helmet, I saw the copy of my own features go puzzled. "You mean a cyber being?"

"You got it."

"Heya, Boss. I know I'm good," Bo protested, "in fact, on some of my better days I approach the awesome. However, I can't assume full operational control of the Mass Driver complex and my own mainframe and stay tactical with the Kens. I'll start bibbling and smoke'll come out of my ears."

"I know, Bo. But to quote a famous doctor from speculative fiction, 'Igor, we must have a brain!' "

"So where in eternity are you gonna get a fast-cyber-to-go-with-a-side-of-fries out here?"

I looked into the doppelganger's face and grinned. After a second, he grinned back. Sometimes you don't have to use a neurolink to be able to read each other's minds.

"Oh, Lil!"

My superior wasn't initially enthused with the concept.

"You want me to assume control of an ore tug?" Through the neurolink, I could sense the lips she doesn't actually have, curl.

"Something to that effect," I replied as Bo and I trudged across the asteroid's surface, heading for the asteroid's cut face and the mass driver's massive push plate. *"Think about it. Ever since our arrival on Cibola, our perp has acted only through the MD-24's computer control systems. If we take those integral computers off-line and operate the tug's systems remote control over a set of our secure data links, we might pull his fangs, or at least maybe force him out into a more obvious form of attack."*

"I concede that it is a valid tactic, Gain, but I am attempting to run a division of a major security agency here. I can't commit that much time and processor power to a single project."

"Aw, c'mon there, Lil," Bo interjected. *"You're all the time kyping about how you never get out in the field."*

"Running a tug wasn't exactly what I had in mind, Lobo," she chilled back.

"So don't do it then," I thought patiently. *"Just get me another cyber or a milspec secure AI with enough thinkin' in it to run this rig on remote."*

"Systems that powerful aren't that easy to come by on short notice, Gain."

"Why not pull Hawk away from whatever door he's propping

open and put him on the job?" Bo put in helpfully. *"Shoving rocks around would be about on a par for his mentality level."*

"Marshal Hawk has prior commitments, Lobo, as do all of the other cybers under my authority."

"It's okay, sweet one," I thought in my best heroically self-sacrificing tone. *"As the senior officer on site, I think that this is the best way to handle this situation, but if I can't get the support I need for this job, I guess I just can't get it."*

Some virulent emotional echoes leaked over the link. *"Can you give me an hour or so to clear my calendar for the next couple of days?"*

"Not a problem." I grinned out into the double-dark. Now I was evens-up with Lil for that short briefing she'd given me.

It took us better than eight hours, not counting a couple of short breaks for eatin' and oxygen. Eight hours of program re-writing, system bypassing, circuit rerouting, compromising, innovating, reinventing and, on a couple of occasions, the physical demolition of expensive and delicate pieces of equipment with a crowbar. The re-design all came off the top of the brilliant heads of Lil and Lobo. I just slithered through an endless series of access hatches and crawlways and followed instructions.

When we were done, Bo and I stood out on the surface of Cibola and watched the mass driver's main antenna array index around and target the distant point in space that held Dawn City.

"All data links are up and I have active control of all tug systems," Lil reported. *"We are holding on marked headings and maintaining the deceleration schedule. We are now fifty-four hours and twelve minutes from Earth orbital insertion."*

"Anything else we need to cover?"

"A little fine tuning and some rough edges to round off the new

systems interfaces, but I think I can handle it all from inside," she replied.

"Good enough, sweet one, and thanks. You came through for me, as per usual."

"It's my job, Gain."

"Maybe so, but still, thanks. We'll disconnect and secure the hardlink from the barge and shut down here."

"Do it next watch. I've already got the link disengaged internally. Go get some rest now. Your bioloads are going yellow." That was a valid observation. My head was pounding from the backwash of Wardrug and adrenaline, my arm ached dully where Wilcox had clamped me, and I'd spent too many hours in-suit and I was becoming sick of my own smell. In short, I was thoroughly wrecked and at the moment I never wanted to ever hear the words "asteroid" or "Cibola" again for the rest of my life.

Unfortunately, the damn place wouldn't go away.

"Status of the bunch on the barge, Bo," I asked as we plodded back to the mainframe.

"All quiet; everyone seems to have settled down for the night."

"Great."

"Y'know, Boss," my partner mused, *"we've been tinkering around with the mechanical brains around here all day; what about doing the same to some of the meat ones?"*

"What do you mean?"

"I'm just thinking. Why not we sneak a touch of tranc gas into the barge's life support system? Then I'll go aboard with my little Doctor Bob medical kit and a couple of temporary neural taps and tiptoe through a few cerebellums. No telling what we might find."

"You're making my mouth water but it's no-go."

"Why not?" he protested.

"Because, you know as well as I do that it wouldn't constitute a legal brain scan. None of the suspects have been formally charged

*with a crime, none of the suspects have access to legal counsel, and
you don't have officially recognized scanner credentials."*

"Since when's that ever slowed us down?"

*"Since I don't want this particular perp to walk out of court on
a technical. This is a blood case, Bo. We're not going to blow it,
even if it does mean having to do it the old-fashioned way."*

We reached the corvette and went aboard through the
belly lock. At the moment, the mainframe was the sole totally secure environment available to me and, as the lock
pressurized, I began to stand down from my mental alert
status. That's why I almost ricocheted off the overhead
when the inner door opened and someone moved inside the
ship.

"It's just me! It's just me!" Nell Rainey said, lifting her
hands in alarm.

"Oh, heavens to Betsy," Bo exclaimed innocently through
the overhead speakers, his persona swapping out from the de-
activating Ken to the ship. "Did I forget to mention that we
had guests? I guess it must have slipped my mind."

"Yeah, sure, you betcha."

"I hope you don't mind," Nell added timidly. "I just
wanted to come aboard for awhile."

"No problem," I replied, guiding her back forward into
the main cabin. "Unless you have one?"

"Uh, not really," she said, trying to fake a good case of ca-
sualness. "I just wanted to get off the barge and . . ."

She hesitated and then blurted out, "Oh Lord and Lady,
why not just tell the truth! I can't stand it over there any
more."

"What's wrong?"

"Someone on the team tried to kill me!"

I had to nod in agreement. "Well, yeah, there is that. But I
don't think this guy is the kind who'd try an overt hit in front

of witnesses. If I'd thought anything else, I wouldn't have left you there without cover."

"I know, but still . . . I go around as nervous as a rooikat. I'm scared to be with anyone, I'm scared to be alone, and there is just no way I'll be able to sleep with just a folding door partition between me and . . . whoever. May I stay here?"

I glanced up at the cabin sensor head. "What do you think?"

"She snore?" Bo inquired.

Nell flashed her smile. "I'm told only in a very light and lady-like manner."

Bo pretended to think it over. "Well . . . okay. She can stay. But remind her she had better re-fold the bath bag after every use or I will be merciless."

While Nell explored the accommodations space, I went aft to the air lock to shed and rack my vacuum gear. I'd been experiencing some pain in my right forearm, off and on, all day and I experienced a little more as I squirmed out of my pressure suit. But it wasn't until my right arm bumped the hatch frame that it really hit. "Ow! Tao take it all entirely!"

"What is it, Gain?" Nell inquired.

"Nothing, just a little reminder of why I took Wilcox out of my Christmas card file."

I went to the foldout couch forward of the galley dinette. Bracing myself down, I peeled my damaged limb out of my suit liner. Like I figured, a magnificent bracelet of purple-black flesh looped fully around the forearm. The snug pressure of my space armor had been keeping the swelling under control, but now it was making up for lost time.

"Ah, I should have chopped that bionic bastard's tin hand clear off."

"Stars! That looks bad!" Nell exclaimed. "Did Gavin do that?"

"Yeah, I must confess that he did."

Nell said, settling down beside me and starting an intent examination of my injured arm, "I initially thought you might have overreacted just a tad in your confrontation with him but now I take it all back."

I winced again at her probing. "By the way, how'd he make out?"

"It took some doing but we got him pried loose from that landing jack and back inboard. It was rather interesting really. A humbled Gavin Wilcox is a novel sight."

Abruptly, she got up again and zipped back into the 'fresher compartment. A few moments later and she was rummaging through the medical stores locker.

I raised an eyebrow at Bo's cabin sensor head.

"Before I'm cut out of this equation altogether," he thought, *"may I state for the record that a thermographic scan of your arm shows no sign of blood clotting and that circulation is more or less intact. It's not going to fall off; it'll just feel like it is."*

"Thank you, oh noble medicine man."

Nell was back a moment later with an armful of first aid stores. Anchoring back down beside me, she flipped open the packet of a cleansing towelet and wiped the antiseptic sheet lightly over the discolored tissue of my arm. She followed it up with a deft wrapping of analgesic gel tape. To say the least, it felt pretty good.

What followed next felt even better.

Nell hesitated shyly for a moment, then tugged my liner the rest of the way down to my waist. Opening another towelet, she slowly began to run it over my bared shoulders and chest, all with a touch as light and as cool as an Earthside sea breeze and all with the same look of sober intentness she'd worn when she had been tending to my injury.

"I . . . think I'll go turn myself off for awhile."

"I think that's a good idea, Bo."

As for me, I just lay back for awhile and let it happen. Not only was the alcohol bite of the rubdown incredibly refreshing and Nell's warm, hovering presence highly appreciated, but there was a definite, masculine ego-boost in effect here. Something on a very primal level; the prime bitch wolf of the pack laving the boss dog. Very addictive stuff.

Too much so maybe, if I let it be.

I reached behind her head. Her stubby ponytail made a convenient handle and I used it to gently steer the tip of her nose to within about eight centimeters of mine.

"You're welcome," I said.

"What?" The spell was broken for her and her eyes came back into focus. I really noticed for the first time that she was that biological rarity, a true brown-eyed blonde.

If you're up for details, honey-brown.

"You were saying 'thank you,' so I said, 'you're welcome' to indicate that we're evens-up."

"What are you meaning, Gain?" she asked, looking puzzled.

"Because before things possibly get a little bit crazy around here, I just want to make sure we're both guarding the same frequency. When I dragged you out from in front of that grinder today, I was doing my job. I would have done the same for Wilcox. Maybe not with quite as much enthusiasm, but I still would have done it."

"Ah," her eyebrows lifted and she relaxed, letting me hold support her quarter ounce of weight. "And you think that I might be . . . acting . . . out of a sense of obligation?"

"I don't know," I replied with stark honesty, "I haven't known you long enough to be able to read you that well. What I do know is that I seem to like you a lot, Nell Rainey, and that

I don't want you to think you have to do anything that you don't want to do for yourself."

She seemed pleased. "I understand, no obligations. And now, please let me go so I can do what I want."

I released her, and her arms came up and circled my neck, her lips closing with mine and her breasts molding against my chest. It was a prime kiss, just as it had been that morning. (Had it just been that morning?)

No obligations she had said. Those were terms I could live with.

I touched the light bar behind the couch, sinking the cabin down into its cool blue night illumination. Then my hand returned to the back of her neck, this time seeking the release tab of her liner. I found it and she gave a low appreciative moan and an involuntary shiver as the fabric parted down her spine.

In micro gee, it was easy to lift her around until she lay on her back beside me on the couch, her head and shoulders cradled in my lap. From there, it was a pleasant chore to help Nell make her transition from clothed to naked, aiding her in peeling her single tight-fitting garment down and off until she could kick free of it, acknowledging each inch of satiny skin revealed with my fingertips. Nell shivered again at my touch and looked up into my face, waiting for what would be next.

Turnabout was fair play. I caught up one of the towelet packets and used its contents as a polishing cloth on her breasts, cooling each hardening nipple and working down across her flat stomach to the shadowy valley of her thighs.

Way back over a century ago, the old master, Arthur C. Clarke, had been right when he had predicted that one of the great advantages of low gee would be that you could really hold someone close all night long without having to worry about your circulation being cut off.

Some time along later, something nudged me back awake. We were back in the sleep cubicle and Nell still lay nestled in the curve of my arm, held in place by the tension of the elastic sheet.

"Lil?"

"Yes, Gain." Her thoughts trickled into my brain. *"Sorry to wake you but there have been some new developments."*

"The tug okay? We still on course?"

"It is and we are. No problems. In fact, I'm actually beginning to enjoy handling this monster. It's a rather novel challenge."

"What is it then?"

"An intelligence report from Earthside concerning that quasi-biblical propaganda that showed up on the infonets concerning Cibola."

I'd nearly forgotten about that stuff. *"What do we have?"*

"Unfortunately, not much. The spore virus that had been creating it has been pretty much purged from the nets. They were never able to fix a point of origin, however, nor were they able to get a positive make on the designer's identity."

"Anything unusual noted with any of the religious radicalist groups?"

"Nothing worth noting. A couple of very minor fringe groups appear to be reacting to the message virus but there is no evidence any of them initiated it. Likewise, Interpol reports no unusual activity by any known terrorist-for-hire operation."

I digested the data. *"Query, any outstanding religious affiliation noted among the on-site Joburg team?"*

"Donna Torveska and Gavin Wilcox both list themselves as Roman Catholic. Paul Zane was born into a Mormon family. However, records indicate inactive membership. The Doctors Nolan show no religious affiliation at all, while Ms. Rainey is a member of a neo-pagan group that, barring a propensity for worshiping out-of-doors in the nude, appears totally unremarkable."

I found myself glancing down at the graceful curves concealed beneath Nell's half of the sheet. No doubt she was a jewel in the crown of that particular congregation. I shook off the intriguing imagery and got back on track.

"Any repeat runs of the spore virus? Any other acts along that line?"

"Negative, Gain. No follow through of any kind. Just the single insertion."

"That's kind of funny, isn't it, Lil? They go to all of the trouble of constructing a sophisticated program like that virus and then they only use it in a single, clumsy propaganda ploy."

"I think it was purely a diversion," she replied, *"and that we can safely drop the religious fanatic angle altogether."*

"I concur; they were trying to fox us off. The thing is, they should've done a better job of it. There should have been some kind of follow-through."

"Don't sound so disappointed, Gain."

"Stay with me on this, sweet one. Our perp is demonstrating a kind of split personality in the way he operates. Sometimes, he's very, very good at what he does, as he was with his penetration of the Joburg computer net and the hacking he's done with the MD's computer here on Cibola. But at other times, he's not so good. As with this diversion and with his attempted kidnapping of Nell Rainey."

I received only carrier touch for a long second as my distant boss digested the thought. *"This could be a valid point of consideration, Gain. Possibly it's a clue to either their methodology or motivation."*

"Or identity," I continued. *"I think we're dealing with an amateur here, Lil. A smart one, but still an amateur who doesn't know all the tricks yet."*

"Again that closes the loop into someone within the Joburg United group itself."

"We shall see."

"Speaking of kidnapping," Lil continued, *"I ran a genie box sweep of the barge a short time ago and I didn't detect Nell Rainey's life signs. I presume she's with you aboard the main-frame?"*

"The only way we could get any closer would be through skin grafting."

"Ah," I felt Lil's amused pang echo through the link. *"I didn't think that poor child would be safe around you."*

"What can I say? It's a gift?"

Lil's thought pattern flicked back to serious. *"Does this indicate you have eliminated Ms. Rainey as a potential suspect?"*

Good question.

"I don't know, Lil. I still don't have any kind of track on a solid suspect yet. I can't afford to eliminate anyone."

I shifted position slightly and my golden-haired bunkmate instinctively snuggled in response. *"I'll confess though, I do hope this fair lady isn't our perp. I admit I would find that seriously depressing."*

"Then I hope she isn't either," Lil's link mellowed out into a mind caress. *"Share joy with her, love, but don't let down your guard."*

"I won't, sweet one. Talk to you tomorrow."

"Tomorrow."

Chapter 9

I awoke the next morning to find my bed pad considerably more empty and less friendly. Nell apparently had slipped out earlier on and I had been too deep under to notice. A pity because I consider a cuddle with an affectionate female as one of the few things that can make the AM hours worth bothering with.

"Time!" I croaked, crawling out from under the restraint sheet.

"0717 hours, oh Lord and Master," Bo replied, his voice issuing from the overhead speaker, "and good morning to you too."

"Okay, okay," I replied, dragging a fresh suit liner out of a locker. "Morning greeting rituals exchanged. When did Nell take off?"

" 'Bout forty-five minutes ago. She very sweetly requested that I not wake you from your swinish slumber."

"Yeah, yeah." I finished dragging on my liner and went out into the main cabin, almost bumping into my doppelganger Ken, who was busy re-cladding into vacuum gear. It's piss-poor Tao when your own dop unit looks better than you feel.

"What's he doing back here?"

"Maintenance problem," Bo replied, switching his commentary from the intercom to the doppelganger's voice box. "Prolonged exposure to the MD's electro-magnetic drive field was making his gyro table start to hunt. I recalled him a

165

couple of hours ago for a recalibration job. Done, and I'm ready to put him out in field again."

"Okay, hang fire and I'll go out with him. Just let me get alive a little." I tossed a coffee pouch into the hot box. "Situational update?"

"All quiet, nothing new to report. Tug functions are nominal, although Lil's reported that a couple of minor glitches have shown up in yesterday's brilliant improvisational work. We'll have to do a hands-on to correct 'em."

"Noted. Navigation?" I retrieved the pouch, juggled it for a second until the surface heat dissipated, and then popped the straw out. Not bothering with sweetener or creamer, I took a pull.

"On course, on sked," the doppelganger replied. "Shortly after zero hundred last night, the Combine entered the Moon's gravity well and began its turn into cis-Lunar space. We're now thirty-one hours, twenty-one minutes to Earth orbit."

"Been picking up anything interesting next door on the genie box?"

"There's just routine breakfast talk going on in the lounge. Mostly Nell and Ms. Torveska with an occasional grunt from Wilcox. Voice stress analysis indicates a mildly raised tension level but nothing out of place given the tactical situation.

"However, I'm also getting raised voices from up forward in the crew's quarters, the Doctors Nolan and Mr. Zane."

"What's their problem?"

"I can't read what they're saying but they appear to be serious stirred up about something."

"Just another thing to look into." I killed off the last of the caff and then started to shake down the rations locker in search of something tolerable.

"Speaking of things to look into," Bo continued, "could I ask you a favor?"

"It's conceivable. What?"

"Next time you feel like heating up the sheets, could you *please* take the lady back to her cubicle? Please?"

"What in the name of Tao entirely is this all about?" I snapped over my shoulder. "I know for fact that they haven't started selling mukluks in Hell yet, so this can't be a belated outburst of hyper-morality."

"Nothing like that, Boss. Far be it from me to deny you the pleasure of that tasty little dollop of trollop. In fact, if she had a link installation, I'd be trying to get on her social schedule as well."

"So hey ho?"

"So having you and Nell thoroughly enjoy each other's company inside my mainframe's living spaces was . . . disconcerting."

"If I was too intimidating for you, why didn't you just turn off your internal sensors?"

"I did . . . eventually. But I couldn't turn off my imagination. Knowing that all those fireworks were going off inside me was kind of . . . well, it was sort of like if you knew that you had a couple of tapeworms busy shagging away in your duodenum."

I deliberately closed the door of the food locker. "Well, that shoots breakfast down right there. We shall discuss this issue further at a later date. In the meantime, I'll gear up and we'll get to work."

The doppelganger Ken was wearing my spare suit setup, so I shared the lock with myself as we cycled outboard.

"Okay," I thought, switching over to neurolink. *"Our first job of the day will be to finish the hardline disconnect with the tug, just in case. Then we'll get on to Lil's system tweaks. In the mean-*

time, our subject of discussion will be Dr. Nolan and his lady. What do we have on 'em?"

"Cross breed your basic marriage-made-in-heaven with your classic local-boy-slash-girl-makes-good plot line and you've got it all," Bo replied. *"He was born in Toronto in the United States. She was born in Biera in the Union of Greater South Africa. Both of them were distinguished, young, over-achievers who scholarshiped their way through college. Our boy Teague receiving his doctorate in Astronomy from the University of Ontario while the then Ms. Rana Mekubara matriculated at the University of Kenya. Their relationship with the law can only be described as virginal. Nothing on record this side of a parking ticket."*

As we conversed, we dropped out of the lock and began the hike across Cibola's surface to the sunglare-silhouetted outline of the lab barge. In that little corner of the brain that constantly processes triviality, I found myself doing a flash-consideration of my actions and surroundings. Here I was, traversing the mythic "soil of the asteroids," something that a scientist or a space-crazy kid of a century or so ago would have sold his soul and a couple of decades of life span to do. And yet, over the past couple of days, this had become a routine. Miracle into drudgery. Figure it. I shook off the mental meandering and refocused.

"When did they meet and how did they get involved with Joburg?"

"The company came first," Bo replied, the dop Ken moving out a couple of paces ahead of me. *"Like I said, they were a pair of bright young things and they didn't have much trouble in picking up a couple of slots in Johannesburg United's Astrography Division. They actually got together about six years ago when Dr. Mekubara was assigned to work with Dr. Nolan on a special project he was developing."*

"Which was?"

"Something like this Cibola thing, a totally wild-ass concept that he'd somehow managed to ram down the throats of his superiors. Nolan had this theory about locating commercially viable geothermal resources on the Moon.

"To prove it out, he developed a computer database that incorporated literally the sum total of all lunar astronomical observations made over the past three and a half centuries, a monumental research and programming job. Then he rigged it to scan for and cross-reference anything that might have been an outgassing event or surface volcanic activity.

"To make a long short, it worked. The end results were . . ."

"The Alphonsis Basin steam wells," I interjected. *"I've heard about them. The only source of natural water on the Moon."*

"Yeah. And, my, didn't the company make money off of that one. The two doctors received a whole stack of major academic awards for proving that everything we knew about lunar geophysics was wrong as well as major promotions within the Joburg corporate structure. They married shortly thereafter."

"Hm," I mentally grunted, *"and ever since then they've likely been trying to figure out how to produce a follow-up act to top their opener. No wonder they're getting a little bent over this rock."*

Without thinking about it, I'd slowed my pace a little, widening the distance between the doppelganger unit and myself. We'd started to angle across to the leading edge of the lab barge where the hardlink had been jacked into the hull.

The hardlink itself was a standard fiberoptics data transfer cable that trailed off across the asteroid to the cut face. From the edge of the cut face it had been allowed to free arc up to a connector point on the MD tug, the cable's weight being irrelevant. But around the landing site it had been suspended on a series of light aluminum pylons magneted to the surface to keep it overhead and out of the way.

"Let's collapse that first pole and do the disconnect from there."

"Rajah, Boss." Bo turned the Ken unit toward the base of the pole.

"Now how about Paul Zane?" I was about five meters behind the Ken.

"Oh yeah. Mr. Zane, our perfect little wage man . . ."

Wage man . . . the trailing end of that phrase somehow seemed to hang on as an echo in my failing awareness as the whole universe suddenly glared blue-white and I was hurled backward on the face of a titanic sledge hammer.

I could have died really easily. In fact I should have died!

The wave front of the explosion threw me right into the Joburg barge. If I had hit the side of the barge itself or had clipped one of the landing legs, that would have been it.

Instead, I skimmed under the barge's hull and crashed into the equipment racks that had been deployed there. The light molytube and glass-fiber strap framing snared me like a drone recovery net, snagged me up short.

I lay there in the tangle and I could feel myself fading out. Whether just from general principles or because the air was leaking from my suit, I could not tell. I could not do anything much about it at the moment either. The last thought I had before I shut down entirely was of Wilcox.

I should have chopped the shagass's head off instead of just his hand.

"Gain . . . Gain?" There was just the darkness inside my mind. I wasn't quite ready to try accessing any of my senses yet.

"Gain, am I reaching you? Can you respond?"

"Yeah, Lil, I'm back."

"Thank all," she murmured. *"Take it easy, love. I'm with you."*

"What happened to Bo?"

"Nothin'. I'm right here too, Boss. I'm okay."

"I thought the damn mainframe had blown up."

"Not so, Boss. I didn't even get my paint scratched."

About then, I gave opening my eyes a shot. The light stabbed through to the back of my skull, triggering a burst of pain. I forced the world to come clear. I was in the lounge of the Joburg lab barge, stretched out and strapped down on a couch section and surrounded by the scattered, battered components of my vacuum gear. Nell knelt by the head of the couch, looking concerned, while Bo stood anchored off near the foot, looking ominous.

The others of the Joburg team were huddled over at the far end of the lounge area. Their uneasy demeanor suggested that Bo had been a little bit moody of late. Mr. Lobo is generally a very genial and easygoing guy, but can be very impressive when he gets moody.

Wilcox was set off a bit to one side. He had about ten meters of restraint tape wrapped around his wrists as well as a massive bruise developing on the side of his face. One that I knew that I hadn't put there. Nell was right, a humbled Gavin Wilcox was something to see.

Gingerly, I tugged open the Velcro restraint strap around my chest and pushed myself upright, cataloging an impressive collection of aches, throbs, and seize-ups. On the end table, Lil's genie box snapped open and its sensor booms and projector heads rigged out. Her hologram materialized a moment later. As with Nell, I seemed to be the primary point of concern, but both females, cyber and human, managed to exchange a few moments of mutual "What the hell are you doing here" examination.

"Okay, Bo," I said. "If you didn't blow up, what did?"

"There was a demolition charge parked under the footing pad of that cable support pole. Somebody used it to try to take you down."

"Link me a replay of it."

"I don't know if that's such a good idea, Gain," my case officer said, her lips synched with the voice issuing from the genie box's speaker. "You've no doubt suffered at least a mild concussion, and a lot of neurolink activity on your part might not be advisable."

"Lil, if my brain was going to fall out, it would have done it by now."

"None the less, let's do this visually."

The genie box's secondary projectors actuated, throwing a half-dome of imagery on the top of the low work surface in the center of the lounge.

It was being called up from Bo's memory, a record recalled from the mainframe's external cameras. We watched in rather morbid fascination as two thumb-sized figures in identical spacesuits appeared, trudging across the miniaturized patch of Cibola's surface. The lead figure approached the slim silver shaft of the support pylon and my stomach muscles involuntarily cinched up.

The charge exploded.

Bo went to hyper-slow motion so we could actually see the bubble of incandescent gas well up from the conical pad at the base of the pylon and expand outward, bits of debris tumbling on its outer surface. It reached and engulfed the figure of the Ken unit, twisting it off the surface and flinging it away. Then it continued to expand, thinning as it did until it touched the figure that had been me.

"Good thing we were on an asteroid, Boss," Bo commented. "If there had been an atmosphere out there to carry the concussion, you'd have been killed seriously dead."

"How'd they blow it?"

"Direct command detonation. A couple of microseconds before the bang, my com scanners picked up a six-digit microburst on a standard EVA data link channel. A standard suit transceiver was used as well. It must have been a pre-programmed trigger code. Someone was standing around with his finger on the button, just waiting for you to stick your head out."

"But you and your doppelganger came out together," Nell almost whispered. "They had to guess at which one to kill."

Across the room, someone cleared a throat. Paul Zane. "As I told Marshal Lobo here, I was up forward in my sleep cubicle when we felt the bomb blast. My quarters are directly across from those of Mr. Wilcox and I immediately went to see if he knew what had happened. At any rate, when I pulled his door open, I found him at his workstation. He had the exterior cameras accessed."

"Damn it! I was trying to find out what the hell was going on, just the same as you were, Zane!" Wilcox exploded. "I never set any charges and I never tried to kill anyone!"

"What about the fight yesterday?" Nell snapped angrily.

"She's right, Wilcox," Dr. Nolan said. "This doesn't look good."

For a second it looked as if the engineer was gearing up for another outburst, but then he subsided, a touch of trapped animal showing in his eyes. Christians 7, Lions 0.

You could read through the body language that his fellow corporates were bailing out on him. My partner, of course, was ready to tear his head off and even Lil was about ready to pass Athenian judgment. Straight data, there was probably only one person in that entire compartment who didn't think that Wilcox was the bomber.

"Cut him loose, Bo," I sighed.

"*What?* What!"

Bo's roar of protest came across both verbally and over the neurolink, triggering another pain-pulse behind my forehead.

Why, oh why, couldn't there be just three fingers worth of brandy somewhere outside of the hundred-kay limit?

"Look, all of you. Superficially, Wilcox does look like a good suspect. I'll even admit that as I was flying away from Ground Zero, his was the first name to come to mind. But if you stop and think about it, the setup just doesn't hold rice."

"What do you mean, Boss!" Bo protested. "Just yesterday the guy tried to tear you in two!"

"Yeah, and today, as the only known explosives man here, he tries to kill me with a bomb. That doesn't compute. The man is a little bit bent where it comes to cops, but he's not foaming-and-pissing crazy!"

"Maybe not, Gain." Lil said with a somber frown. "But it wouldn't the first time a perpetrator had acted in an illogical manner."

"You want more? Then let's try this. Bo, access your area scan memories. Have you been keeping the immediate mainframe environs under continual observation since my frag up with Wilcox?"

"Yeah."

"And during that timeframe has Wilcox or anyone else gone near that cable pylon?"

"No." I could hear the "What-the-hell?" creeping into his voice.

"That thud you just heard was the Wilcox revenge theory hitting the floor. Now, have you been keeping those same environs under continuous observation since we first landed here?"

"Again yeah, except for that couple of minutes when I had to go out to collect you and Nell."

"And during that timeframe has anyone at all messed around with that hardlink cable setup?"

"No again."

"Hey ho. That bomb was probably planted before we ever landed here. Probably it was intended to cut the control hardlink to the MD tug at some inopportune moment. They used it on me just because it was already there and convenient. Just like they used the cutter head yesterday."

"Valid possibility, Gain," Lil said. "But that still leaves Wilcox as the only trained explosives hand here."

"That doesn't count for all that much for a simple little shot like that, Lil. Thanks to the infonet, every human being has instant access to the sum total of human knowledge. That includes how to build every infernal device ever invented, from Greek fire to a red mercury fusion bomb."

I made an all inclusive gesture to the compartment. "Anyone here could put an effective device together. It's just a matter of nerve and a little 'insert tab A into slot B.' I repeat, turn Wilcox loose."

Bo shrugged and crossed over to the bound engineer. A sharp chemical bite came to the air as he sprayed a jet of debonding agent over the tape circling Wilcox's wrists.

Freeing Wilcox seemed to free up the others a little as well. There was that self-conscious flurry of coughing, shifting, and glancing around that follows the slacking off of tension. Nell possessively flumped down onto the couch beside me and fired a challenging look at Lil's image. My boss replied with an enigmatic smile. Only the tug pilot, Donna Torveska, remained pretty much as before, leaning back against the bulkhead as wary and watchful as a Fate.

"Let's forget the bomber for a second and study on the bomb itself," I said. "Bo, was there any chance to recover physical evidence?"

"Surely you jest, Boss. You know how it is with an explosion in a micro gee environment. Boom! Whoops, next stop Alpha Centauri! There's no bits and pieces left to recover. I did get a flash spectrograph of the blast though. K series industrial explosives. The standard stuff all the mining outfits use in the field."

I looked over at Dr. Nolan. "Do you have explosive on board?"

He shook his head emphatically. "No. None at all. Our expedition profile didn't call for any demolitions work whatsoever."

"I can confirm that, Marshal," Torveska said. "There were no explosives listed on the loading dockets."

"But no," Mrs. Nolan spoke up, a frown crossing her attractive golden-brown features, "there were explosives put on board. I saw them."

"Where away?" I demanded.

"The forwardmost exterior locker on the port side. I saw a dock crew loading a case with explosive warning symbols on it just before we launched from Dawn City."

Bo didn't bother with a spacesuit. He could take hard space bare for a while. He was in the air lock and cycling outboard before Mrs. Nolan could finish her last sentence.

"Can you remember anything more about this case, Mrs. Nolan?" I asked.

"It was rectangular, metal, a little more than a meter long, and it had a yellow stripe around the sides."

Wilcox spoke up. "That sounds like one of our standard seismic exploration packs." He'd got himself unwound from the inerted restraint tape and I noted that his manipulator hand was operational again, with a neat patch sealed over yesterday's damage.

"What would be in it?" I demanded.

"Thirty ten-CC seismic testing charges, a couple of rolls of demolition tape, and eight liters of K-5 blasting gel. That plus a full set of detonator tabs and firing kits."

"Joy for fraggin' everlasting." That was plenty more than had been involved in the charge targeted on me.

Bo checked in across the link a couple of seconds later, compounding my positive worldview.

"I'm on site, Boss, and the locker's empty. If there was ever anything here, it's long gone now."

I couldn't think of anything to say other than to recall him back inboard. Rubbing the back of my aching neck, I tried to will my brain back into full clarity. I had another injector capsule under my skin that was guaranteed to make a three-day dead corpse jump out of its coffin and sing an aria from *Madam Butterfly* but I didn't want to pop that one yet. Not yet.

"Okay," I said finally. "I've heard that you asteroid miners sometimes use explosive charges to make the final orbital adjustments on these rocks. Would the size charge we're talking about here be enough to divert Cibola off of its flight path?"

"Not near enough," Nell replied promptly. "A steering shot would be something like a whole pallet-load of K-10. Two or three hundred liters worth. Occasionally, we even use small nuclear engineering charges. The explosives pack we're talking about wouldn't even constitute a love tap."

"But it'd be more than enough to snap the spine of the mass driver," Wilcox rumbled. "Or to blow this barge to bits."

"Well," Lilith said thoughtfully. Her image looked off into space for a moment as her distant mentality assessed the new development. "This references with a complaint the Joburg operations center received from one of their Lunar prospecting teams. A supply shipment dispatched from Dawn City shortly after this vehicle's departure turned up short one seismic testing package. Your perpetrator must have tampered with the loading documentation."

"That does it," Paul Zane said abruptly. "I don't know about the rest of you but this finishes it for me. I'm going to contact company headquarters and advise that we abort the project."

"What?" Dr. Nolan came to his feet so rapidly his soft boots almost broke deck contact. After floundering for a couple of seconds, he managed to fix the administrator with an angry glare. "What are you talking about, Paul? We're almost home!"

"It's like we were talking about this morning, Teague. Our lives are not only at risk out here but the company is at stake as well. If something goes wrong on this rock as we transit the Earth-Moon orbits, the litigation potential is staggering. Johannesburg United could be wiped out. I say that under these circumstances we can't afford to take the chance."

"It's a bit late to think about that, Zane," I interjected. "You're already falling into the Earth-Moon gravity well and your mass driver tug doesn't produce enough thrust to power you back out again. You're committed to transit."

"That's correct, Marshal. But on our current trajectory, Cibola will be carried through the Earth-Moon confluence without crossing the path of any orbital facility. If we don't execute the final phase-braking maneuver, Cibola will pass between Earth and Luna, slingshot, and return to a free solar orbit."

"And the company loses the opportunity of the century!" Nolan reached down and gripped Zane's shoulder. "Come on, Paul, we can't give up on this now!"

Zane shoved Nolan's hand off. "We're not giving up on anything, Doctor. We'll just be resetting things a little. We've established first landing claim on Cibola and the rock's new orbit will be a near parallel to Earth's. A year or two from now, when all of this sabotage business has been resolved, we can vector another tug out and try for another recovery."

Nell looked over at me with a lifted eyebrow. "You know, he could have a point. If we undock the tug and evacuate the surface, what could the saboteur do?"

"She's right," Rana Nolan added, "they both are, Teague. I know that you have worked so hard on this project but it is not worth the risk, to us or to anyone else."

She extended a hand out to her husband but Nolan pulled back. For a few seconds he held himself and his anger separate from the rest of us.

I let him be and looked over to the one person we hadn't heard from yet. "Captain Torveska, currently, you are the command pilot and towing master of this combine. Under UN space transit authority, you've got the discretional warrant to break off the tow. What's your word?"

She shrugged. "We are on course. All major systems involved in the tow are functioning within acceptable parameters. Our stocks of consumables are sufficient and we are adequately crewed. I can see no justifiable reason to terminate this operation."

I held her eyes for a second and gave her an acknowledging nod and she replied with the first, faint touch of a smile I had ever seen on her face. If we walked away from Cibola, so could the saboteur and the killer of her lover. If we stayed and played it out, so would he.

"That's it then," I said. "We take her in, all the way."

"Yes!" Nolan exclaimed fiercely.

"Just a second here, Marshal." Zane said with an equal share of intensity. "We're not under your command here. This is a civil project initiated by Johannesburg United and you haven't any right to say if it's to be continued or halted."

"No, Mr. Zane." My blood was circulating again and

while I didn't necessarily feel that much better, I was at least getting more functional. "This was a Joburg operation. Now however, it's a crime scene. Here, I boss the show. Go ahead and file your abort request. I can file a report too, one stating that you're a hopeless hysteric and that your fears are groundless. By the time your board of directors can make up its collective mind, this thing'll be over. One way or another."

Zane deliberately leaned forward. The face job he'd had done on himself didn't quite fit right when he scowled. "I don't believe this! Ms. Lilith, I suggest you get your man here back under some semblance of control."

Lil smiled gently and crossed her ethereal arms. "I'm sorry, Mr. Zane, but I make it a policy to never second-guess the senior officer on site."

"Y'know, Boss. This is really interesting." Given the flare-off going on in the lounge, no one had paid much attention to the lock cycling. Now, Bo's Ken was leaning in the hatchway. His skin had that slightly leathery look it gets when he's been exposed to hard vacuum but he was also wearing that patented hungry predator grin of his. "Right along, we've had someone out here working to stop this operation. And now, all too suddenly, we have Mister Zane going all officious on us and also saying that this operation should be aborted. Oh, if I had a suspicious mind."

"No! That doesn't mean . . . I was only thinking of the company." His voice trailed off and a sickly pallor crawled across his face. He looked at Bo as if he expected his personal Ken to sprout horns and spit fire.

"Forget it," I said, gingerly floating up to my feet. "We know you were likely just thinking of the company interests, Zane. Everybody's friends again. Let's just get this thing done."

"Sure, Chandry." It was Wilcox. The big man had his

head down and was fingering the now limp restraint tape with his meat hand. "However this job turns out, thanks for believing me on this one. Sometimes I'm an ass. I owe you for it."

"Oh, forget it, Wilcox. Maybe when this is all over we can chase up Becky Thatcher and go hunting treasure in Injun Joe's fraggin' cave."

Chapter 10

I don't know why we'd started to do our brainstorming sessions out on Cibola's surface. Maybe the vista helped to keep in mind what was at stake. The Moon was a great silvery sphere behind my right shoulder and the Earth was a marbled billiard ball, about as big as you would see it resting on your palm at the end of an outstretched arm. The tapering tower of the mass driver was indexing slowly across the ink and silver of the sky and was coming to bear on that distant blue target like a titanic gun barrel.

Bo was back in full vacuum gear and I had also shifted to an issue Sanyo Aerospace. After the bashing my personal suit had taken, I didn't want to trust it until it had undergone a maintenance survey, and my back-up rig was wrapped around the wreckage of my doppelganger Ken, drifting off in some skewball orbit.

Lil had joined us through the medium of an exterior holograph generator on Bo's mainframe and she didn't need a suit at all. She looked incredibly exotic standing out on the airless nickel-iron in nothing but a white silken gown, a space siren born in a low-oxygen fantasy. Her conversation was centered on a far more prosaic level, however. *"You could try testing for chemical trace elements. You might be able to fix on anyone who's been handling explosives recently,"* she linked.

"Thought of it. Forgot it," Bo answered. *"That's a well-used mining barge over there. There are traces of K-series residue all over its internal environment. Everyone aboard would likely trace*

positive. The best my chemosensors can do is tell you that there are currently no primary explosives on the barge."

"Beyond that, we've got more important things to worry on," I said.

"*Such as?*" A cybernetic wind ruffled Lil's hair and she brushed back a silvery lock that had curled down across the bridge of her nose. Even in a crisis situation there was always that touch of art with her.

"*Like what our perp really wants.*"

"*I thought the whole thing was about stopping this rock,*" Bo replied. "*That's what you were saying back on the barge.*"

"*Yeah, but that's not all of it, Bo. We know that he has the makings for at least one pretty good-sized bomb. We have to assume that he already has it planted somewhere where it can do a lot of damage. If all he wants is to disrupt the capture of Cibola, why doesn't he just push the button? What is he waiting for?*"

"*Maybe this is some kind of terrorist event,*" Bo said. "*Maybe he's going to try and drop this rock on somebody just as soon as it gets in close enough.*"

"*That possibility has been considered, Lobo,*" Lil said. "*We're already preparing counter-moves should that be the case. In fact . . .*"

Bo's head snapped around, and he stared out along our line of flight, adding the eyes of his Ken to the sensors aboard his mainframe. "*There's a ship out there! It's just dropped out of stealth mode and it's matching vectors fast!*"

My partner bared his fangs and raised his ruff.

Beyond us, the mainframe rose up on its landing gear from "grounded" to "ready/alert" posture. Up forward, light blazed on the mirrors of the chin turret as the anti-missile lasers pre-heated, while on the spine mount, the barrel of the 10mm rail gun pod jerked back, then forward into train, as a spike jacked into the exciter chamber.

It's kind of scary to see that big of a chunk of metal take on a fighting jag, even when it is on your side.

"Easy, Lobo," Lil thought. *"Stand down. This is one of those counter moves I was mentioning."*

I could see a new star in the sky now, one that pulsed and flickered amid the chill steady-state glow of the constellations.

It was the exhaust plume of a ship, decelerating hard on its main engines. It grew in size rapidly, falling back along the spine of the MD until, with a final intense flare of sun-fire, it matched vector with us, running parallel about half a kay over our heads.

Even without visual magnification, I could make out the blocky sleekness of a UN Space Defense Force cruiser. I could also make out that it was operating in boomer mode, packing a strategic strike pod.

"We've got a cyber aboard that ship requesting neurolink access, Boss." Bo still hadn't gone off guard.

"Let him have it, Bo."

A couple of seconds later, an unfamiliar thought pattern began to overlay on my mind.

"Marshal Chandry, this is Captain Saber of the SDF Atalanta. We are reporting on station and I have been instructed to contact you for a situational update."

"Acknowledged, Captain. My case officer has just notified me about your assignment to this mission. I assume that you are here to serve as a Nemesis over-watch?"

"That's a roger, Marshal. We'll be tailing you all the way into Earth orbit, just in case that rock gets away from you."

"Understood. The situation has escalated down here, Captain. We now think we have a bomb deployed somewhere on the combine."

"Can we be of assistance? I could land a couple of my ordinance technicians."

"*Negative,*" I replied. "*I think we've still got a handle on it. No sense in risking your people. I'm just advising you in case we lose things down here.*"

"*As you wish,*" the coolly hyper-professional tone replied. "*There is one thing I'd better get clear right off the top, Marshal. My mission is to insure this asteroid can present no threat to Earth or to any of our major orbital facilities. I'm carrying a load-out of variable yield fusion warheads and I've been given pre-authorization to arm and fire at my discretion.*

"*As we close the range with Earth, I'll be constantly projecting escape and diversion trajectories for Cibola. If that rock drifts even fractionally off course, I have been ordered to blast it back out into deep space.*"

"*Understood, Captain.*"

"*Then I hope you also understand this, Marshal. If Cibola starts wandering, I may not be able to give you and your people much time to evacuate the surface. If I say to get off in five minutes, I will not be meaning five minutes and ten seconds.*"

"*Understood again.*"

"*Very well. Good luck, Marshal. I hope that rock is worth it.*" The cruiser's retro-thrusters burned and it began falling back into our trailing slot.

Bo began to ease the mainframe out of its defensive posture. "*Saber, huh? He was one of that big batch run off early on during the war. I've never taken to any of those guys too much. They always seemed to be a little humanity short.*"

"*They're good enough folk, Lobo,*" Lil replied. "*They just tend to be rather task-oriented. Accordingly, you might want to take his words to heart, Gain . . . Gain?*"

I was taking the SDF cyber's words to heart. Just maybe not in the way he had figured. I had dropped down on one knee, intently studying the gray metallic surface we stood on.

Several hours later, the air lock on the mainframe hissed and slid open, allowing entry for Nell Rainey.

"I'll take that for you, M' Lady Gold," Bo said, accepting the pressure-proof lab case she carried.

"Thank you, Bo," she replied, lifting off her helmet. "I've gotten what you asked for, Gain, but it wasn't easy. I couldn't pass this lot off as a spare liner and a pouch of mouthwash."

"Did anyone ask any questions?" I inquired, starting to help her pop her hardsuit latches.

"Nobody got the chance. I put it all together in the lab and then sneaked it out to the air lock when no one was in the lounge."

"Good moves."

I lifted her out of the suit and she replied in kind with a quick hug and a friendly nuzzle. "Okay, small and pretty," I said. "You know what I want to get done. So, can we do it?"

"This isn't exactly kitchen sink chemistry, Gain. The book says you need at least an acid proof glove box to work with aqua regia in micro gee."

"But you can still manage?" I insisted.

"Well, if I'm extraordinarily careful, yes." She went over to where Bo had clipped the pressure case down onto the galley work surface. Opening the seals, she began to set out her equipment and chemicals. "I still don't see why though. I've already tested the ore from Cibola. It's the real stuff."

"Maybe, but the samples you used were collected before we arrived. Maybe they were doctored somehow."

Her eyes widened. "Doctored?"

"Yeah. I've been recalling about how, back in the old days on Earth, if somebody had a loser of a mine they wanted to unload, they'd sometimes fake the ore quality."

"It was called salting a mine," she replied. "You think someone could have somehow salted this asteroid?"

I shrugged. "The possibility has occurred to me. At least it's something we should cover."

"Salting an asteroid. Now that would be quite a trick," she mused. "But how? And why? Joburg United doesn't have any intention of selling Cibola."

"I don't know, Nell. It is a wild shot. But right now I am grabbing for anything." I retrieved a rack of sample tubes from a locker. "Bo and I have personally collected this ore from random points all over the surface. No way it could have been compromised. I'd like you to check it out, just to be sure."

"All right," she said with a dubious frown, "but I'm going to have to work slowly so this will take awhile."

As it was, it took until damn near zero hundred hours. She went through sample after sample while Bo and I hovered over her shoulders and watched. Each time around, the result was the same.

Finally, Nell removed her gloves and eye shields and began stowing the lab gear back into its case. "That's it. Unless someone has figured out a method of electro-plating an asteroid, Cibola is just as advertised. A noble rock with a remarkably consistent gold ore percentage."

"Yeah, well, I guess that's one wild notion we can discard," I said, sinking back down onto the cabin couch.

"What now?"

"I don't know, Nell. I definitely don't know. I'm dead-ended on all points of the investigation. There's nothing left to do but wait it out."

"So being it, why don't we get some sleep?" She eased down beside me. "You look a little faded."

"Being blown up does that to a person. As for sleep, forget

it. I'm going to be running on stay-awake patches and caffeine until we get this rock put in its hole."

"You're staying awake, hm?" Nell leaned languidly against me. "Well, I can help with that too."

"Is this where I'm supposed to turn myself off again?" Bo asked plaintively from his position, parked in the dinette.

"No it isn't and no, we're not, damn it. I have to conserve what minimal reserves of energy and concentration I have left," I said, running a finger down Nell's arched spine. "You go doss out, small and pretty, while my faithful partner and I here do our duty."

"If it must be. See you in the morning." She rose and stretched, accidentally-on-purpose giving her hips a seductive shift. Then she started pushing away aft to the sleep cubicle while I sat and silently swore at the fates and circumstances.

There wasn't much to do for a while after that. Bo just went neutral and I dug down into the containment pouch at the head of the couch section and produced *Astounding Science Fiction* again. It seemed like an awfully long while since I'd started the old magazine and now would be as good a time as any to finish it. As I read, I kept an ear tuned to the little noises Nell made as she riffled around in back, readying herself for bed. Eventually though, things went quiet and I turned the last couple of pages to the purring whisper of the air in the ventilator ducts.

I closed the little magazine and studied its faded cover for a moment. The heroes in these old SF yarns had it pretty easy. Their problems were pretty much out front and hard-edged: alien invasions, new technologies, the struggle of men trying to live in new places. They also generally didn't have a whole lot of personalities lying around to clutter up the situation.

Easy work if you can get it.

I put the book back in its protective envelope and then I reached up and pushed a button on the overhead. An emergency oxygen mask popped out of its compartment and I fitted it to my face.

"Bo, put a shot of tranc gas through the environmental system. Not too much. Just enough to make sure that Nell doesn't wake up for awhile."

This is what having a good partner is all about. He didn't even ask me why.

"She's down deep," he reported after awhile, *"and I've got the tranc purged out of the cabin environment. What now?"*

Removing the oxygen mask, I stood up and dug out a second set of ore samples. *"Now, those tests are going to be run again. Except that this time, we're doing them ourselves."*

Chapter 11

I hooked an arm over a girder and hung in place, resting for a second. We'd been searching for the bomb since 0600 hours that morning and I'd already burned through my second life support recharge and my fourth thruster pack refueling.

Earth dominated the sky now, half sun-lit, half in reflected moon-glow and girdled around with the bright beads of the powersat belt. On her darkened side, you could make out the glittering gem patterns of the major cities. It looked like they might be having a big time down in Tel Aviv tonight.

If I twisted around in the other direction, I'd be able to see the Moon, also half in light and darkness, and maybe, gleaming in line with the lunar terminator, the spark that marked Dawn City holding stable at LaGrange 1.

Six kays away aft, Bo reported in. *"Got the steering bell checked out. Nothing to report."*

"How's your EM scanner working now that the drive field is down?"

"Still no good. The latent field effect from the primary magnets are still killing any fine returns. I'd have to be sitting practically on top of anything thing before I'd get a trace."

"Okay. Frag it and drive on, Bo. Proceed to the next search zone."

"Rajah."

I closed my eyes and shut out the stars for a second. In our particular situation, finding a big bomb was going to be a tougher proposition than spotting a small one. To knock out something as huge and as redundancy-heavy as a mass driver tug, there are only a few areas where a small shot could be effective. A big bomb though, something powerful enough to actually bust up the structure, could be almost anywhere.

Maybe I shouldn't have been so quick to turn down Captain Saber's offer of those extra ordnance hands. Maybe for a second there, I'd bought into the myth of Free Marshal Infallibility.

Baaad move, Chandry.

"You know, Boss," Bo thought tactfully, *"maybe it's time you back off out of here. Getting my Ken bent is no big deal but if you're outside on the rig when that bomb blows, it might not be so good."*

"I'm still okay for awhile, Bo." I opened my eyes and checked the time hack glowing in the corner of my helmet visor. *"I've got at least another two hours and fourteen minutes."*

"How can you be sure 'a that?"

"Because that's how long we have before we initiate the final phase braking program. I figure that if our perp is going to shag things up, he's going to want to really shag it up right."

That meant he'd wait. Currently, the Cibola/MD-24 Combine was snaking through the Earth-Moon system in a shallow S-curve. Turned inward by the pull of Luna's gravitational field, it was cutting diagonally across cis-Lunar space. Soon, Earth's gravitational influence would be swinging the asteroid through another partial arc around the planet before breaking free again into deep space.

If it was allowed to, that is. By shaving off just a scootch more of Cibola's speed, the rock could be dropped into its target slot in a geo-synchronous Earth orbit some thirty-seven thousand kays over the Pacific.

That final burst of deceleration would have to wait until just about the last second though. As we crossed the main cis-

Lunar flight corridors, Lil had been forced to shut down the mass driver's propulsion system. Its thousand-kay-long metallic exhaust plumb would've cut across too many heavily trafficked orbits otherwise.

She would have to execute a restart just as we were coming around the far side of the Earth.

If that final braking burn was interrupted in mid-thrust, Cibola would go into some kind of wide eccentric orbit within the Earth-Moon system and Tao knows where it would end up or what it would run over. There'd be no choice but to Nemesis the rock and blow it back into deep space.

The hot point was why this one outcome was more important to our saboteur than the other.

"I hope you're right, Boss," Bo broke me out of my musing. *"But our perp might also have a command detonator on his main charge, just like he did on his first bomb. And our scopin' around out here might make him nervous."*

"Maybe."

That was a cause for valid concern. However, short of chaining the entire Joburg crew to a bulkhead or feeding them a load of tranc, there wasn't much I could do about it. The best I'd been able to manage had been to order them all to stay put aboard their barge while Bo and I conducted our recon.

I released my hold and dropped back down inside the thrust member framing. A trickle of power from my thrusters sent me ghosting between the driver coils and the girder structure. I had a set of work lights clipped to my helmet and I swung my head in a regular up-down, right-left pattern, sweeping illumination through the shadow patches, looking for whatever might not look right.

"Okay," I linked, *"let's go over our list of suspects one more time. I think we were back up to Paul Zane again."*

"Born, La Paloma Arcol, South California, United States of North America. Age: thirty-two. Education: UCLA and U of C. Degree in Business Administration. Currently single with one contract expired marriage on record. Split career in the metals and mining industry. Four years with Yakoshima-Ignesto, operating out of their Brazilian division, then six with Joburg United. Modestly successful career so far. No sign of a blotted copybook yet. Also no sign of a criminal record barring a few minor traffic violations and one charge of driving under the influence of a controlled substance."

"Another pathetically average individual," I commented, pitching out and doing a slow inspection roll around a junction box.

"Yeah. Too bad it ain't the good old days when the villain had a black mustache and a perpetual sneer."

"They still leave a trail though, pal. They still leave a trail."

"Heya, Gain. Ever since last night, you've been making sounds like you've got some ideas going."

"It happens I do," I replied.

"Then how about . . . Wait a second . . ." Bo broke off, then continued. *"We've got action at the barge. We've got a cycling air lock . . . and a suit comin' out."*

"Ah nuts!"

I keyed in to the suit EVA frequency to find someone waiting on it for me.

"Marshal Chandry, this is Torveska. Wilcox has just left the ship."

"We've got him spotted. What in sweet damn all is he up to?"

"He would not tell us. He just said that he had something to check out. We tried to stop him but he refused to listen. He's a difficult man to . . . work with," she finished apologetically.

"Understood," I replied. "Did he say or do anything beforehand? Did he give any indication of intent?"

"I know it has something to do with the bomb. He's been talking about it all morning. Asking questions. Studying technical data on explosives. What do you want us to do?"

"Nothing much you can do. We'll handle it. Just stay put and stand by."

"Wilcox has grabbed a thruster pack and it looks like he's headed for the mass driver," Bo reported. *"I've got firing locks on him from the mainframe. You want him hammered?"*

"Negative, negative! Just track him and expedite your Ken back here."

"Rajah. Moving out."

I jetted clear of the driver frame and then headed forward, hosing out fuel to build my speed. I was a couple of kays out along the frame, however, and I couldn't move quite fast enough.

"Damn! He's reached the driver and I'm losing him in the superstructure!"

Nothing is ever easy in this profession.

"Acknowledged, Bo. Keep all of your eyes open and report if you pick him up again."

As I approached the bow of the driver and the asteroid, I reduced speed and switched all of the thruster pack's operational functions over to the left-hand controller grip. With my right hand, I drew my sidearm and keyed the Norinco's heads-up sight into my helmet visor display. Tagging someone out amid the light and shadow geometry of the driver's frame could prove to be a challenge.

Slowly, I began to set up a spiral search path around the central thrust member. Just like a bomb, a hiding man could be a hard thing to find.

194

As I prowled, I let the back of my mind free-run, trying again to place Gavin Wilcox into the pattern I was building.

At long damn last, this case was coming together. But there were still some ambiguities out there, and Wilcox was one of them.

I missed him on the first pass. I reached the tug's bow plate butted up against Cibola's surface, then reversed vectors and headed back out. Several kays distant along the spine of the driver, I could make out the lights of Bo's suit as he came in to join me. Then, suddenly, a second set of suit lights bobbed up into my line of sight a whole lot closer.

I had Wilcox targeted in my helmet crosshairs before I could make a conscious thought of the act. I started to challenge him, then I noted what he was doing.

The engineer had lifted his hands from his thruster pack controllers and had them cupped on either side of his helmet. Deliberately he shook his head from side to side. It was spacer's sign language for a failed suit radio.

Or a request not to use one.

Wilcox drew a coil of communications cable out of a harness pouch and tapped the side of his helmet again.

"Bo, be advised I've found Wilcox. He wants me to jack into a hardlink with him. I'm going to do it."

"Have you gone certifiable!" my partner yelped. *"If you get within grabbing reach of that tin hand of his, he'll rip your liver out!"*

"I don't think so. Not this time."

I drifted in closer to Wilcox. While I no longer held the Norinco on him, I didn't reholster the pistol either.

Wilcox plugged one end of the hardline into his helmet jack and tossed me the other. I snagged the line with my free hand as it floated past and connected up as well, direct linking his com system with mine.

"That should do it," I heard him say into my earphones. "I figure we shouldn't let everyone in on this conversation."

"Okay, Wilcox. What's this all about?"

"It's that bomb, Marshal, I'm out after it the same as you are," he replied, sounding mildly amused. "The only difference being that I know where it is."

"You shaggin' me on this?"

He shook his head again. "Straight data, Lawboy. If we're to bring this rock home, we don't have time for games. Come on, I'll take you to it."

I hesitated for a moment, then re-holstered my gun. "Let's go."

"How did you come to know where it was?" I asked as we jetted off aft, still connected by the hardline.

"I didn't know, not for sure," he replied. "That's why I had to come out here. I wanted to be certain before I said anything."

"Being certain is my job. So what did you see?"

"Nothing all that much really. Just someone hanging around where they had no cause to be. It was shortly after we'd landed here and before you people arrived. I spotted some suit lights out on the mass driver. Captain Tran and I were slotted to do all of the systems check-out work and there wasn't any real reason for anyone else to be fossicking around on the rig. I didn't think much of it at the time and it didn't come to mind again until a little while ago. I tried to shake that lot on the barge down to see who it might have been, but nobody owned up. So I EVA'd to see for myself. It was there all right, but you'd never have spotted it in a million years."

"So why couldn't you just tell me about it?" I demanded.

"I don't work that way, Johnny Law," he replied with gruff humor. "I thought you'd figured that out by now."

He'd gotten one up on me again and he was enjoying himself. Neither of us realized it at the time, but he was having the last couple of seconds of feel-good in his life.

I heard a querulous grunt in my earphones and I saw Wilcox twist his helmet like a man trying to shake off a fly. Then his first scream overloaded the com circuit.

We'd been running along side by side and his first wild flail sent him crashing into me. The collision tripped the thruster controllers on both his backpack and mine, sending us both into a berserk, three-axis tumble. The communications hardline that had linked us, now lashed us together in a tangled snarl.

The universe whipped past—black sky, gray hull, black sky, gray hull—and still Wilcox howled.

I hit the kill switch for my backpack's thrusters, slowing the increase of our spin rate and I grappled for the engineer.

"Damn it, Wilcox! What's wrong?" I got a hand on his helmet ring and twisted him around towards me.

Inside the clouding visor of his helmet, Gavin Wilcox's face was disintegrating.

"Bo! Get the mainframe up here now! Wilcox has acid in his suit!"

Another go-round. Black sky, gray hull, *close!* We crashed into the girder structure of the tug and deflected off. For a second, I thought I'd busted a rib. After a moment though, the edge went off the agony and I could conclude that it was only bent.

I found and hit the kill switch for Wilcox's thrusters and I caught fragmentary glimpses of both Bo's suit lights and the lights of the mainframe lifting off Cibola's surface.

"Wilcox, listen to me! We're getting you some help out here!"

He didn't hear. All there is in his universe is the searing agony and the need to be free of it. Instinctively, he clawed at what was left of his face and I could see that metallic manipulator hand of his coming up.

"Wilcox! Don't!"

It's no good. He no longer knew or cared where he was. I grabbed for his arm but I . . . couldn't . . . quite . . . do . . . it. He was running on pain-stoked adrenaline and my arms were partially snared in the hardline. I couldn't get the leverage to force his gripper claw away from his helmet visor.

Acid-weakened, Wilcox's faceplate blew out. A geyser of blood, atmosphere, and pulped lung tissue spewed into space and our wild tumble twisted off at a new angle as his suit's life support system vented its entire oxygen store in a vain effort to maintain internal pressure.

Something else crashed into us: Bo. With a few quick thruster burns he killed our spin rate. Too late though, by a lifetime's worth. Wilcox convulsed one final time and then there was nothing left.

Bo snapped the tangle of hardline and I drifted back a couple of meters. With my teeth clinched and my eyes shut, I clamped down on the surge of nausea boiling within me. Wilcox had died about as bad as a man could, but drowning in your own puke would be right up there with it.

After about a minute, my equilibrium settled and I could open my eyes again.

"How you doing, Boss?" Bo was parked a short distance off with one hand laced through the harness of Wilcox's limp suit. The mainframe hovered nearby, playing its searchlights over the scene.

"I'm surviving." I reached up and backhanded away some of the freeze-dried stuff smeared on my visor. *"Watch yourself around his helmet. The agent had to be concentrated aqua regia.*

The same stuff we used in that ore testing. Nothing else could be that mean."

"What happened?"

"It's easy enough to figure," I replied grimly. *"Wilcox had seen something, but he wasn't a subtle kind of guy. He talked up about going after the bomb and he made somebody worried. They slipped a vial of acid into the liner padding of his helmet just before he went outside. When the stuff ate through the stopper in the vial . . ."*

"Stars!" Bo mentally murmured. *"It kind of makes a guy glad he wasn't born with skin."*

"Not fun, pal."

I unplugged the hardline jack from my helmet and brought my suit radio back up.

"This is Chandry. We just lost Wilcox. Don't ask questions, I'll brief you all later."

"Acknowledged." Donna Torveska's filtered voice came back tonelessly.

"Also put all hands on notice. If anyone else attempts to leave the barge without my express permission, it'll be shoot to kill. I mean it."

"Understood."

At least I knew now which side the engineer had been on, and I allowed myself a couple of seconds to be intensely sorry for how this line had played out.

A couple of seconds was all I had to spare. *"There is a bomb, Bo. Wilcox saw it."*

"Did he tell you where it was?"

"No. He was showing me when he was killed. We've got to figure out how to backtrack him there . . ." I checked my time hack again. One hour and twenty-four minutes left. *". . . and we'd better do it fast."*

The only crime scene we had to examine was Wilcox's body itself and so we went to work on a hasty post-mortem, floating parallel to the mass driver frame. Trying not to look into the charred interior of the helmet, I began to examine his vacuum gear for any clues to where he might have been.

A field terminal? No. Any hardcopy charts or schematics? None. A camera? Any special tools? Any service bay access keys? Nothing, nothing, and nothing. I checked both of the forearms of his suit. Some of the engineers I've known use the white hardshell there as a convenient slate for note writing. Negative.

We were burning time and without getting anywhere. Slowly, I rotated the body, scanning the surface of his suit for any unusual marks or damage. The rotation was almost complete when I spotted the smear on one shoulder, just about where a man might brush against something squeezing into a narrow space.

It's a thick, cream colored substance, speckled with darker spots and streaks. The unusual thing was that it was still soft and slick, even exposed to hard vacuum.

I swiped it off with a finger. *"Look at this."*

"Silicon grease," Bo replied promptly. *"Heavy duty stuff too."*

"And old. This has been partially discolored from prolonged exposure to straight sunlight. This has got to be from somewhere on the mass driver. Bo, access the rig's maintenance documentation and find out where they use this kind of compound."

"Doing it. . . ." He came back with the data in only a second or so. *"Two places! The antenna array gearing drive and the guy line winches! It's got to be the antenna array, Boss! Blow that and Lil'll lose control of the rig!"*

That seemed logical but I hesitated, turning the problem around my mind, examining it from all sides. We weren't going to be able to squander time on a mistake. *"No! Wait a minute! Like the other one, this bomb was probably planted before we arrived on Cibola. The perp would have no idea that we were going to shift the driver over to remote control so he'd have no reason to wire the antenna array. It's got to the winch heads!"*

We secured Wilcox's body in an exterior cargo compartment aboard the mainframe. It wasn't elegant but it was the best we could do at the time. Then we jetted towards the winch deck, the ship trailing along behind us like an obedient pet whale.

The winch deck was a girder structure platform that circled the main thrust member of the tug, about a kay back from the bow pusher plate. Tapering up to it from the surface of Cibola were the KevlarX guy lines that kept the mass driver braced into position. Blow something here and the rig would topple off axis.

Spaced around the platform perimeter were the power-driven winches that kept the mooring cables taut. One of the few non-solid-state-technology blocks aboard the tug, the whole deck area was a magnificent tangle of heavy machinery. A perfect hiding ground for a destructive device. Bo and I separated, circling in opposite directions. The secret to a search like this is to develop a feel for the local technological environment, a sense of what's right and in its proper place and what isn't, and you have to develop it fast.

As I had done inside the frame, I drifted along over the assembly, countering Cibola's faint gravitational pull with an occasional burp of my jets and setting up my search sweep. Something else kept tugging at the corner of my eye though, the clock hack reflected in my visor, marking the bleed-away of our time.

It took us twenty-four minutes to spot it. I, and likely any other human being, would have missed it altogether, but Bo has a cyber's perfect eye for gauging and processing size and distance. He noticed that one of the deck's massive foam-aluminum girders radiating out from the central thrust member was exactly twelve centimeters longer than any of the others.

Like all of the other technical aspects of this crime, the bomb was a masterpiece.

Put together a solid-state timer-detonator pack, then take it out and glue it into the center of the outside end of the beam. Set your timers, then fit a frame coated with Teflon or some other anti-adhesive over the end of that beam and pump it full of demolition gel. Wait a few minutes while the gel cures and hardens and then pop the frame off and spray-paint to match the background color of the beam. Not only do you have an infernal device that's harder than sweet damn all to find, but once the bomb is found, there isn't a whole lot the finder can do about it. The detonators, power source, and everything else that you need to get at to disarm the device are solidly encased in high explosive plastic.

Bo hovered off the end of the beam, looking as grim as he could within his design specs.

"This is all of it," he thought. *"The volume here would take about the full amount of K-5 listed in that explosives pack."*

"Small blessing," I replied, hovering up beside him. *"We only have the one to worry about then."*

"And I think that one is going to be plenty. You'd better get out of here, Boss. I suspect this is going to be a flamin' howler to tinker with."

I smothered my instinctive refusal. This was Ken work. *"Okay, pal. Your baby. Don't get sloppy though. We don't need any more trashed hardware on this month's expense account."*

The mainframe and I both backed off a couple of hundred meters and I went into station-keeping on the far side of the ship from the potential blast. Given the size of the charge, I'd have to watch for shrapnel even this far out.

It was a weird, weird, feeling. I knew, I *knew* that Bo, the real Bo, was right here beside me snug in the mainframe, as safe as a government entitlement program. That the thing back there on the winch platform was just a super-sophisticated puppet. And yet, my gut instincts were still screaming that my partner was out there with his neck on the block. It just goes to show which wins in a conflict between logic and emotion. *"What are you getting in the EM spectrum?"* I asked. I could picture Bo's personal Ken hovering over the device, his hands outstretched to it like a gypsy with a crystal ball.

"Two distinct, identical, modulated sources," he replied. *"Timers, I'd say."*

"Two of them?" I queried.

"A primary and a back-up, maybe. Let's take a look at her through the infrared and see what we find."

"Okay. I'll be plugging into your vision block for this."

"Be my guest."

I accessed in to the Ken's visual sensors as Bo began tuning them across the energy spectrum, seeking for a band that would let him see through the structure of the bomb.

"Well, the thermal range isn't doing too much for us," Bo commented judgmentally. *"Not enough contrast and that paint seems I-R absorptive. Let's go up to passive microwave and see what happens."* That managed it. In my mental visualization, the bomb casing became cloudily transparent. We could now see the cluster of components that made up the detonator package, some of them glowing dully from the current they carried.

"Here we go, Boss. I was right. Two timers but nothing I recognize as a radio receiver or a command detonation circuit."

"Yeah." I surveyed the synthesized image in my mind's eye. *"Hot spit and hurrah for that. Still I wonder what those two timers could be about?"*

"Like I said, a back-up."

"Maybe. On the other hand, it may not be that simple. Let's do a full go-round before we come to any conclusions."

"Okay. Doin' it."

The image began to rotate almost as smoothly as a computer graphics scan as Bo edged around the bomb.

The whole detonator package could probably be held in the palm of your hand and yet it had so much potential to lay so much grief in the laps of so many. Next time you hear someone say, "Don't sweat the small shit," you may assume that they don't know what they are talking about.

Then I spotted something even smaller and my belly cinched up. *"Hold it!"*

"What is it, Boss?"

"Tell you in a minute. Just back the Ken off real slowly by about five meters. Very light on your jets."

I jacked out of Bo's vision system and blinked my own eyes a couple of times to get them working again.

"Okay. What's going on?" he demanded.

"Bo, what's just about the worst thing a bomber could do to us in a micro gravity environment?"

"I don't want to know, but tell me anyway."

"Check out that little cylindrical jobber in the lower right-hand quadrant of the detonator package, the one with the hot leads going in at the top and the bright metallic return at the bottom. Given the way it's oriented along the Cibola gravity axis, I'd put out serious cash that somebody's rigged a mercury switch anti-tamper."

Bo brain-groaned. *"Profane comments too numerous to enunciate. You're right, Boss. We're shagged and fragged."*

A brief lesson in the laws of physics and terrorism. A mercury switch is one of those dirt simple, old fashioned, absolutely foolproof little dinguses that anti-bomb people hate because they can't be finessed or tricked with. It consists of a glass or plastic tube with a set of electrical contacts at one end that contains a blob of mercury. Hold it upright in a positive gravity field and the mercury is held at the bottom of the tube and the circuit is left open and inert. If you tilt it over, however, the mercury rolls up to the electrical contacts and the circuit closes.

Bomb disposal hands still refer to them as "Mormon" switches in honor of a long-ago series of bombings in which they figured prominently. Bad enough though they are on Earth, they don't really start to shine until you get them out into low gravity. In positive gee, that mercury blob will at least just lay there. In micro gee, any movement, any vibration, any little tap at all will send the mercury bouncing around into the contacts. Stare at it hard and it could go off. As an anti-tamper device, it was near as perfect as you could get.

"That's what that second timer was about, Bo," I thought. *"It wasn't connected to a detonator, but an actuator. Something that armed the anti-tamper system after the bomb had been planted and the mercury switch had been given a chance to settle down."*

"How about we try cold soaking it?" he suggested unenthusiastically.

"No joy, it's already been out here for several days. If it was going to freeze up, it would have. The detonator's power cell is throwing off a heat trickle and the plastic explosive is insulating everything." I rested one hand on the flank of the mainframe and kicked into long range link. *"Lil, got another problem here."*

"I'm current, Gain. Lobo's been feeding me situational updates. Should I scramble a bomb-disposal team?"

The time hack indicated forty-seven minutes to the start of final deceleration.

"There's no way they could get here in time and nothing they could do if they could."

There was one of those pregnant pauses before Lil replied. *"I concur. I had to make the suggestion just for form's sake."*

"Frag it, sweet one, I think they got us beat."

"It happens, love. I suppose we'd better begin considering damage control. For a start, we'd better evacuate Cibola."

"Yeah, I'll inform the Joburg team." I'd been deliberately keeping them in the dark on the off chance that our perp had, as Bo had suggested, rigged a command detonator circuit on top of everything else. Now that didn't matter a damn anymore. *"All we can do is let her go and wave good-bye."*

"I could undock the tug and use its secondary engines and whatever time we might have left before the explosion to nurse the tug into some kind of Earth orbit. That would make it easier to salvage at least."

"Forget it. All that's holding that mercury ball in place is Cibola's pull. The second you try a braking burn outside of this rock's gravitational influence, she'll blow."

Lil's thoughts went thoughtful. *"I might be able to execute a skew-flip turn under continuous power. That would replace the gravitational pull with constant acceleration along the same axis. That might keep the switch safe."*

"Yeah, might."

I hadn't been paying to much attention to this conversation, the bulk of my concentration being focused on being royally honked off. Suddenly though, something pushed a button.

"Wait a minute . . . Wait a minute . . . Maybe we can still pull this thing out. Maybe we can use acceleration to save the whole package."

I felt Bo and Lil press close mentally. *"What do you mean, Gain?"* my boss demanded.

"We don't fool with the bomb itself. Instead we cut loose the en-

tire section of superstructure it's attached to. Then, we use power pots to throw it clear of the mass driver. As long as we can keep that mercury switch under constant positive acceleration, we can keep it from tripping."

"I can see your angle," Bo mused. *"It might even work. It's going to be a damn fiddly job though. But I'm willing to give it a shot."*

"We both are, pal," I replied. *"It's going to take more than one set of hands to make this work."*

"Wait a minute," Lil's thoughts flared almost painfully. *"I don't know if I can permit this, Gain. I can see your concept, but I don't know if it's a certain enough thing to risk a life on. The slightest vibration or shock while you're cutting that beam loose or the slightest bobble while you try and get it moving and you're dead. Replacing a Ken unit is one thing; a sentient being is another matter."*

"Heya, sweet one. I'm open for alternative options if you have any to offer."

She didn't. A wave of darkness suddenly swept across us, leaving nothing behind except the stars and the pattern of the tug's running lights. The Earth was eclipsing the Sun and Cibola and the MD-24 were passing into its shadow enroute to the deceleration point. It might not actually be an omen, but it sure felt like it.

I collected the gear we'd need. A work laser and power cells. A power pot and igniter kit. Damage control adhesive and a couple of portable grab bars. On top of everything else, I noticed that my thruster pack had just about gone flat again and I had to do another recharge. Finally, I got back out to the winch platform.

Bad as it was, this project is going to be a little bit trickier than described. You see, this bomb was mounted on the end of a girder extending out at a right angle from the main structure of the tug. However, that damn mercury switch was set so that its "down" was oriented forward on the tug, towards the mass of the asteroid the tug was shoving.

That meant we couldn't just flip the bomb and girder combine laterally away from the ship. That could trip the anti-tamper. What we'd have to do was to detach the girder, move it out parallel to the vehicle frame, and then curve it away into space, at all times keeping that critical "down" going in the right direction.

We glued the grab bars into place on the section of beam we intended to cut loose and mounted the power pot at the section's central point of balance. This power pot was a small, industrial-use rocket motor. Little more than a solid fuel-lined combustion chamber and exhaust nozzle, its ten-second burn time should be enough to carry the bomb clear of the rig, not to mention us.

Then came the cutting. Bo's Ken would be the key here. He'd be as good as a heavy machining clamp for holding that beam steady while I handled the laser. He might also be able to yell a warning if I started to shake things up.

First the mesh decking over the girder had to be peeled away. Then the lateral connectors to the beams on either side had to be cut through at both ends and very gingerly maneuvered clear. Then some odds and ends of cabling and duct work had to be trimmed back. I hadn't even started the main cut when a glare came from off my right shoulder. It was the Sun, crawling back out from behind the black curve of the Earth. We were leaving the shadow cone and down the line, the mass driver's double row of huge solar arrays began to trim themselves to the light like the sails of God's yacht.

Lil came in urgently over the link. *"Gain, we are at point of initiation. I have to start final phase braking now!"*

"I know. Do it."

"That bomb could detonate at any time from this point on . . ."

"Acknowledged."

". . . and the deceleration will reduce the margin of error on that anti-tamper!"

"Lil, you're not telling me anything I don't already know."

"Gain, I don't like this!"

I had to smile a little. Lilith doesn't get shrill too often and I had to smile at her doing it just now.

"I thought you made it a policy to never second-guess the senior officer on-site."

Any further planned protests collapsed into a jumble of frustration/fear/anger/concern. I wish I had the time to thank her for always giving a damn, both as my boss and otherwise.

"Very well," she thought abruptly. *"Initiating engine start now."*

Bo was doing his statue act with his hands clamped onto the beam and all of his motor functions locked down.

"Do I get any input on this situation?" he asked plaintively.

"No," I replied, squeezing in on hands and knees toward the cutting point of the girder, striving earnestly to not bump it or Bo's solidly planted legs.

"I was just going to suggest we give 'em a yell back on the barge . . . just in case."

"Valid point."

I keyed in my suit transceiver. "Captain Torveska, you still there?"

"Still here, Marshal."

"I advise that you bring your engines to hot-start standby. If you feel any heavy bumps or bangs over the next couple of minutes, lift off immediately. Don't worry about us, just head for a lower orbit with all the delta-vee you can pull. Watch out for wreckage and for that SDF cruiser. He'll likely be setting up a firing run on the rock."

"Will comply, Marshal. And good luck with whatever you are doing."

The mass driver came on-stream. Its push was running counter to the pull of Cibola's gravity and in my hyper-sensitive state, I thought I could feel it paring away the minute amount of mass left to me. That bead of mercury would now be weighing far less than any bit of dandelion fluff you could imagine.

I activated the work laser and began the cut at the mark Bo had made. Foamed aluminum went incandescent under the touch of the coherent light and began to boil away into the vacuum. My spacesuit was fully insulating me but my senses pretended to feel the heat.

As I worked, my eyes kept flicking up towards the other end of the beam. In all of the entertainment VRs, the bombs all have these neat little clock readouts prominently displayed so that the hero knows just exactly how much time he has left. Real-world explosive devices, like this one, are seldom so co-operative. The only people around here who knew when it was going to go off were the ones who had planted it, and they weren't talking.

"Holdit, holdit, HOLDIT!" Bo link-yelled.

I cut the laser and waited to die.

I couldn't say how long the next couple of seconds lasted before Bo spoke again. *"Thermal stresses were putting a little tick in the metal. It's okay now but you'd better even things out some by back-cutting from the other side."*

"Yeah, will do. There's not much more left."

I mashed my face into my helmet liner to absorb some of the sweat and started burning again.

Finally.

"Okay, just about there . . . 'nother couple of millimeters . . . that's got it!"

Brief pause to wait for loud noises.

Nothing. Bo and the girder stood as immobile as Tycho's central spire.

"You want to take a breather for a second, Boss?" he asked levelly.

"Nah," I replied, backing clear. *"Let's just get it done."* There was no sense mentioning how I was going to start trembling uncontrollably in another couple of minutes.

I kicked loose from the superstructure and drifted up to the top of the beam. Carefully, I fitted my left hand around the grab bar we'd positioned there, while my right went to the controller of my thruster pack.

"The big deal is that we've both got to step off at the exact same instant," Bo said. *"Do you want me to call it?"*

I swallowed, hard. *"Yeah."*

"Okay, accelerate on my mark. Three . . . two . . . one . . . mark."

I came forward on my controller grip and we were moving, ghosting along parallel to the tug's frame. A few centimeters away from my shoulder, the little mercury ball jiggled and danced at the bottom of its glass tube, waiting for its chance to kill.

"Starting to angle away now."

Bo increased power, toeing the end of the girder out and away from the tug. Acting as the pivot, I did nothing except watch the tug drop away and the stars fill all of my field of vision.

"That's got it. Line of flight looks good. Ready to ignite?"

"Hit it."

"Okay, Boss. On my mark again. Grab loose as you feel her start to pull and watch out for the exhaust plume. Three . . . two . . . one . . . mark!"

The power pot fired. I let the grab bar pull out of my hand

and I ducked and twisted away to take the buffeting of the rocket wash on my shoulder. I tumbled for a couple of turns and then the thruster pack gyros pulled me upright again. I could see the flare of the little engine as it shoved the girder away into the distance and I could hear Bo counting. *"Five . . . six . . . seven . . . eight . . . nine . . ."*

There was a dazzling, blue-white flash against the stars and a broad sphere of incandescent gas expanded and dissipated. A moment later, a chunk of warped metal came spinning back out of the dark and ricocheted off the driver's frame.

I rotated and looked at my partner. *"Was it my imagination or did that thing blow before the power pot burned out?"*

Bo shrugged broadly. *"What difference does it make at this late date?"*

"Absolutely none." My partner and I grinned at each other and we crossed wrists again, sharing that unique exaltation you feel when you've managed to ass-shag the Fates one more time.

"What do we do now, Boss?" Bo asked as we started back to the mainframe.

"First we finish taking care of Wilcox. And then we start setting up to make the bust. It's time to end this thing, pal. It's time to close out this whole sliming deal, all the way."

Chapter 12

Lounged back in the command chair, I listened to Lil's voice coming in over the traffic band.

"We are approaching target slot. . . . We have trajectory and velocity convergence. . . . Ten . . . nine . . . eight . . . seven . . . six . . . five . . . four . . . three . . . two . . . one . . . Engine shutdown. . . . Onboard instrumentation indicates we are station keeping in geo-synchronous orbit. Pacific Rim Track, can you verify?"

"MD-24. We verify you as stable in geo-sync."

"Atalanta, do you concur?"

"Roger, MD-24. You are stable with no drift noted on any axis."

"Thank you, Atalanta . . . Pacific Rim Track, this is MD-24. We are registering arrival in Earth orbit and we are closing out our flight plan."

"Acknowledged, MD-24. Your arrival is registered. Welcome home."

And that's all there was to it.

In the four-odd hours since we'd gotten shed of the bomb, I'd had a bath, a meal, and I'd worked on rehydrating myself after my prolonged EVA stint. I'd also thought a few things over with my case officer and partner. Mostly though, I'd rested and tried to recharge my personal batteries for what we had to take on next.

"Thank you, Pacific Rim," Lil replied. "It's been an interesting trip."

"Congratulations on a successful mission," the cyber skipper of the Defense Force ship interjected. "It looks like we weren't needed after all."

"You were our insurance policy, Captain, and we thank you for your assistance."

"The pleasure of the Force, Ms. Lilith. This is the Atalanta, returning to base."

The fire plume of the cruiser cut past us out to starside. Captain Saber was pulling heavy delta vee again and I decided that I'd hate to be a meat rating serving on that guy's decks.

"All right, Gain," Lil switched over to the security of the neurolink. *"We have arrived."*

"Right," I replied. *"Next step is to get the tug clear."*

"Acknowledged. Un-docking now."

There was a brief delay as the tug's cutter heads returned into their garage bays on the bow plate. Then, out on Cibola's surface there was the flash of an explosion. A whole string of them followed as explosive bolts severed the guy lines that moored the mass driver to the asteroid. Eye-achingly brilliant dots of blue-white light then flared in rows down either side of the driver as the tug's auxiliary plasma engines fired. For a minute or two, nothing seemed to happen as the thrusters strained at the mammoth vehicle's mass. Then, ponderously, she began to back clear, her mooring cables reeling in like the tentacles of a giant jellyfish.

Deprived of the techno-spire of the MD tug, Cibola was a different place. Even though we were cuddled up in orbit around the mother world, the rock now seemed smaller, colder, and lonelier.

"The tug is clear and answering on secondary propulsion systems," Lil reported. *"Where do you want her?"*

"Park her in a parallel orbit and stand by. Bo and I will be heading out to make the first move now."

214

"Good hunting and take care."

I closed my eyes and triggered my other subcutaneous injector, this one a broad spectrum bio-sustainer. As it hit my blood, I could feel the fatigue fade out of me like the memory of a bad dream. When I opened my eyes once more, the world had an almost supernatural vividness and clarity to it.

In using the sustainer, I was writing another humongous overdraft on my physiology. I was also guaranteeing myself at least a half an hour's worth of the "Dangers of Excessive Booster Drug Utilization" lecture from medical division when I went in to get recharged. I didn't have much choice though; I had to be ultra-clear, at least for the next couple of hours. Bo had his Ken already geared up and waiting back in the main cabin. He tossed me my helmet and a grin. "Ready to take 'em down, Boss?"

"Down to the dirt, Tin Man."

Maybe for the last time, we made the crossing from Bo's grounded mainframe to the Joburg lab barge.

When the inner lock door opened, we found an abbreviated celebration underway in the barge's lounge. The Nolans and Paul Zane were experimenting with pouring non-alcoholic champagne in micro gee while conversing with that highly-brittle gaiety you get when people force themselves into what they think is an appropriately upbeat behavior pattern.

There was more naturalness to Nell. She bounced over to me and threw her arms around my neck. She had a little trouble with the hug because I hadn't un-geared, but there seemed to be a genuine, spontaneous joy in her.

"We've beat them, Gain!" She lightly nuzzled my face through my open helmet visor. "We've brought her home, all the way."

"Most of the way, small and pretty," I corrected gently. "Just most of the way."

To her puzzlement, I peeled her loose and parked her to one side.

"Hello, Marshal," Dr. Nolan said, trying to contain his non-booze in its plastic goblet. "I know this might seem in rather bad taste considering the losses we've taken in our personnel but, well, we've been working on this project a long time now and we felt that some kind of celebration was in order. I hope you understand."

Donna Torveska should have been the one to be asked. She was leaning back in her usual corner, her face absolute stone.

"It's none of my affair, Doc," I said. "I'm just here to conduct some business."

I brushed past him as well and confronted my objective.

"Paul Zane, I am invoking the United Nations law enforcement mandate and I am placing you under arrest for murder, barratry, terrorism, and criminal conspiracy."

Bo had him flanked and had a hand clamped onto the back of his neck before the shock wore off.

"What in the hell are you talking about!" Zane had gone fishbelly pale at my declaration, and he strained to rise against Bo's grip.

"Gain, no! You don't mean it!" Nell exclaimed, looking just about as flabbergasted as the company man did.

"I do," I replied. "I knew from the start that there had to be at least one insider involved and this gentleman's the one. Paul here has been moonlighting on you. Not only is he employed by Johannesburg United, but he's still on the books back at his old outfit, Yakoshima-Ignesto. He's an industrial double-agent, one who's been selling out your company for years."

"That's a lie, God damn it!" Zane yelled with more enthusiasm than I would have given him credit for.

"Belt it up, wage man," Bo growled, ramping up his grip slightly. "Presently, I'll be reading you a bunch of stuff that will include your right to remain silent. Start practicing."

"God," Dr. Nolan whispered. Champagne forgotten, he stared at his teammate as if he had just sprouted a spare head and a set of tentacles. "I know what you said, Marshal. And logically, I knew that you had to be right. But still . . . Is this certain?"

"Our people back on Dawn City have his contact in custody, and Interpol has seized his pay-off accounts back on Earth. It'll just be a matter of time before we get the full story, but the scenario as we read it now is that Yamashita-Ignesto was afraid of the enhanced profit margin Johannesburg United would be bringing in from Cibola. It'd permit Joburg to move into certain critical areas of the metals market that Y-I had been dominating. They ordered their agent here to make sure that didn't happen."

"This is a fantasy!" Zane exploded. "You're making the same mistake with me that you made with Wilcox!"

"The mistake made with Wilcox," I continued smoothly, "was in turning him loose. He was your man, Zane. He had the hands-on technical expertise you needed to sabotage the tug, so you bought him.

"The only thing was that after the death of Captain Tran and the attempted murders of Ms. Rainey and myself, Wilcox must have started to freeze up. He hadn't counted on outright murder and so he decided to bail out. He was trying to hunt me up to cut a deal, wasn't he, Zane? He was going to turn state's evidence on you, so you burned him . . . literally."

Zane attempted another protest but my partner turned him off.

I nodded to Bo. "Get him ready to move out."

"Rajah." He heisted Zane to his feet. "C'mon, slimer.

Let's get you packaged up. And you're breathin' on the tax-payers now so keep quiet and don't waste the oxygen."

Zane instinctively tried to struggle. A banana would have had more chance in the hands of a hungry gorilla.

I turned back to Teague Nolan. "I guess that should about do it, Doctor. A UNILAW court officer will be contacting you and your people within the next few watches to collect your official statements on what's happened here. Routine stuff. Unless you're called up for testimony at the trial, that should wrap things up."

Out of the corner of my eye, I kept track of how Bo was getting along with suiting Zane up. We had to get moving before the shock of our action wore off.

"I've been ordered to immediately transport my prisoner back to Dawn City," I continued. "Sorry I have to dump things back in your lap like this but you should be okay until your own people can catch up to you."

"Oh, of course, Marshal." Nolan caught up with himself and straightened. "We'll be fine. Thank you." He paused for a second. "That seems rather inadequate considering you've saved my future and that of my wife."

I shook my head. "Forget it. I just wish that I could have saved Tran and Wilcox while I was going about it. So long, Doc . . . ladies."

As I turned to follow Zane and Bo to the air lock, I let my vision pan across the others in the lounge, noting each expression, each posture, in turn. Rana Nolan sat unmoving on one of the lounges, coming out of the same nightmare as her husband. Donna Torveska, still against the bulkhead, targeted all of the cold, silent hate a human could generate on the back of Zane's head. Nell Rainey looked after me with an expression of hurt bewilderment on her face. As for myself, I just kept my best poker face latched down like a helmet visor until the lock door closed behind me. Then I could breathe. No one had noticed that I had "accidentally" forgotten Lil's genie box again.

"Initial phase successfully completed, Lil. Proceeding with phase two."

We towed Zane across to the mainframe. Bo had popped the antenna on the company man's suit to keep him quiet but he started in on us again as soon as we got him aboard and back in atmosphere.

"I can guarantee you one thing, Marshal," he snarled, tearing off his helmet. "I will see you in court on charges of false arrest. That you can bet on!"

"Well, if you're going to whine about it that much." I reached over and flicked him on the forehead. "Omni omni difar, you're un-arrested."

Zane goggled at me. "What?"

"You heard me. Arrest revoked. Go forth and sin no more, my son."

"But, what about those accusations of industrial espionage, sabotage, murder? Where did all of that come from?" he bleated.

I shrugged. "Mostly from my imagination. Look, as far as I can tell, you're just a butt-average, middle-management kiss-up, guilty of nothing beyond wasting your company's time and money by joy-riding along on this expedition. I sincerely apologize for having to shove you around back on the barge, but Bo and I urgently needed an excuse to get out of there, and you, like a public 'fresher, were convenient."

"I don't understand?"

Thick as radiation shielding.

"It's this way, Mr. Zane," I replied with more patience than I really had. "Right now, our real perpetrators think that I'm about to haul out of here taking a mistake to the lock-up.

219

They've just been given one last miraculous chance to wreck things with Cibola and I'm betting they'll take it."

Zane's brows came together. "It's a trap?"

"You got it," I replied, starting to riffle through the gear lockers that lined the air lock access passageway. "When they go active, I'm going be waiting for them."

"Wait a minute. Do you know who they are?" We were tight on both space and time, and so Bo had started to nudge Zane politely but implacably forward into the crew space.

"Sort of. I'm cop sure, but not court sure. I'm going to have to bust these guys with a blood chit in their hands to guarantee that they take the fall. Relax and flow with it, Mr. Zane; you're just along for the ride."

I clipped a communications booster module to my suit harness and snapped a full fuel cartridge into a light-duty maneuvering pistol while Bo secured our passenger. Then I felt the vibration of the secondary thrusters firing, and I had to balance myself against the tug and sway of the mainframe as it lifted off the asteroid's surface.

Bo returned aft to the passageway just as I ducked back into the air lock.

"I got our boy bolted down. What else do you want me to do with him?"

"I don't know. Give him a pouch of coffee. Tell him some of your old war stories. If he wants something to read, there's a pretty good magazine in the containment pocket of the couch. Mostly just keep him out of the way."

"I don't much like leaving you back there without backup," Bo brooded.

"There's nothing much we can do about it."

There wasn't either. The special broad-band data links you need for operating a Ken only had a carry of about twenty-five kays and Bo would be going a long way beyond that.

"Guess not. Watch your ass, Boss."

The inner lock door slid shut and I braced myself off on a couple of handholds as we maneuvered. Bo was going to loop out and cut back under Cibola on the far side from the moorage of the Joburg barge, just as if he was just setting up a routine departure trajectory. However, during the few seconds we'd be concealed by the asteroid's bulk, I'd go over the side in a combat debark.

"You set?"

I snapped down my helmet visor. "Yeah."

"Okay. Setting you up. Setting the angle. Green light . . . Go!"

The exterior hatch slammed open and the air burst carried me tumbling into space.

Bo had kicked me out just right. A few jets of the maneuvering pistol and I was stable. A few more and I was touching down on Cibola again. By the time I had the chance to look to the sky, the mainframe's engine flare was just another star in the darkness.

I'd studied the photo charts of the asteroid so it didn't take long to orient myself. Soon I was double-timing back around the rock to the Joburg landing site. I'd also studied up on the stats of the barge and towboat combine as well and I'd learned that its exterior camera coverage was minimal right aft. Accordingly, I'd preselected my route to bring me in along that angle. A half-hour's hike later, and my objective appeared over the close horizon.

Everything looked quiet. The MD-24 hung in the sky like a model of itself, and nothing else moved on the surface.

I hunkered down and deployed the communications module, letting the antennas extend until they had line-of-sight on the barge. That would guarantee me neurolink contact with the outside, suit radio as well if I needed it.

"Bo, Lil, I'm back at the barge. Anything up?"

"Only a little radio traffic," Lil replied. *"Dr. Nolan filed a brief report on the Zane situation with his company headquarters. Beyond that, he stated that they had arrived at destination and that all was well."*

"Nothin' much from me either, Boss," Bo added. *"Like you figured, I'm being tracked out by the barge's radar."*

"Right. I'm moving in."

Keeping to the blind zone, I crept up on the barge, at least as well as you can creep in space armor. Sliding in under the curve of the towboat's exhaust bell, I went to ground again. There was no reaction from within the ship.

After another quick double-check of my surroundings, I closed my eyes for a second and tried to link-access the genie box.

Nothing.

It wasn't that there wasn't anything coming in over the sensors, the sensors just weren't there. No contact.

"The box is down."

"I checked it just after you left with Mr. Zane," Lil thought back. *"It was functional then."*

"Okay, sports fans. We could be off and running."

"You want me to turn back?" Bo queried.

"Negative. Hold your course. If they're nibbling at the bait, we don't want to spook them off by moving too fast."

The problem was we didn't want to move too slowly either. If we had bad guys aboard this ship, we also had innocents. People I didn't want to see get hurt.

Balancing necessities in this kind of situation is not fun at all.

I didn't have to wait long though.

An alarm tone sounded in my helmet phones and a red flag warning flashed on my visor.

"This is it!" I reported. *"I've got a radiation flare here. It's got to be coming from the towboat's propulsion system. I'm going aboard now."*

And I'd better not drag my feet either. Given the way my rad counter's gradient display was ramping up, something very peculiar was going on in that engine room.

I eased up into the barge's belly lock, moving carefully so my backpack wouldn't clank against the hatch rim. I secured the hatch with the manual dogging lever and then pressurized the lock with air from my own life support tanks. By not activating any of the lock systems, I could hope not to attract any undue attention. I shed my suit then and strapped my gun harnesses back on over my suit liner.

I'd debated about that. Out here, in an unstable situation, getting separated from your vacuum gear isn't such a plus idea. On the other hand, as I said, you just can't be sneaky in a spacesuit.

The first thing I noticed when I cracked the inner hatch was the biting metallic smell in the barge's atmosphere. Something had dumped a big load of free ions in here.

It didn't take me long to spot what it was. A massive hole had been burned right through the lid of Lil's genie box. The filter screens over the lounge's air circulation intakes were also disintegrating after pulling in the residue of the spray. Aqua regia can dissolve gold and silver like sugar in water. Aluminum and composite don't put up much of a fight at all.

Anyone who would mistreat a ship's air revitalization system in that way wasn't planning on staying around long.

Nothing else was going down in the lounge area so I moved aft, towards the control center. I didn't want my boot soles to rasp on the Velcro decking, so I took advantage of the faint gravity and armed myself silently along the handrail.

Ahead of me, I heard movement and I drew the Norinco. I

already had a set of barrels loaded with frangible inner-ship rounds mounted in it and now I set the firing options selector to burst fire.

I reached the hatch at the end of the passageway and, keeping myself back behind the hatch rim, I gingerly peered into the control center.

Two figures were propped back against the starboard bulkhead, mouths, wrists, and ankles tightly taped, not with official police restraint stuff but with the good, old-fashioned duct variety. One of the figures stared at a third party, out of my line of sight across the compartment. The other figure glanced in my direction and a desperate hope replaced the fear in her eyes.

I guess it was time to announce my presence.

"Doc! Mrs. Nolan! This is Gain Chandry! Give it up! It's all over!"

I heard a gasp of shock from within the compartment and I risked a quick look around the hatch rim. Rana Nolan cowered back in the far corner of the control center. The air of composure I had come to associate with her was gone. There was a wildness in her eyes and the skin was drawn skull-tight over her fine-boned features. The weeks and months of tension and evasion had eroded her shell of control and the hysteria inside was breaking through.

She held a weapon in her wavering hands. One glance at it made me glad I hadn't tried a fast rush-and-grab. It was a heavy-gauge industrial spray gun, self-powered and presumably acid-proof. The aqua regia from the ship's laboratory stores had served them well as an armament before and it was doing so again now.

"Teague!" she shrieked. "The marshal is back aboard the barge! He's here now!"

The transit hatch leading back into the towboat had been

latched open and her voice reverberated down the connector tunnel.

Doc Nolan's reply cracked back over the ship's intercom, "Keep the spray on Rainey and the pilot! He can't do anything while we have hostages!"

There was an interphone station just across the passageway from my position and I reached across and tapped the mike key with my pistol barrels.

"I wouldn't count on it, Doc."

"What are you doing back here, Chandry? How did you figure it out?" The same kind of broken-glass hysteria I'd seen on his wife's face was in his voice. Like her, he was breaking up fast internally, a non-monstrous man who had done monstrous things.

"It was pretty easy, Doc," I replied. "The tug's reactor was your last chance. Triggering a low-yield nuclear explosion was the only way you had left to knock Cibola out of orbit. It was the only way you had left to hide the fact that there's no gold on this rock and there never was."

"Have you told them? Have you told the company?" He almost whimpered the question.

Whoa, Chandrey. Better consider that reply for a second. A few meters away, an unstable man was tinkering with an unstable gaseous-core reactor. If I cut Nolan off from hope too rapidly, he might develop a bad case of the don't-give-a-damns and there could be a five-kiloton period at the end of my next sentence.

"No, Doc, I haven't told anyone yet. I had to be sure first. I told Bo I was staying behind to cover you."

Any straight-thinking perp would see through that line in a second, but I figured that the Nolans might just buy it because they'd so desperately want it to be true.

Nell and Captain Torveska were seated on the deck almost within grabbing range of me. I might have considered trying it too except for the loops of tape leashing them to the bulkhead hand rail. The trusting expectancy in their eyes as they looked at me was a little disconcerting. The law was here and as far as they were concerned, everything was going to be all right.

I wish I was that confident.

"Lil. It's all going pretty much like I figured, just worse. Dr. Nolan is trying to blow Cibola out of orbit by triggering a detonation of the towboat's reactor. I've also got a hostage situation going with Rainey and Torveska."

"Acknowledged," Lil replied. *"We've been monitoring the situation through your vision and hearing. If you have to, can you take down Mrs. Nolan?"*

"Not easily. The problem is that acid jet they've rigged up as a weapon. If I accidentally clip that pressurized tank with a round, all of our eyeballs are going to collectively fry in here."

"Boss, can I please turn around and get back there!" Bo pleaded over the link.

"I'm not sure you could make it back here in time, pal. Nolan's either going to have that reactor ready to blow soon, or he's going to do an oopsy and have it blow a whole lot sooner than he figures. Either way, Bo, you'd better stay clear. And Lil, you'd better put Cap'n Saber back on stand-by. We could have a runaway rock out here at any moment."

Better talk up the bad guys a little bit. Can't let them start thinking too much.

"I don't think you really want to be doing this, Mrs. Nolan," I said. "Somehow I don't think you ever planned on having to hurt anyone."

"We didn't!" she quavered. "Not at first. But it grew! It all grew, Marshal!"

"How about that, Doc?" I aimed my voice at the intercom

mike. "It started with just a little computer tampering, didn't it? You had to hide the fact that your figures weren't coming out quite the way you wanted. Isn't that how it went?"

I heard the clatter of a fumbled tool over the circuit. "That's right. I was sure Cibola was a noble rock. My figures all indicated it. The micro-deviations. . . . Then the tug made intercept and the navigational data was skewed. . . . I was sure it was just a minor error in my computations so I altered the files. I didn't want the directors to know until I'd worked out the correction. But the mass wasn't there. It just . . . wasn't . . . there!"

And they kept trying to hide the fact. First they'd made their brag, and then their lie, and then they couldn't admit that they'd been wrong after their company had committed hundreds of millions on their word. They'd have been ruined. The whole flash life they'd built for themselves would have caved in.

And so they kept on concealing and hiding and building the lie. Eventually though, the lying alone just wouldn't do it any more and the sabotage had to start.

That's what the Nolans had never understood, that once you start a conspiracy like this, you can't get out of it again. You just keep sinking in deeper as more layers get added on and the best you can ever hope for is to just keep your head above the surface. They were failing at that now, and the waters were closing over them, leaving them without even enough air for one last good scream.

Poor, pathetic little murderers.

"Doc, listen to me. For the sake of your wife and yourself, put this thing down and walk away from it, now. It's the only way out for you."

"No, I just have to get rid of Cibola," he chanted back. "With Cibola gone nobody will know. Rana and I can get away in the towboat's escape module. They'll think Paul Zane sabotaged the reactor before he was taken into custody."

Something had come into Nolan's voice that made the hair on the back of my neck stand up. You hear it sometimes in the cop business, usually in the barricade and suicide situations.

It's a flatness, a lifeless tone that means the rest of the Universe has ceased to exist for that particular individual. There was just his own mind left and whatever he's got crawling around inside of it. Hostage Negotiation specialists refer to the phenomenon as "flipping the switch" and when it happens, there's no calling them back.

"Lil, I'm going to need a distraction down here and I need it now."

"What do you want me to do, Gain?"

"Is there any iron left in the propulsion ducts of the mass driver?"

"A few tons, yes."

"Okay, then use the driver as a rail gun and target the engine compartment of the towboat . . . Lilith don't argue!"

She snapped off the link for about two seconds and then came back on stream under cold steel control. *"I have no dedicated fire control to work with, Gain. I could do it easily enough with a real weapons system, but as it is, I can't make any guarantees on accuracy. I could blow you all right off the face of that asteroid."*

I tried to dredge up a little humor. *"That's what's going to happen here presently anyhow. Heya, sweet one, I trust you."*

"It will take a few minutes to train the tug around and develop a firing solution. Can you stall them?"

"I'll have to."

"I hope you know what you're doing, Boss," Bo added. *"Be-*

cause it'll be a real ache in the ass, having to break in a new partner."

I hoped I knew what I was doing too, but at this point I wasn't going to make anybody any promises. The only thing I was certain of was that I was running time and options short.

"Heya, Doc," I said aloud. "Here's something to consider. Maybe we can at least get your wife out of this mess without anyone else having to get hurt. We could set up a plea bargain, maybe get her a suspended sentence in exchange for voluntarily turning state's evidence. Think about it!"

"No!" Rana Nolan screeched explosively. "Teague, don't listen! We started this together because we had to. We had to! I'm not going to leave you now!"

True love is a beautiful thing, but just now I'd swap a bargeload of it for just a little enlightened self-interest on somebody's part. I took another peek around the hatch rim and found that Mrs. Nolan now had the acid spray aimed in my direction instead of at the hostages. That was some sort of an improvement I guess.

"If you don't want to think about yourself, Mrs. Nolan," I said desperately, "then think about your husband. Will another handful of murders do him any good? I'm just the first one to figure this thing out. There'll be others. Please, Mrs. Nolan, you can't win!"

She didn't answer. Commitment. She'd flipped her own switch.

Over the intercom system and echoing down the access corridor I heard a new set of warbling alarm tones from the distressed reactor system. *"Lil, where's that diversion?"*

"I'm still turning the rig and running firing simulations. I need more time."

"Maybe so, but I don't have any left! Fire as you bear!"

I tried to come up with some more brilliant arguments,

some psychological insight that would give me a handle on the hyper-stressed minds of the Nolans. Tao, even for a little bullshit to sling around to buy Lil some extra seconds. But my brain was suddenly as dry as my throat. All I could visualize was that mass driver slowly pivoting in space. The most titanic sniper's rifle ever conceived and Lil was going to have to fire it with absolute precision first crack out of the box.

Some plan, smartboy.

Nell Rainey still had her eyes on me, patiently waiting for that miracle.

"Rana," the Doc called out over the intercom. "I've got the reactor safeties off and I'm setting the spiking program now. Get back into the access tunnel and lock the hatch behind you. Then get into the escape module."

"Don't try it, Mrs. Nolan," I yelled. "I'm warning you!"

She hesitated and I edged forward a little, getting the access tunnel into full sight.

"Rana, come on!" Nolan called again. "We have to leave now!"

"Damn it, Doc," I yelled, "if she moves toward that hatch, I'll cut her in half! I mean it!"

"Use the spray gun, Rana," Nolan said in his empty voice. "That will keep him off."

So that was all the time we had left. None.

"Lil!"

"Firing now!"

A shock whiplashed through the barge an instant later and its hull rang as millions of minute projectiles impacted on it like a hailstorm from hell. An instant more and the hull had been eaten through.

I'd been hoping to just poke a hole in the towboat's engine room. I hadn't planned on blowing the whole back end off the thing.

I thought I heard Doc Nolan scream over the first explosion of air out into space. Then a heavy-gauge tornado was trying to fight and claw its way out through the transit tunnel hatch, dragging us all along with it.

The internal lighting went down, to be replaced by the yellow-white glare of the emergency lamps, and the racing air filled with dust and hard copy sheets and every other kind of high-velocity shit you could imagine. Over the roar of the escaping atmosphere, you could hear a higher-pitched shriek. The drop in pressure had tripped the blowout bottles in each of the compartments and they were venting their air as per their intent. Five seconds after that sound stopped, we'd start to die.

I had planned to dive across the control center and slam the access tunnel hatch shut after the towboat was hit. Unfortunately, I didn't make it.

I'd started my lunge, but just clear of the passageway, Nell plowed into me. With her hands bound, she hadn't been able to make a holding grab at anything when she'd been torn loose from the rail and now she was being sucked toward the tunnel. We crashed into the chart table in the center of the compartment and I got one arm around her and one hand on the table's grab rail. Donna Torveska collided with us a couple of heartbeats later and I managed to wedge her against the table as well.

I was pinned. I couldn't get to the hatch without turning loose the two women and if I did turn loose, one or both of them would be dragged out through the hatch before I could get it closed, and I was unwilling to live with that.

Terminal lock up. No positive resolution existent.

I tried to shut down the neurolink. No sense in making Bo and Lil experience my death.

It was Rana Nolan who saved us, although I don't think

231

she had it planned that way. I heard her shriek thinly over the roaring of the air as she lost her hold and flew across the compartment. There was a meaty crunch as she struck the open hatch door and then she was gone, whipped away like a dry autumn leaf. I hope she was dead before she was sneezed out into space.

The impact of her body had released the latch on the airtight door though, and now the vacuum pulled it shut with a slam like an explosion.

As quickly as it had come, the hellish drag of the air was gone. My eardrums popped and suddenly I could catch a real working lungful of breathin'. Nell, Donna, and I all drifted down to the deck. Both women were bleeding from the nose as, I guess, I was, and I hastily stripped the tape from their mouths so they could breathe without choking.

"Gain, are you all right?"

"Yeah, Lil, I'm fine. So are the hostages. Both perps died trying to escape. Situation resolved."

"Acknowledged, Marshal Chandry. Situation resolved."

"Hey, Bo?"

"Yeah?"

"Now you can come a running."

"Already underway, Boss. Be there in a short."

Around us, the barge made the sounds of a dying ship. Creakings and moanings, the hissing of minor air leaks, the electronic whimpers of a couple of still functioning alarm systems. One of those was a radiation warning. Most of the gaseous uranium in the reactor core had probably vented into space when the engine room was breached, but there was enough left to cause creeping contamination.

I finished freeing the two ladies and we headed forward for the suit lockers and the air lock.

We'd wait out on the surface for Bo's return.

Chapter 13

There were new stars in the sky. Stars that blinked and flared and occulted each other as they jostled closer to Cibola. They were the running lights and thruster glows of the incoming Joburg convoy and they marked the end of my time here.

Over at the initial landing site, a salvage ship had already settled down over the wreck of the laboratory barge and its crewmen were snubbing off the towing straps that would be used to lift it off and away for decontamination and repair.

"Incoming call from the salvage hauler, Boss," Bo said over the living space speakers.

"Okay, let me have it."

I flipped the dinette access screen over from exterior view to communications.

" 'Lo, Captain Torveska. You getting ready to move out on the salvage ship?"

"Yes, Marshal," the lady replied, her face filling the little monitor. "But I am not a captain currently. I have nothing left to command."

There was a touch of humor coming back into her. A good thing to see.

"You'll get another ride soon enough," I replied.

"Maybe not so soon. I'm thinking about moving on from Joburg."

"Where away?"

"I'm still considering," she said. "I might go back to

233

school for awhile for my unlimited tickets and then maybe try out for one of the deep space haulers. Something new."

"A little closure?"

She nodded and smiled. "Essentially. I think I may be finished with this part of my life. But before I make any final decisions, I'm going to go Earthside and take a little vacation."

"In Singapore maybe?"

She nodded again. "You were right. Co and I have talked and there is an understanding. Maybe we can lean on each other a little bit to get through this time. We'll see."

I nodded and smiled to her. "Yeah. Well, get out there and find some more happiness, Captain. Bo and I will be wishing you well."

"And I shall do the same for you, Marshal. Thank you, from all three of us."

"Another satisfied customer," Bo commented as the screen went blank.

"Yeah. And even after I managed to let her lover get blown away," I said. "A very forgiving lady."

"Are you going into your usual post-mission mullygrubs?" Bo demanded.

"Just acknowledging some failings and weaknesses, pal. Start your pre-flights. We'll be getting out of here shortly."

"Not before I find out a few things," Nell said, slipping into the dinette beside me. "Like how you ever figured out that the Nolans were sabotaging their own project."

She was fresh out of the bath bag and her skin was cool and water-sweet. After I'd kissed her, I held her face against mine for an extra moment more, just to enjoy the sensation.

"Mm, I'd never have believed it was them," she finished.

I arched an eyebrow. "Well, you weren't supposed to. That was the whole idea. The Nolans had a couple of very powerful things working in their favor and they used them well. One being that we had them visualized as primary victims of the crime. Your victim is seldom also your perpetrator. It made a great shield to work behind."

"I can see how it would." Nell frowned. "Among other things, as executive staff in the Sciences Division, they had access to most of the primary key codes in our computer net, including the updates we made after the security audit."

"Exactly. It also gave them an insider's edge on all the rest of your cyber security as well. That's why we seemed to be fighting the hyper-hackers of the Universe. They never had to crack into your system; they were inside to begin with."

"What was their second edge?"

"The fact that they were genuinely brilliant people," I replied. "They used the same kind of scientific methodology they would have used in a research project in planning their sabotage campaign."

"Scientific methodology?" Nell asked, puzzled.

"Sure. I've talked to the Interpol team that went into the Nolan's quarters dirtside. They had a complete database assembled on this project. Operational checklists, stats, and schematics on the MD-24 and the crew barge, police procedural texts, and UNILAW investigations doctrine, even performance parameters on outsider cybers."

"Nosy parkers," Bo muttered through the overhead speakers.

I ignored the interrupt. "They also had personnel files. When Doc Nolan said he'd hand-picked this team, he meant it. You were all apparently integral parts of the plan."

Nell's brows drew together. "You are kidding?"

"Nope. Think about it. For example, Gavin Wilcox, a good field engineer but with a world-class bitch-on where it comes to cops. A perfect irritant and distraction for any security element deployed to Cibola.

"Then there were our towing masters, Captain Tran and Ms. Torveska, good people again but with a strong personal tie between them. Take one down and you emotionally cripple the other. Two for the price of one. That was the theory at any rate. Come to find out though, friend Donna was tougher than they figured."

"I wonder what they thought my glaring weakness was?" Nell said ruefully.

"Don't know for sure." I traced a finger down her cheek. "Maybe they figured you would serve as a distraction as well. Or maybe they just figured that you'd be an easy mark to put out of the way when the time came. Only you turned out to be tougher than they projected as well."

"Too right!" she snorted.

I used the same finger to riffle her hair. "Interesting thing. The kidnapping attempt on you was one of the first things that made me suspect that something was bent about this setup."

"Why?"

"Well, if this was some great cosmic conspiracy masterminded by some terrorist outfit or corporate cadre, why'd they rely on a bunch of fumble-fingered station snotties to put the bag on you? Why didn't they import some professionals for the job?

"The answer's simple. The Nolans had no operational experience in the criminal environment. They had no idea about how to go about finding a pro kidnaper, much less hiring one."

"I, for one, am pleased about that," Nell replied emphatically. "The enthusiastic amateurs were bad enough."

"No argument. But that was another one of the things that kept throwing me off. I couldn't find a conventional criminal motive. Who'd gain by disrupting the Cibola project if this wasn't a terrorist strike or a hostile corporate action?

"In the end, I had to invert the equation to make it make sense. They weren't trying to gain anything, they were just trying to hold on to what they already had."

I pulled back the memory of those last few minutes in the control center of the barge. "Doc Nolan said it started as an error and there's no reason to think it was anything else. He and his wife were convinced that Cibola was a noble rock and they produced a set of orbital calculations solid enough to commit your bosses to an intercept attempt.

"However, once the tug docked up and started shoving, something showed up wrong. Like the Doc himself said, 'The mass wasn't there.' Cibola turned out too light to have an appreciable gold content.

"That was bad enough, but the Nolans had to go and make things worse. They figured that they'd just dropped a decimal place somewhere and that they just needed a little time to redo their arithmetic. So they started cooking the tug's navigational files, altering the data feed so it would match up with their original projections.

"Unfortunately, they kept coming up with the same bottom line. No gold, no silver, just plain old iron. Not only had they been wrong, costing the company a whole mountain of cash, but now they were also guilty of falsifying company documentation to conceal the fact."

Nell nodded thoughtfully. "They wouldn't just be finished at Joburg. No other spaceside corporation would touch them •with a four-meter pole."

"Yep," I agreed, "they'd be permanently derailed off the fast track. Their only chance was to get rid of the evidence. Which, considering we're talking about a four and a half cubic kay block of solid metal, was going to present quite a challenge.

"They almost made it though. They were smart enough to

start turning their liabilities into assets. When the security audit turned up their file tampering, they used that as a jumping-off point to create their fake terrorist threat. That gave them the excuse they needed to get out to Cibola."

"What I can't figure is why they didn't blow the rig when they first arrived," Bo interjected. "They had every opportunity in the world before we got there."

"Not really, pal. Just sabotaging the tug wasn't enough. By the time they could get to Cibola, it was almost in a parallel orbit with Earth. There was too much chance that a couple of years down the line, Joburg or somebody else would salvage the rock and they'd be found out.

"The Nolans had to wait until the asteroid was actually coming in to Earth orbit before they acted. Then they could be certain that the UN would call in a Nemesis strike that would blow Cibola back into deep space. The rock would be cast into some wildass eccentric orbit and would be rendered radioactive from the fusion bombing as well. Nobody would ever likely bother with it again and they would have been clear. They just had to keep us all diverted until it was time to fire the shot."

"Huh," Bo snorted. "I wish there was time for you to tell us another story, Daddy, but the Joburg foreman's barge is on final approach. Our guest desired to be notified."

"Oh Lord and Lady, yes!" Nell slipped out from behind the dinette. "I've got to get out there."

I helped her suit up. It wasn't until we were standing in the air lock access passage that other topics of conversation came up.

"Gain, what about us?" she asked quietly. "Where do we go?"

"Well, for me, I have to head back to Dawn City for reassignment. You're welcome to come along."

She shook her head. "I can't. Until we get Cibola on stream, I'll be shuttling back and forth between here and company headquarters. At least for the next two months."

"Hey ho. In two months' time I could be anywhere between here and Venus."

Nell drooped a little. "So, this was just a short term thing," she said, a tinge of bitterness coming into her voice.

I tilted her head back up and I kissed her again. Even unhappy, it was a prime kiss.

"Short term by necessity, small and pretty, but I don't think 'just' comes into the equation. We each have someone new we can count on if we need. We each have accumulated some green memories and we each have a 'maybe some day' to carry around with us for possible future redemption. It seems to me like we're already doing better than three-quarters of the male-female relationships recorded in human history."

That lifted a chuckle out of her. "I guess you're right. And I'll remember that 'maybe some day,' and you."

"Heya, what about me?" Bo protested over the intercom.

Nell reached out and patted the bulkhead with a gloved hand. "Lobo, you would be impossible to forget."

She started to don her helmet, then paused. "One last thing, Gain. How did you figure out there wasn't any gold here on Cibola? I double-ran the tests and every one indicated a good ore concentration."

"Oh, that. Something somebody said back there when I was groping around in the darkness keyed me to it. It occurred to me that while we had been testing the ore, we hadn't tested the test. As you science johnnies phrase it, we hadn't established a control. So, on that nightwatch when I had you bring your assaying kit over here to the mainframe, Bo and I kept fooling around with it after you had dossed out. And one of the things we did was to run an assaying test on some filings we'd taken from a bar of aluminum stock. According to the results, it'd be worth Joburg's time to stake out a claim on our spare parts locker."

"How did the Nolans manage that?" she asked.

"Easy. Before we ever arrived on Cibola, they contaminated all of the aqua regia in your laboratory stores with minute amounts of gold. When you ran your tests, it'd precipitate out as if it had been part of the ore sample. You could've assayed a polish sausage and would have read out as being worth mining.

"That's also why they staged that attack on us with the cutter head. We were just secondary targets. What they were really after was the spectrographic analyzer. It would have revealed the truth about Cibola."

Nell fingered her helmet. "I wish the Nolans could have done that on their own. It would have been a setback to them, certainly, but our board of directors are mostly old mining hands. They know that every strike doesn't pan out."

"I guess it was a risk they weren't willing to take, so they tried running a different kind of risk that got them killed. Bad judgment."

As I helped Nell lock her helmet down onto its mounting ring, something occurred to me. "What are you going to do with this rock now that you're stuck with it?"

"Mine it of course," she replied through her open visor. "Cibola is still a perfectly good little nickel-iron asteroid, just what the MD-24 was originally designed to go after. The company will make good money out of it. Maybe not as much as we had hoped, but then you can't have everything."

"I guess not, small and pretty."

Ten minutes later, we made a final low pass over the surface of the asteroid and Bo dipped his wings in response to the slight, white-suited figure who waved us farewell.

Elsewhere on the rock, flares were burning to mark the touchdown points for equipment pallets and barracks pods and all of the other hummers and bumpers that would be needed to start sawing Cibola up into salable chunks.

There'd be a natural progression to it. First the mine would come on stream. Then a couple of metals-hungry industrial concerns would move their platforms out to this point in geo-sync to reduce transportation costs. Then a habitat station would be needed to provide more living room for the growing number of personnel. Then service industries would appear to serve that population. Soon, there would be another island added to the little archipelago of human and cyber civilization.

Maybe that would be the best testament that could be left for Captain Lee Tran and Engineer Gavin Wilcox. Maybe for Teague and Rana Nolan too.

Bo headed back to Dawn City over the thinly traveled polar trajectories, arcing us high over Earth's northern ice pack. Twenty hours in flight and, as usual, I'd probably spend most of it working on my backlog of sleep and bureaucracy. For the moment though, I was content to slouch in the command sphere and think.

Specifically, about a lady called Nell Rainey. She was attractive and tough and smart and not inclined to be excessively clingy. Out here in cis-Lunar, you could put together a pretty good life with someone like that.

Which is why I was kind of glad I got out of there when I did.

You see, there's a reason that the lawman always used to ride off alone into the sunset at the end of all those old western flatscreens. That being that the only cops who ever hang fast to anything permanent are the stupid ones.

The smart ones are like me. They stay free and focused on the job, getting it done across the years until they harden up and chill off and stop worrying about things like a home and maybe a family.

Unfortunately, about then, they may also start reconsidering their definition of "smart."

"Good operation, Marshal."

Lil's holograph, wearing the image of a sleeveless white suit liner, had materialized silently in the other command chair.

"I was slow," I replied, "and I let the Nolans lead me around by the nose. If I'd worked it out faster, Wilcox might not have had to die. Maybe Tran wouldn't have had to either."

Lil quirked up an elegant eyebrow. "We're only human, Gain."

"Speak for yourself," I grunted. "I'm supposed to be invincible."

"Maybe. Be that as it may, the Authority is satisfied with this team's performance."

"UNILAW or just you?"

"It's interchangeable."

I grinned a little and settled deeper into the command chair. "Did you timeshare like this just to tell me I'm not fired?"

She shook her head. "No. I just suspected that with your houseguest gone, things might seem a little lonely. I thought you might like some company."

"What am I supposed to be, chopped liver?" Bo protested.

Lil rolled her eyes toward his speaker. "You are the junior officer present and should be seen and not heard."

"You know, I feel a bad case of receiver failure coming on."

"Heel! Both of you!" I said. " 'Preciate the thought, sweet one, but I'm not sure how much company I can be in return. I feel like I could sleep all the way home and for three days thereafter."

"Two," Lil said in a small voice.

"Oh, I'm gettin' that ooold feelin'," Bo moaned.

"I'm sorry, Gain," she continued. "The most downtime I can give you is two days, if that. There's some idiot soapboxing revolution out on one of the L-4 stations and I might need you to lead an intervention group."

I sighed. "Where do the bad guys get all of their energy? Okay. No rest for the weary."

"You know, Gain," Lil coaxed. "You could extend your R&R a little by sharing a reality pocket with me. By tweaking the time perception I could stretch a couple of hours out into a long weekend."

"That's a possibility," I acknowledged. "What did you have in mind?"

"Oh, skiing on the Hilo Continental or a visit to the beach resorts in the Marianas. Or maybe something a little more exotic."

"Such as?"

"Ancient Rome. The Emperor Caligula may have had his limitations as a statesman, but the man did know how to throw a party."

Tao take it all anyway. A cop doesn't need a family, he just needs a partner. Or maybe two.

About the Author

James H. Cobb lives in the Pacific Northwest, where he writes both the Amanda Garrett techno-thriller series and the Kevin Pulaski fifties suspense mysteries, not to mention the occasional odd bit of historical and science fiction. When not so involved, he enjoys long road trips, collecting historical military firearms and learning the legends and lore of the great American Hot Rod. He may also be found frequently and shamelessly pandering to the whims of "Lisette," his classic 1960 Ford Thunderbird.

James may be reached at DDG79@AOL.COM. All criticism and commentary gratefully accepted.